CW01086027

Soldier of the Queen

Book 1 in the Soldier of the Queen Series

By

Griff Hosker

Soldier of the Queen

Published by Sword Books Ltd 2022

SWORD
BOOKS

Copyright ©Griff Hosker First Edition 2022

Soldier of the Queen

Dedicated to Terry Bermingham- a true artist. Thanks for the figures.

Contents

I
The Charge of the Light Brigade

Half a league, half a league,
Half a league onward,
All in the valley of Death
Rode the six hundred.
"Forward, the Light Brigade!
Charge for the guns!" he said.
Into the valley of Death
Rode the six hundred.

II
"Forward, the Light Brigade!"
Was there a man dismayed?
Not though the soldier knew
Someone had blundered.
Theirs not to make reply,
Theirs not to reason why,
Theirs but to do and die.
Into the valley of Death
Rode the six hundred.

III
Cannon to right of them,
Cannon to left of them,
Cannon in front of them
Volleyed and thundered;
Stormed at with shot and shell,
Boldly they rode and well,

Into the jaws of Death,
Into the mouth of hell
Rode the six hundred.

IV
Flashed all their sabres bare,
Flashed as they turned in air
Sabring the gunners there,
Charging an army, while
All the world wondered.
Plunged in the battery-smoke
Right through the line they broke;
Cossack and Russian
Reeled from the sabre stroke
Shattered and sundered.
Then they rode back, but not
Not the six hundred.

V
Cannon to right of them,
Cannon to left of them,
Cannon behind them
Volleyed and thundered;
Stormed at with shot and shell,
While horse and hero fell.
They that had fought so well
Came through the jaws of Death,
Back from the mouth of hell,
All that was left of them,
Left of six hundred.

VI

When can their glory fade?
O the wild charge they made!
All the world wondered.
Honour the charge they made!
Honour the Light Brigade,
Noble six hundred!

Alfred, Lord Tennyson

Prologue

Crimea 1854

Private Griffith Thomas, Taff to his mates, had never regretted joining the army for he loved the life and the camaraderie. He endured the brutal discipline of some of the non-commissioned officers who seemed to enjoy inflicting pain and he could cope with the incompetence of young officers who had only joined the cavalry so that they could ride to hounds as often as they liked. He had witnessed floggings but avoided being punished himself. He did not mind the food, growing up in a poor part of North Wales meant that the dull diet was nothing new to him. What he did not enjoy was the climate of this land to which he had been sent. The Crimea was far too hot and while he knew that he would need the warmth of his woollen tunic in winter even now, in autumn, it was still too hot. The flies and the disease were also a problem and no one enjoyed a good night of sleep under canvas.

His tent mate was Henry Ramage and he suffered just as much as Taff but the two of them found some solace in their shared misery. They also shared a love of horses. It was why they had both joined the Second North British Regiment of Dragoons. Neither had any idea why the regiment had been renamed. Everyone knew them as the Scots Greys, named for the white horses they rode and it was the name everyone used when speaking of them. Famous for their wild charge at Waterloo almost forty years earlier they were big men riding huge horses, Henry and Taff had both joined up on the same day and for the same reason. They stood out amongst the rest of the enlisted men for most were from the northeast of England or Scotland. They seemed to speak a different language to Taff who was Welsh and Henry, who came from Manchester. They were fortunate, or perhaps, unfortunate in that the RSM, John Grieve, was also not from the far north. It was fortunate in that he liked them but that also made it unfortunate for he gave them no leeway whatsoever. He expected them to perform better than the rest of the squadron and he drove them both hard. That was life in the cavalry. The two men were part of a famous regiment but that was broken down into squadrons and then troops. Now that they were on active service it was also broken down into tentmates, messmates they called each other, like the sailors on the ships that had brought them halfway around the world to the Black Sea. There were two kinds of cavalry. There were the light cavalrymen, the lancers and the flamboyantly dressed hussars wearing braided pelisse and dolmans. They were the peacocks. Henry and Taff belonged to the heavies. The Scots Greys apart, the heavy cavalry wore metal helmets. They carried long straight swords capable of taking off an arm and they knew how to wield them. The regiments in the Crimea were the wild Inniskillings, fierce Irishmen known for their ability to fight and the Royals, the household cavalry. They were the ones who guarded Buckingham Palace and Windsor. They were the Queen's guards. The two cavalry arms had little time for one another. The light cavalrymen were, in the opinion of the heavy cavalry, too showy and flamboyant. The heavy cavalry saw themselves as the descendants of the knights of old. Certainly, their new swords were longer, straighter and heavier than the flashy sabres of the light cavalry.

They had landed in the exotic land of the Crimea and then spent time helping their animals to recover from the long and gruelling sea voyage. If they thought they would be sent to battle immediately then they were wrong. The infantry had fought battles almost from the moment that they landed but the cavalry, that most valuable of arms, had merely been spectators. It seemed they were too valuable to waste. With the war almost over it seemed that the cavalry would have sailed halfway around the world and for nothing. Up till now the war for the light and heavy brigades of cavalry had been a series of patrols and vedette duty, but on that October morning with the army close to Sevastopol and the town of Balaklava, the bugler's call was more urgent. The Russians were attacking.

Taff and Henry knew what to do and they prepared for war. Some of the equipment, like the sabretache, was archaic but the troopers understood the need for tradition. Taff carried his bearskin to the horse lines as donning the headgear would be the last thing he would do. He had much to do to ensure that Caesar was also ready for war. Taff and his horse, Caesar, were a good combination. The horse, named by the troop commander, Captain Pullein, was one of the larger horses in the regiment but Taff was a good rider and could handle the powerful beast. There was no reason why he should have been as the only soldiers in the family had joined the 24th Foot but as well as having a natural affinity for horses Taff also had natural ability. Others had tried to ride Caesar but failed. Private Thomas made it look easy. He slipped the gnarled apple he had found into Caesar's mouth as he saddled him.

"There might be a little action today, Caesar. Now remember that while you might be the best horse in the regiment, you needn't show it. Just stay in line, see? No need to get ahead of the others." The horse whinnied and Henry Ramage shook his head as he, too, prepared his horse. It was as though the two could talk to each other.

"How do you do that Taff?"

"Do what?"

"Talk to your horse and he answers you."

Taff shrugged, "Don't know. I just do."

RSM Grieve's voice boomed out, "Less chit chat, ladies. It looks like today we might actually get to see some action. We want to show the rest of the Heavy Brigade that we are the best regiment Lord Raglan has. He will be looking on from the heights. There are some Russian cavalry regiments forming up and they are threatening our guns so look lively eh?"

There were two valleys before them and the British High Command was on the heights overlooking the two valleys. They afforded a fine view and they could see the British and French redoubts that were there to discourage Russian attacks. They could see that the Russians had launched an early attack and were attempting to take the guns from the redoubts. The allies had been caught napping.

The two men did as they were ordered and finished preparing their mounts. The last thing that they donned was the bearskin they wore. Neither man was confident that the cumbersome headgear would stop a sabre cut but it might cushion the blow a little. They led their mounts to form their lines before the order was given to mount. The Heavy Brigade was made up of the elite horse regiments in the Crimea. The Light Brigade liked to think that they were but they were all show. As Henry's Manchester mum might have said, 'fur coat and no bloomers.' There were five regiments in the brigade although, thanks to the voyage and the climate, none were at full strength; 4th (Royal Irish) Regiment of Dragoon Guards, 5th (Princess Charlotte of Wales's) Regiment of Dragoon Guards, 1st (Royal) Regiment of Dragoons, The Royals, 6th (Inniskilling) Regiment of Dragoons and of course, their regiment 2nd (Royal North British) Regiment of Dragoons, The Scots Greys were commanded by Lt. Colonel Henry Griffith. The commander of the Heavy Brigade was Brigadier General Scarlett and he was a cavalryman through and through. He rode at the front and endured all the dangers of the men he led. His only problem was that he was the most short-sighted man in the whole army. Lord Lucan commanded the cavalry but as he and the commander of the Light Brigade Lord Cardigan did not get on Lord Lucan tended to pay more attention to the Light Brigade rather than the Heavy Brigade as he liked to nitpick with his brother-in-law. It suited the heavies.

It took time for the regiment to form up and by the time they reached the empty camp of the Light Brigade, the Russians had started their attack. This was a thinly defended section of the allied lines. There were Turkish regiments but only one British one, Highlanders. The gossip in the camp was that the Turks were somewhat unreliable and as the Russian cavalry formed up for what was clearly an attack every soldier in this sector knew that any battle would be hard-fought and the outcome in the balance.

Heavy Cavalry had a specific purpose. They were intended to charge and break up enemy formations and it was always the infantry who endured the worst of the fighting. They were the ones who stood in line and keep an enemy occupied. The cavalry always had the luxury of forming lines at their leisure. The 93rd Highlanders were in line with a Turkish Corps. As Taff looked to the northeast he saw the Light Brigade forming up close to the Sapoune Heights. Lord Raglan and his staff were on those heights. There was some comfort in that. Between them, the allies could muster a thousand cavalrymen although Taff estimated that they were facing two thousand Russians.

Henry chuckled, "I see Lord Cardigan is still absent."

Taff nodded, "Aye, he likes to sleep aboard his yacht." Taff did not blame the commander of the Light Brigade and given a choice he would have slept on a ship. There were no biting insects at sea.

Henry nodded, "Ey up, the Russkies are getting close."

"Aye and the Turks look like they don't like it."

The Turkish regiments were edging back away from their positions. They were not fleeing but everyone, the Russians included could see that they had no appetite for a fight. The horsemen were close enough to hear Sir Colin Campbell's reaction. Rather than going into a square, which would have been the normal manoeuvre in the face of three thousand horsemen, Sir Colin kept a two-deep line. "Men, remember there is no retreat from here. You must die where you stand." The men cheered. The 93rd was a tough regiment of hard Scotsmen and retreat was not a word in their vocabulary. They would be isolated and in danger of being massacred as the Turkish Corps no longer provided protection for their flanks. There was just a thin red line to slow down the two thousand and odd cavalrymen who were forming up.

As cavalrymen, Taff and Henry knew the qualities of the men they faced. There were Cossacks, Uhlans and Hussars. This was their land and their terrain and they knew every fold and rock. It would not be easy for many of their enemies were born to the saddle. British guns supported the 93rd as well as some marine batteries on the heights but the Scottish soldiers were outnumbered by seven or eight to one as the Russian cavalry charged. The Turkish soldiers would not face so many horsemen and began to fall back even faster than before. Even if the Heavy Brigade joined in then they would still be severely outnumbered.

Henry leaned in to speak to Taff, "I wonder if Raglan will bring the Lights to support us?"

"Not sure it would make much difference, you know what they are like. Think they are riding to hounds." Both men laughed.

They were close enough to hear the order from Sir Colin Campbell for the Highlanders to open fire. Neither trooper was an expert in the use of rifles but it seemed to them that the order had been given too early for not a single animal or Russian fell.

"Ey up, Taff, Lord Lucan himself is coming over to us. I think things are going to happen soon."

Both men slid their sabres in and out of their scabbards for they did not want them to stick when the order was given to draw sabres. The 93rd fired a volley along with the cannons from the slopes and the marine batteries and this time men fell from horses. It seemed inconceivable to both horsemen that the 93rd would stand. Only a fool faced charging horsemen when not in a square but the Highlanders seemed determined. At the third volley, the Russian horsemen suddenly stopped and that too was inexplicable. If the Russians continued their charge they would simply sweep the brave red-coated Scotsmen away.

Both men were close enough to hear the conversation between the Lieutenant Colonel and the RSM, "Strange, RSM, why have they stopped?"

"You have me there, sir. Perhaps they think it is a trap what with us and the Light Brigade being so close."

"Sergeant Major, you may not have noticed but there is a camp between us and the Russians and then a slope. I think this is what they call, in chess, a stalemate. We can't move while they are there and they can't advance while the two brigades threaten them."

Just then a florid Lord Lucan rode up to General Scarlett and screamed, "Charge! I order you to charge! I want the Heavy Brigade to move! The honour of the cavalry is at stake."

General Scarlett threw a contemptuous look at his superior officer. Even ordinary privates knew that you had to dress ranks and prepare properly for a charge. The Heavy Brigade would not move until their commander gave the order.

Lord Lucan turned to his trumpeter, Trumpet Major Joy, and shouted, "Sound the charge!" The strident notes rang out and not a man in the brigade moved for we all knew that cavalry needed to be organised into ranks to make a charge.

General Scarlett said, calmly, "The brigade will form ranks."

The Scots Greys and the Inniskillings were on the right and, as the three squadrons moved forward to join the others, it became clear to both Taff and Henry that they would be engaged first. Moving troops into position was never quick and it had to be done right. The Royals and the Dragoon Guards had to manoeuvre around the Light Brigade camp and then form up to the left of the Scots Greys. General Scarlett and Lord Lucan were with the Greys and the Inniskillings. The order came to draw sabres and the collective hiss of two hundred basket-hilted swords being drawn sounded like an enormous snake. When General Scarlett was satisfied, he turned to Trumpet Major Monk and the order to charge was sounded. This time the whole brigade trotted forward as one. The gap between the Russians and the Heavy Brigade was so narrow that had they both charged at the same time then they would have met at a walk. Amazingly the Russians did not move. Taff marvelled that even though they were going into action against many times their number there was neither panic nor fear amongst his comrades. Still, for a few moments more, the Russians did not move. It was as though they could not believe that they were being attacked uphill by a force that was a fraction of their own. When the Russians' trumpet did sound then the Heavy Brigade had managed to reach a trot.

The Inniskillings were wild warriors and to a man they gave their battle cry, '*Faugh a Ballagh*', to clear the way. The Scots Greys did not have a battle cry as such but they began a wailing moan as they headed towards the Uhlans, Hussars and Cossacks. Taff was pleased to see following in the wake of the Greys was C Troop of the Royal Horse Artillery under the command of Captain Branding. They would have artillery support but he wondered if that would be enough, for now the Uhlans and Cossacks with their lances charged into the flank of the Greys. The charge came at more of a walk than a gallop but the slope helped them. Lieutenant Colonel Griffith was one of the first to be hit but neither Taff nor Henry had time to take that in for they were both fighting for their lives. Out of the corner of his eye, Taff saw General Scarlett struck on the helmet but he continued to fight the Russian horsemen who surrounded him.

Taff and Henry had to focus on their own battle. First blood went to the Uhlan whose lance rammed into Taff's knee. The pain was excruciating but even as the Russian screamed in delight Taff stood in his stirrups and brought his sword across the face of the Uhlan. The Russian's scream of delight turned to a scream of pain as half his head was taken off. With the Colonel dead it was left to the adjutant to take command and he did so but the Russians were now trying to take the standards knowing the effect it would have.

All order had gone from the two sets of horsemen who were mixed in flowing lines that went back and forth as more men joined the battle. Henry shouted, "Taff, they are trying to take the colours!" He spurred his horse and despite the pain from his bloody knee Taff tried to follow. As Caesar laboured up the hill Taff knew that the lance had struck his mount in the side too. He did not have the strength to carry on after his friend. Another Uhlan, seeing his chance rode directly at Taff's wounded side. Taff would have been skewered and died had not his natural abilities come to his aid. He let go of the reins and he grabbed the head of the lance as it was rammed at his side. The Uhlan kept coming and this time Taff's sabre almost took off the Russian's arm. Dropping his lance the wounded Russian turned and fled. Taff saw that the RSM and Henry were fending off more than seven Russians as they defended the colours.

"Come on Caesar, we can't let the boys down!"

The gallant horse laboured up the slope and Taff was able to bring his sword across the back of the Cossack who was trying to get behind Henry. Taff's sword was sharp and he laid open the Cossack's back to the spine. He fell from his horse. Taff felt Caesar stumble and, half turning he saw a Russian Hussar leaning forward in his saddle with his sabre held before him. The curved sword was a weapon that was flexible and could dance around a heavy cavalry sabre like Taff's. Taff had worked as a labourer before he had joined the Greys and he had arms like oak saplings. What he lacked in sword skills he more than made up for with power and his sword smashed the sabre away as though it was a hazel twig. He then lunged with the tip. The 1853 pattern sword had only the slightest of curves and the end went into the Hussar's chest, tearing through the dolman and waistcoat as though they were paper. The blow that came from Taff's left was not blocked and the Ukrainian sword sliced into Taff's left arm and then into Caesar's side. Had he been able to, then Taff would have stood in the saddle to deliver a mighty blow that would have killed the horseman. As it was, he had to twist, bringing more pain to his right knee and then slash across the face of the Kyiv horseman. Taff was lucky for the horseman was young and as he flinched, pulling his reins back, his horse reared and both rider and horse fell to be trampled by the maelstrom of horsemen who were all fighting for their lives. They were almost through the first regiments of Russians and as Taff saw the Cossacks about to charge, he heard the adjutant of the Greys shout, "Rally the Greys! Rally the Greys!"

It was a command drilled into every heavy cavalryman in the Scots Greys for their failure to do so had cost them many men at Waterloo. They reined in their horses and, whilst still fighting, backed their mounts so that they formed a solid wall of steel against the Russians.

Taff risked looking for his friend and saw that the RSM and Henry had managed to save the colours, slaying more than ten Russians in the process. Just at that moment, out of the corner of his eye, Taff saw the Royal Horse Artillery unlimbering their guns. Miraculously the Russian cavalry commander, General Ryzhov, decided that enough was enough and they ordered the retreat. As the survivors of the attack headed back to their own lines the exhausted Heavy Brigade could not pursue but every eye went to the Light Brigade that had sat and watched the battle just five hundred yards away. They did not move and appeared as disinterested spectators.

When men are in battle they can become oblivious to bugles and orders. Not all the Russians fell back. The cavalryman who slashed down with his sword to kill Trooper Thomas mistimed his stroke or else Taff might have not just been wounded across the cheek and eye but would have lost his life. The sword caught Taff's bearskin and then his brow. The razor-sharp edge ripped down his cheek. It was a miracle that he did not lose an eye. Slashing at the Russian Taff shook his head and then felt himself falling forward. Caesar's legs had gone from beneath him. Even though he was wounded his training did not desert him and he kicked his feet from the stirrups and rolled clear. It would not do to be crushed by almost half a ton of horseflesh. The RSM and Henry galloped to him and after despatching the Russian, both leapt from their horses. Henry took a belt and made a quick tourniquet for Taff's leg while the RSM, a real horseman too, knelt by Caesar.

When Taff saw him going for his pistol he knew what was going to happen. Shaking his head he said, "Give me a minute, Sarn't Major."

The RSM nodded and said, "Be quick. This animal is in pain and we don't let them suffer."

Taff put his bloodied hand on the white neck of his horse and stroked it, "Caesar, I shall never forget you. You are more than a horse, you are my friend and I shall never have another like you." The horse was looking directly at the man he had carried for three years. Taff put his mouth to the horse's muzzle and nodded. The sound of the gunshot deafened Taff and he felt the life leave the gallant animal.

As Henry helped him to his feet, he saw that the horse had been speared on more than one occasion. He had kept going beyond all reason. RSM Grieve said, "He was a good horse and he had a good man on his back but," he looked at Taff's leg, "your days as a cavalryman are gone, Private Thomas. I shall be sorry to lose you."

Standing on that bloody battlefield, even as the Light Brigade was beginning its fateful and fatal charge at the Russian guns, he wondered what he would do now that his life, like Caesar's, lay in tatters on that Balaklava battlefield. His friends were the regiment and his best friend, Caesar, lay dead. What would he do with his life now?

It was when he was lying in the hospital and they were bringing in the huge numbers of wounded men of the Light Brigade that Taff realised he had been lucky and that he had retained his leg. He would do something important with his life. God had granted him life and he owed it to God to make it a good one.

Chapter 1

St Helen's Lancashire 1866

I am Jack Roberts and I am putting my story on paper so that my children might know what I was really like and the journey I took to get where I am today. How would I earn money and what would I do with my life? My father had made it quite clear, on the odd times he was sober, normally a Thursday night, that I would either work or he would throw me out on my ear. I knew we were better off than most families for we rented a house on Central Street. Many of my friends lived as boarders and whilst our home was cramped, we shared it with no one. I confess that there appeared to be nothing that I wanted to do. The choices were stark. Had I been a better reader and writer then I might have become a clerk. It did not pay well but at least it was safe. The main three industries for me were the mines, the glass factories or the chemical industry.

My dad, John Roberts, worked at Pilkington's glass factory and served the mighty furnaces. He worked hard, ten hours a day and, as I later discovered, the work was hot and created a thirst. While at work he drank gallons of tea but such was his thirst that he called at the *'Feathers'* for a few pints each night. The night before payday was the only time you could guarantee his being sober for funds would be low. Like my little brother, Billy, and my two sisters, Alice and Mary, I had learned to stay away from him when he was drunk. The days he did not go to the pub saw a different man to the one who growled and barked at the slightest dissension.

I had found a haven away from his drunken temper when I was six when my mother took us to Sunday School. Her mother, unlike my father, had been quite religious and my mother attended church each Sunday. Parish Church had a hall on Birchley Street and on Sunday we could go there for two hours. It was peaceful and we learned to read and write as well as hear the stories from the Bible. There was no school for the likes of me but at Sunday School I was taught to read. It was also where I met Trooper Thomas. He was a carter and had a gammy leg as well as a wicked scar down one cheek. I liked him because he was gentle. He was a good teacher and very patient with me. He needed to be for I was not a good student. He taught me to read using the stories from the Bible. I loved the story of David and Goliath. When my Mother got used to him she allowed him to take me for a long walk home where we would walk through the countryside and they were the best walks for he told me of his time in the army. He had been a cavalryman and that was why everyone called him Trooper.

"Why do they call you Trooper?"

"You know, Jack, my rank was Private but because I was in the cavalry and I still work with horses, everyone gave me the nickname Trooper. It has stuck with me."

"Why do you teach Sunday School?" The other Sunday School teachers were all what we called, posh girls. As I came to learn, most just gave a few months to teaching Sunday School and then disappeared. Trooper Thomas was the one constant along with Mr Martindale, the lay preacher who played the harmonium and led us in the singing of hymns.

"I nearly lost my leg in the Crimea and when the doctors were debating if they ought to cut it or not, I prayed to God that if he saved my leg, I would do good. They didn't amputate the leg and I chose to give any spare time I had to the Church. He had looked wistfully to the east, "I would have been a missionary but they said they didn't need a cripple." He had shrugged, "They are right and they weren't nasty about it. They said that life in Africa was harsh enough without having a one-legged man." He had looked sad, "You know I loved my life in the Army but the Crimea did for me. When I enlisted, I had a sweetheart and I hoped she would wait for me but she didn't. When I came back to my village she had married and had children. I think my injury would have put her off in any case but she just didn't wait. That was when I came here. I needed to earn a living and there is plenty of work for me here."

He not only taught me to read, but he also taught me about life. Like me, he had had a hard upbringing in North Wales. He told me how he had walked many miles, sleeping rough so that, when he was old enough, he could join the cavalry. "The real reason I joined up was not to be a soldier but to be close to horses. Strange isn't it, Jack? Still, I met some good blokes in the army. Most are dead but the comradeship is still here." He had tapped his heart and his head."

"Were the battles glorious, Trooper? Like in that poem, 'The Charge of the Light Brigade'?" I had heard the poem many times. My mother, a gentle woman, loved poetry and she had memorised it when she had been a young girl. I could quote huge chunks of it.

"I was only in one real battle so I am no judge. All I know is that a cavalry charge is a messy affair. Men come at you from all sides. You do the best you can but you just have a sword and if men are trying to spear you with pig stickers, well." He shook his head, "And it is a terrible waste of horses. No, Jack, I was a soldier of the Queen and we did our best work when we were not charging into battle. The sight of a red coat often stops trouble. Besides, the generals we have are not the best. Raglan was a good chap by all accounts but as a general he was useless. It is men like the RSM that make the British Army what it is. The politicians send armies to take places and it is not the generals who take them but ordinary soldiers and their sergeants."

I was disappointed. After hearing the poem I had dreamed of being on a mighty charger and with a sword in my hand slaying all the enemies of our great empire. I had pictured the generals as being great heroes who led men to victory time after time. Trooper told me of the setbacks the British army had suffered so I had a more realistic view. I think he was trying to dissuade me from following in his footsteps.

"I only learned to read when I was older, Jack. I wonder how different my life would have been had I been able to write. When I joined the army, I could only make my mark. It was RSM Grieve who taught me to read and I am still grateful to him. A man who can read has a passport to the world."

"What is a passport, Trooper?"

He laughed, "It is what the great and the good have to travel the world. If you can read then you need not leave your own fireplace to visit the world."

I was not convinced. I wanted to see the world nor had he dissuaded me from emulating him. I was a clever boy, my mother had told me that and she was always truthful. I saw his plan. That was always one of my faults. I was, as my father often said, too clever for my own good.

As the years passed so I came to know him even better. I would see him in the streets where he sat on his wagon pulled by his horse, Caesar. He didn't like to overwork the beast and so when I saw him, he would get off the wagon and walk next to me, talking. I learned that he was up at five every morning and he went to the Sefton Arms for a nip of whisky and a gill of bitter. Unlike my father, he was able to limit himself. As he said to me a man had no right to be in charge of a horse and wagon if he was drunk. I liked his horse. I helped him to look after Caesar and I mucked out his stall. He even let me ride the huge beast. He taught me how to approach a horse and what to do to put one at its ease. Caesar was a lovely horse and very gentle. This was his third, Caesar. One had been killed in the Crimea and his second had been old and just died. "This one will be my last one, Jack. When this Caesar is too old then I will be too."

"What will you do then, Trooper?"

He rubbed his scar, "Everyone thinks that the gammy leg was the worst wound but the really bad one is here. The reason the doctors left me my leg is that they didn't think I would last the year. A piece of the sword was lodged in my skull and they didn't want to operate. I have been told that it is working its way deeper into my head and one day..."

That had terrified me. I didn't have many friends: Marjorie and Geoffrey Allerton lived next door and we played together all the time. Trooper was even closer to me than they were. I had not thought of him dying. He only had a few grey hairs and he didn't seem that old. After he made that confession it made our conversations and talks even more precious. As I became older, I helped him with the wagon whenever I could. He coughed a lot. I blamed the pipe he kept constantly in his mouth but he had laughed that off as being foolish. He told me every soldier smoked.

I begged him for every detail he could give me about his life in the army. I knew the story of the Battle of Balaklava inside out and back to front for I never tired of hearing it. I learned that he had been lucky to join the Scots Greys.

"When I went to join the Queen's soldiers, I went first to the regiment my brothers had been in, the 24th. It was pure luck that the Scots Greys were recruiting too and they found me first. They reckoned I had the strength to handle one of their big horses. The Queen always has need of soldiers. We have an Empire and it needs defending."

"I think I should like to be a soldier."

He shook his head, "It is a hard life, Jack. Punishments are severe and they flog men, even in peacetime." I thought of my dad and his drunken rages and did not think that whatever the army did could be as bad. "And you get sent to some awful places. One of my brothers was killed during the Indian Mutiny and life out there is hard for us. The people who live in such places can cope with the heat but not us."

"It would be wonderful to see all these strange places."

"Aye, well, most of the time you are in a barracks drilling for half of the day and spending the other half keeping your equipment in perfect condition."

"What is the alternative?" I remembered when I asked that question. I was just eleven and knew that I would have to get a job sooner rather than later. Already my father was making enquiries at Pilkington's to see if he could get me taken on.

"There is plenty of work in St Helens. There are a couple of glassworks and foundries as well as the chemical works."

I had seen what that had done to my father and I did not like the idea. "Could I work with you?"

His face told me that he liked the idea but he shook his head, "I would love that, Jack, but I make barely enough money to feed Caesar and pay my rent at Mrs Sharratt's. Besides, I don't think your father would like it."

He was right. My father had a plan for each of us. Alice and Mary were both good with their hands and one of his friends in the pub had a wife who was a tailoress. She was happy to take on the two girls as apprentices. Bill was my father's favourite. Like me, Trooper had taught him to read but he had learned far quicker than I did and seemed to enjoy it more. He was a natural student and my father recognised that. He had already spoken to Mr Pilkington about having him taken on as a clerk when he was old enough. I did not resent my brother. I liked him. Unlike me, he was not pugnacious. I had saved him from a beating on more than one occasion. I knew how to fight and I was more than handy with my fists. Trooper did not like that side of me.

"It is not God's way, Jack."

"I can't turn the other cheek, Trooper, I just can't. Are you saying I should have let Harry Stanley hit our Bill and done nothing?" Harry Stanley was a bully and enjoyed hurting others. He was wise enough not to try that with me but my little brother was another matter. He had learned the error of his ways and he would not bully anyone for some time.

Trooper shook his head, "If you had just stood in front of your brother would he have tried to hit him?"

"No, but he would have waited until I was not around and given him an even worse beating. This way I have cleared the air."

"And what if you meet someone bigger and tougher than Harry Stanley?"

I grinned, "I am the cock of this area. There might be someone up Parr way or Windle who can beat me but I doubt it."

I was confident in those days.

It was just as I was approaching my twelfth birthday that everything went wrong. My father told me he had a position lined up for me at a local iron foundry, Pritchard's. I headed for Trooper's house on North Road for I wanted to tell him and, perhaps, ask his advice. My father had come directly from work. It was Thursday and he would not be paid until the next day. I had not seen Trooper since Sunday School as I had been asked to help around the house while my mother spring cleaned. Mother rarely asked for my help but she had been ill and I had to forgo my normal pleasures to be that rarity, a good son.

I knew Mrs Sharratt for I had visited the house before. I knew that something was wrong as soon as she saw me. One hand went to her face and the other to my shoulder, "Eeeh, I am sorry, Jack, I should have told you. Things have been so hectic and…"

I felt sick. I knew what she was going to tell me and yet I did not know how. My question was a vain one posed in the hope that I had got things wrong, "What should you have told me, Mrs Sharratt? Trooper is alright, isn't he?"

She shook her head and her bony fingers gripped my shoulder, "He died two nights ago. He just slipped away in his sleep. The doctors are flummoxed."

I said, quietly, "It was his wound."

"His leg?" She looked confused.

"No, Mrs Sharratt, it was the piece of metal in his head. He knew it would kill him one day. He viewed every day on this earth as his last."

"Well, I'll be blowed. He lodged with me for fifteen years and I never knew." She smiled at me, "He liked you. He often spoke about you."

"Can I see him?"

Her mouth opened and closed but no words came out. She put her thin arms around me and hugged me, "I am sorry, Jack. He was buried this morning, in Parish Church cemetery." She stopped squeezing me and looked me in the eyes, "There was just me there and a couple of other old soldiers who used to drink with him at the Sefton. I should have told you. I know you live close to the railway but…"

It was not her fault. It was no one's fault. Bad luck was what Trooper would have said. I suddenly remember Caesar, "And where are his horse and wagon?"

"Old Fred Foster bought both of them. He will look after Caesar. He was a mate of Trooper's" She looked guilty, "He needed a coffin and his rent was due and…" She suddenly stopped and said, "Wait here." She quickly returned and there was a small, battered, metal box in her hands. "These are the only things he had except for the clothes we buried him in. They might just be junk but I think he would have wanted you to have something to remember him by." I knew I needed nothing to remember Trooper by for he was in my heart and in my head. I wondered if I was the son he never had with the sweetheart who had abandoned him.

She handed me the box. I nodded, suddenly aware that tears were forming in my eyes and I was too big to cry. I turned and ran towards the cemetery. It was a mile or so from where we lived but I ran until I thought that my lungs would burst. I saw the grave as soon as I entered the tiny cemetery. The freshly turned earth marked it as clearly as any gravestone. I ran to it and dropped to my knees. I wept, grateful that there was no one to see me. I would have been fetched a clout from my father had he seen me but I would have endured the blow for I had to grieve

"I should have been there, Trooper, and you should not have died alone. Your whole life you were alone." I put my hands on the clods of soil hoping to feel something from beneath them. "I know you had your horses but I thought that we were friends. What shall I do now? I am alone." Even as I said the words, I knew I was not. Even gentle Trooper would have chastised me. I had a family and I knew that I had to be grateful for that but I felt alone, even if I was not. "What do I do now? Where do I go to get the advice, I need?" If I expected an answer, I got none. No words came from beyond the grave into my head; I had hoped that they would I sobbed myself out and then stood. "I will bring some flowers when I can and if I see Caesar, I shall say hello."

I suddenly remembered his tin and I opened it. It contained a strange mixture of objects. The first thing I saw, bizarrely, was a broken pipe and I wondered why he had kept it. I took it out and placed it on the lid. There was a gilt button with a grenade on it. I looked closely at it. Trooper had told me of his uniform and I guessed that this was the socket on his bearskin that had held his plume. When he had been hit at Balaklava the sabre had sliced through the bearskin and plume. He must have kept it as a memento. The other objects were hidden by a stiff piece of bloody cloth. I knew exactly what it was. It was the piece of cloth his friend, Henry Ramage had tied around his wounded knee. Trooper had been sentimental. I picked it up and folded it. Clearly, Mrs Sharratt had not searched it, for inside I found a golden guinea with a portrait of Queen Victoria upon it. That was a fortune! The landlady was a nice lady but I knew that the temptation to take it would have been too great. I put that on the cloth with the dried bloodstains. I saw more treasure. There were the buttons from his Scots Greys' tunic. They were worth money but the most valuable thing of all was his Crimea medal. Just one and a half inches across with Victoria Regina and the face of the Queen embossed upon it, there was the Balaklava clasp. I returned all the items to the tin except for the pipe. It had meant something to Trooper and I had no need for it. I placed it on the grave. It did not seem much to mark a life but it was a marker.

As I headed back to Central Street, I swore that I would do something to honour Trooper. Everything I had in the box told me to do one thing, become a soldier of the Queen. I even convinced myself that Trooper's voice came into my head and told me to do it. That was my imagination. I cannot blame Trooper for the decision that I made in Parish Church cemetery. I was too young yet but when the time was right, I would join up. I would become a cavalryman like Trooper.

Chapter 2

My father took me to *'The Feathers'* to meet with Joe Stafford, the foreman from the foundry. Father only worked half a day on the last Saturday of the month and it coincided with my meeting. Joe was a florid faced fellow with, like my father, a beer gut. My father had worked as a young man at the foundry but left for the higher pay at Pilkington's. With the higher pay came more danger and two of my father's team had died as a result of accidents. One, when a bucket of molten glass had fallen and the second, when a large sheet of glass had also fallen. It meant there were two widows and their families without a breadwinner. They would either have to seek a relative or the almshouse. It was rare for a widow to have the skill to bring in money. That was another reason that my sisters were going to become tailoresses. To be fair to Joe, he was a pleasant enough man and I got on with him. I am not sure if that was because of my father but when I began work at Pritchard's I saw a harsher and more cruel side to him.

"So this is the young lad you want me to take on, John?"

"Aye. He needs to learn a trade and as he has nowt up top, he shall have to use his hands."

"Well, he looks strong enough." He put an enormous paw around my arm and squeezed. "Right son, you start on Monday. You work six days a week, eight until six and the pay is sixpence a day. You get an hour off for your dinner. Bring your own. You will be the tea lad and general dogsbody until we can train you up in the Iron Gang."

Inside I groaned, I had gained my first military title but I would be at the bottom of the heap and at everyone's beck and call.

"Eventually, when you have grown a bit more, we shall have you working with the Iron Gang. They don't need brains just brawn. If I think you have any aptitude then I might give you to a tradesman." He looked at my father, "No promises, John. This is a favour to thee."

"And I appreciate it, Joe. He won't let you down." He turned to me, "Now off home. Your mother will need to get your clothes ready for work. I have an old bait tin for thee."

Whenever my father and his mates got together then his words became more old-fashioned. He never used thee at home but I noticed that in the pub and when he chatted on the corner with other men then he sounded more Lancastrian. I suppose I noticed because I was used to Trooper's lilting Welsh voice. I walked home feeling strange. I had left the world of children and was now entering the world of grown-ups. Many young men my age had been at work for a number of years. Marjorie had been working since she had been ten. She was a rag picker for the nimble fingers of young girls helped with the work. I suppose that I had been cosseted by Trooper. I had not noticed the lads I knocked around with going to work. His death and employment would change my life. Of course, I knew that I would not be keeping the three shillings and sixpence I would be earning. I would be given some but it would be handed over to my mother and she would take board and keep from it. I would retain a shilling if I was lucky, and the rest would go into the upkeep of the family house.

I told my mother what my father had said. Nodding she said, "I have some old work trousers of your father's. They are a bit ragged at the bottom but Alice and Mary can cut off the worst and make you a new hem. You have still some growing to do. The same with your father's old shirts. The girls can put in pleats." She held my shoulders in her hands and looked me in the eye. Mother always looked weary but when her eyes held mine there was a sparkle there, still. "I know you are upset by the death of Trooper but look on this as a new chapter of your life. You begin anew. Starting work is like being reborn."

"Is that how you felt when you began work, Mother?"

The sparkle disappeared and she turned to stir the pan that was on the stove, "Bless you, I never got the chance to work. I looked after your granddad while he was ill and then your father married me and I had you." Her back to me, she waved a wooden spoon around the tiny kitchen. "This is my work and this is my world."

I went behind her and put my arms around her. I knew that she was crying and that she had little in her life, "You deserve more, Mother."

She sniffed and her back stiffened, "Aye, love, but deserving and getting are a world apart. It will be hard for you but stick in. Do what you are told and don't answer back. Pritchard's is a good firm and you could get on." I don't think she believed what she was saying but she was a good mother and was saying the right thing.

The girls and Billy bustled in, having been playing in the street. I turned, "Right you three, time to get washed up for tea."

Alice put her hands on her hips, "And who are you to tell me what to do Jack Roberts?"

I grinned, "I am your big brother and as I start work on Monday, then I am a wage earner so you mind your manners."

The three of them were excited. They knew that starting work meant more money coming into the house. We might get a bigger piece of meat for Sunday lunch and they might get a sliver more of it. Mother might be able to buy more sugar and make treacle toffee or tea loaf. The possibilities for the extra coppers were endless. Of course, the four of us would still have to share a bed. The house would not suddenly grow but life would be better and that pleased them.

Pritchard's was dirty and it was clear why I had been employed. I learned I had more duties than just being the tea lad. They called it the can lad as when I made the tea, I carried it around the foundry in a large can. It was fortunate that I was strong. I also had to sweep up their work areas. At first, it terrified me as sparks flew and tiny pieces of molten metal could splash. I learned to avoid such dangers. I also had to run errands. There was an office there and if the clerks needed anything at all then I would be sent to the stores to get it or, failing that, nip into town to buy it. I never stopped and there was always someone calling my name. In many ways that helped me as the days flew by and time passed quickly. When the hooter went for lunch, I was ready for the bait my mother had made for me. The first week was the same diet, thin slivers of cheese on homemade bread with an apple but as my money began to come into the family then there was thinly sliced ham and homemade biscuits. I ate better as I grew older.

We had a routine in our house that went from the food we ate to the tasks my mother and now my siblings completed. As payday was Friday then we enjoyed fish and chips on Friday night or if she could get some from the fishmongers up North Road, fish with potatoes and a white sauce. Saturday was usually ham, potatoes, and peas with a white sauce my mother made. Sunday was the highlight of the week. We would have Sunday dinner: meat, roast potatoes, Yorkshire pudding, cabbage, and veg. As I started to earn money so we would have a suet pudding for afters. Monday was leftovers day and the meat and any veg left over would be put into a pan with other vegetables and the left-over gravy to make what my mother called lobscouse. Tuesday was usually sausages, mashed potato and gravy or sometimes liver and bacon. Wednesday was getting towards the end of the week. We had bacon scraps, fried eggs and chips. Any sausages that were left would be given to my father and we looked enviously at his laden plate. Despite the fact that I was earning money my portions did not increase. Thursday, the end of the week, financially, usually meant liver, kidneys or tripe; some kind of offal. It was cheap and there was plenty of it. With the best gravy in the world and mashed potatoes, it was one of my favourite meals. Mother made loaves every day and there was always bread to fill up on.

The weekly tasks were also regimented. Monday was wash day and it was all hands to the pumps. It was not until I sailed to South Africa that I learned that was a nautical expression. We had clothes to boil and I was normally, until I began work, given the task of using the three-legged posser to turn the clothes, it was backbreaking work. The clothes would all be rinsed and then passed through a mangle before being rinsed and mangled a second time. We always prayed that Monday would be fine and blowy so that the clothes would dry. If not, we would have to endure the damp smell of the clothes and my father hated that. Tuesday would be ironing day with the iron heated on the fire. Wednesday was baking day although my mother baked bread every day. Wednesday saw her making biscuits and pies. When apples were in season then it was apple pie. If there was any lobscouse left over from Monday's meal then it would be a meat and veg pie. Thursday was cleaning day upstairs while Friday saw downstairs being swept, washed and scrubbed. Saturday was shopping day for my mother had money to spend and we would all head down to St Helen's market. Sunday was the day we were all scrubbed and dressed in our best clothes and taken to church. Father never came but we all marched with mother to church and while we went to Sunday School she would walk home and begin work on Sunday dinner while my Father drank in the pub and played dominoes with his mates.

That first year at Pritchard's passed quickly. We had a tiny bit more money coming in when Alice and Mary began work as apprentice tailoresses, for Joan Stretch. She lived around the corner in Gleave Street and it was handy for the girls were able to walk to work with Joan. She and her husband, Albert, had no children of their own and it did all three of them good. They were given a shilling a week each and poor Billy, the youngest, was the one left at home to do all the chores the four of us had done the year before.

I learned a great deal at Pritchard's. I learned to weigh people up. My life was fairly solitary as I was by far the youngest. The others all smoked pipes and went to the pub. They gambled. I did none of those things. I wondered when I would be allowed to smoke a pipe. Many youths my age did so but my mother was adamant that I would not. I was almost invisible in that crowded foundry that was full of noise and people. I watched. Trooper had told me not just about the battle he had been in but about life in the army. He was preparing me for a world of work that would last a lifetime. He had told me to watch people before I judged them.

"You will see folk, Jack, who are lazy. They look like they are working as hard as the next man but they are not. Be wary of such men. They cannot be relied upon. Look for those who knuckle down and keep working no matter what the difficulty." He had sighed, "And then there are them as are less than honest. They steal even when there is no need. Watch out for them. If they steal then they have no scruples or morals."

I soon saw what he meant. Going around with the tea I saw men slipping some of the work they had made into their aprons.

They would sell it later on. I was not so foolish as to inform on them but those that did get caught, normally because they were incompetent, were sacked by Joe Stafford on the spot. It was just such a sacking, a year after I had begun work that led to my promotion and more pay. It was an important lesson. Bob Harrison, who was sacked for thieving, had recently married and his wife was carrying their child. The last thing Bob needed was unemployment. As I was promoted to join the Iron Gang, I realised that the money he would have had for the door fittings would have been a shilling or two. He lost a shilling a day for his crime. Before I had begun work I had not known what the Iron Gang was. I learned that they were the labourers who did all the heavy lifting. If a machine needed to be taken out and cleaned in an acid bath then they would have to lift it, put it on a bogey and take it out to the baths. My muscles grew every day for the work was hard and more than a little dangerous.

I was not paid a shilling a day as the pay was age-related. Although I was doing the same work Bob had done, I was only paid nine pence a day but overnight my pay had increased. Even my father was pleased. It was Friday night when I was given the news and I could not wait to tell him, although when he came back from *'The Feathers'* he had already been told by Joe. It took some of the gloss from my story.

"Then tomorrow I shall take you with me to have your first pint in *'The Feathers'*. Just the one mind."

My mother's glowering face told me what she thought of that. My mum didn't drink. Bearing in mind that she was Irish and her father died of drink, that was no surprise. I gave an apologetic shrug of the shoulders. I determined that it would be just the one.

The last time I had been in the pub had been when I had been given my first job. This time it was even busier and filled with the stink of pipe smoke and spilt ale. My father took me to the bar and, for the first time, seemed almost proud of me, "This is my son, Jack, and he is going to have his first pint." I saw him look down the bar at the pumps and it seemed to make up his mind. "Give me a pint of the usual, Harry, and a pint of mild for the lad."

The landlord, a grim, dour-looking man who in all the time I knew him, never smiled, pulled my father's pint. It was a light brown beer with a foaming head that rose high above the glass. I had seen beer before and even tasted it, for when he was ill once I had been sent to *'The Miner's Arms'* to buy a jug of beer and I had sampled it on the way back. That beer had seemed flatter. My beer was a black beer and, disappointingly to me, the head barely touched the rim. I was handed my beer and my father said, "Cheers."

I think that day was the closest I ever came to my father. He talked to me, that day, about his hopes for me and my future. He had sent me to work at Pritchard's, not as a punishment but as the first steps to becoming a man. My father equated hard work with being a man. He also hinted at the schism between him and his family. I knew that he and his father had rowed about something. Each year, at Christmas, we made an annual pilgrimage to Thatto Heath where his mother and father lived with my Uncle Tom and his family. I did not like my cousins and the visit was to be dreaded. In contrast, my visits to Liverpool with my mother, my father never came, were a delight. Mary Hogan was a wonderful little old lady who lived with her unmarried daughter, Sarah Ann. They lived in a house the size of ours and it seemed palatial after ours for there were just two of them and six of us lived in ours. My nan used to make her own butter and lemon curd. Her bread was even better than my mother's. We visited her three or four times a year. Her birthday, Boxing Day and Easter. I looked forward to all of those.

After one visit, on the way back to St Helens on the train I asked, "Why hasn't Auntie Sarah married?"

It was an innocent question but patently upset my mother, who was normally happy on the way home having seen her sister and mother. She glanced at my brother and sisters who were busy with their noses pressed against the steamed window making faces. She sighed and hissed in my ear, "I suppose you are old enough to know but not a word to anyone else."

I was intrigued. This sounded like a secret and who doesn't like a secret? I nodded and made the sign of the cross over my heart.

"There was a young man who took advantage of your auntie and then left her." She paused, "Broke her heart and put her off men."

I had wondered why she always looked so serious and wore black more often than not. "But she has a good job."

Mother nodded, "She threw herself into work and was promoted. She is in charge of one of the offices at the British and North American Royal Mail Steam-Packet Company." Having got that mouthful out my mother smiled, "She is well thought of and earns a lot of money. That is rare for someone from our background and for a woman... I am proud of my sister. She has done what I did not do, make something of her life."

I thought about that, "But didn't you look after your father? Was that not something to be proud of?"

"That is the duty every child owes its parents and was a Christian thing to do. You cannot be proud of doing what is right. We all should."

And that ended the conversation. It was also a mark of my progress to becoming an adult for she had given me the respect of the truth, unpalatable though it might be.

My world changed again six months after I had turned seventeen. There was an accident at Pilkington's. There were always accidents but they had never touched us. Perhaps my father was getting slow, or old, perhaps the drink and his pipe-smoking had got to him, but, whatever the reason, when the bucket strap broke on the molten glass above his head and his gang managed to escape, my father did not. Mr Pilkington was genuinely upset and the £10 compensation he gave to my mother was unexpected but my mother knew it would not be enough. He also paid for the funeral. We had to do things right and so a pound of the compensation was spent on the food for the wake. As we laid him in the ground I glanced over and saw that Trooper's grave was covered with grass and indistinguishable from the other markerless graves. I felt guilty for I had not visited since I had placed flowers there the week after he had died.

Father had little to leave. I was given his clothes for they were too big for Billy but Billy was given his pocket watch. I didn't mind for a clerk would have more need of such a gift than a labourer in an iron gang. After the funeral, as darkness came and the last of the mourners had long gone, my mother sat with the four of us. She had been a rock after my father had died for

Billy, especially, was broken-hearted and she had not cried in public. The night before the funeral, when my father had lain in his coffin on the table in the parlour I went downstairs and heard my mother sobbing over the corpse of my father. It was a sealed coffin. The undertaker had said that it would do no one any good to see the body. It was a measure, I think, of her love for him. I did not intrude but when she left and came to go upstairs, I held my arms open and she put her head on my chest and cried some more. It was then I realised how much I had grown for she seemed small.

"Don't worry, Mother, I will be here for you. Don't fret. I am earning better money now."

She had looked up at me and nodded but her eyes were sad, "Perhaps."

As we sat, all in our best, me wearing my father's second-best suit and a black tie bought especially for the funeral from Tyrers in the town, I realised that I was now the man of the house. I was seated in what had been my father's chair, by the fire. Someone had brought half a bottle of brandy to the funeral and I saw something unique. My mother was sipping a small glass of it.

"Well, your father has gone and with it, I am afraid, is our home." None of us had thought of that. We were too caught up in the death of John Roberts. My mouth dropped open and she put a hand on my knee, "Even with your wages, Jack, and the little the girls bring in we can't afford the rent. We have to move."

I had heard of earthquakes but never experienced one. I think my mother's words gave me a glimpse of what one was like. I was sat down but my legs felt like jelly and I was finding it hard to breathe. I had only ever lived here. Where would we go? My nan and Auntie Sarah had been the last to leave and the three of them had been deep in conversation and when she spoke, I realised why. "Aunt Sarah said we can live with them but it means moving to Liverpool."

She had a sip of brandy. There was more to come. "Billy can sleep in Nan's bed and I shall sleep with Auntie Sarah. Billy, she says there is a position for an office boy. It will lead to a job as a clerk. Your father would be pleased."

I looked at my sisters. They had not been mentioned, nor had I.

Mother looked at the girls, "Alice, Mary, you get on with Mrs Stretch, don't you?" They both nodded for I could see that their eyes were brimming with tears. Both were on the cusp of being women but this was something hard to bear. "She is happy to have you as lodgers so that you can continue to work for her. She is happy with your work and she will board you as well."

Alice seemed to find her voice first, "But we won't be living with you."

Mother nodded and I could see how hard this was for her. I heard the catch in her voice as she spoke. Whatever she said to me I would make the best of it. "I shall come over, with Billy, every Sunday on the train and we shall spend the day together and I will always be there for you." Her voice cracked, "I didn't want this but I am doing the best that I can. I don't want us to get in debt. The money Mr Pilkington gave us will soon go. I shall have to pay my way at our Sarah's." She downed the brandy.

I stepped up and became the man, "Don't you worry, Mother, we know you are doing the best, don't we, girls?"

I think the downing of the brandy was sufficient enough of a shock for them to nod and then smile, "Mrs Stretch is a nice lady. It is not as though we are going to the poor house is it, Mary?"

Mary was younger, just thirteen and she put on a brave face, "And we will see you every Sunday, won't we?"

"Of course."

She was silent and all eyes turned to me. It was clear to me that I didn't fit into the picture. I knew that Mrs Sharratt still had rooms and it might be fitting if I lodged with her. I made it easy for the others, "I shall be fine. I will see Mrs Sharratt and ask if she has a room available."

Mother looked relieved but her words showed her concern, "Are you sure? I mean you could sleep in Nan's parlour."

"But my job is here and I don't fancy the ride to work every morning. No, I am a man now and I need to make my own way. I will be fine."

"There are all your dad's old clothes and…" She stopped, "We buried him in his best suit…"

I smiled, "I wouldn't worry about that. I don't go anywhere I would wear one. Don't you worry about me."

I knew she would. Just as Billy had been my father's favourite I was my mother's, and as we spent the next week packing up our belongings I caught her glancing at me often. She would touch my hand gently or stroke my hair. We sold the furniture to neighbours and they collected it on the Saturday morning when we left. Mrs Sharratt had a room for me but it would take half of my wages. Any hopes I had of saving money would be dashed. I might have to use trooper's guinea. The girls' belongings were already at Joan Stretch's and we had a tearful goodbye as we parted. The three of us didn't have far to go to Central Station but we were laden like pack animals. We had less than a mile to walk from Lime Street Station to Tibley Street but we had to stop often. Billy and I were carrying all that we could but my mother was struggling.

It was dark by the time we finished unpacking and Nan said, "You can't go back tonight, Jack. Sleep in the parlour. I have made a nice cow heel stew."

I did not need much persuading for Nan's cow heel stew, made with a couple of calves' feet and served with Nan's legendary mash was persuasion enough but, in truth, I was loath to say goodbye. It was all very well saying we would meet up every Sunday but quite another to expect it to last.

I didn't drink much but, after we had eaten the meal mother said, "Why don't you nip out for a pint, Jack? We can make up your bed while you are out and it will remind me of your father."

Auntie Sarah said, "Aye, Jack, you look just like your father did when he wed our Mary. The *'Red Dragon'* on the corner is not a bad pub. Just stay away from the ones by the docks. The pubs are alright but they have women there!"

Mother said, "Our Sarah!"

"Well it is true, Mary, and there is no denying it. Jack is a good-looking young man and the trollops who frequent those kinds of places would have him on toast for breakfast."

I smiled. The whole family had a low opinion of women who went into pubs. I had been a regular in *'The Sefton Arms'* and the only women who frequented that pub were three widows who sat in the snug and drank milk stout, slowly.

I nodded and picked up my jacket, "I'll just have the one."

The three women all laughed and Auntie Sarah said, "And if you do then you will be the first man to do so."

I went outside to the gas-lit street and headed down to the pub on the corner. It was as I neared it that I saw the flash of red uniform. There were soldiers here. I had seen the Loyal Lancashires recruiting in St Helen's occasionally but that had not been for some time. Trooper had told me that after every major war the army got rid of surplus men, to save money. Often, regiments were reduced to one battalion. I wondered which regiment this was. I saw them accosting the men who approached the pub. Trooper had already spoken to me of the devious methods that might be employed. They would invite you in for a drink and then slip a coin, sometimes into the beer, or if they were deft enough, your pockets and you would be a soldier of the Queen. It was as I neared them and heard them speak that I quickened my step. The sergeant and the private had Welsh accents and reminded me so much of Taff that I cared not if they tried to trick me into signing up. I knew my own mind and I could not leave my mother so soon after my father's death.

As I drew closer to them, I saw that their collars were green and had the Sphinx with the clasp Egypt. It was the 24th. Trooper had described the uniform to me once as one of his brothers had been in it. The three of them wore their forage caps at a jaunty angle. It was the regiment that Trooper had tried to join. They were not watching me for the officer drawled, "I don't think, Sergeant Bourne, that we will find any recruits here. It seems like a waste of time to me." I noticed that the officer spoke overly loudly and had to cup a hand around his ear to hear the sergeant's reply.

"Patience Lieutenant Bromhead, these things take time. We have been here barely an hour and the chaps will be coming to the pub after work."

Just then I was seen by the private, an older soldier than the officer and with a grey flecked beard, "Here is a likely lad, sir. Look at those shoulders. He would make a fine soldier."

The officer looked bored but the sergeant smiled, "You are right Private Cooper. What do you say, lad, do you fancy a fine red uniform to attract the girls, eh? See the world and leave Liverpool far behind."

I know now that it was a stupid thing to say but I answered, "I come from St Helen's."

The officer rolled his eyes but the sergeant grinned even more, "Excellent, young man, you like to be precise and those are the qualities we seek in the 24th Foot. We are soon off to South Africa and the chance for glory."

"I have a job," I said weakly for I could not take my eyes off the red uniforms. I had kept polished the buttons and the plume clasp in Trooper's metal box and seeing the gleaming buttons on these three uniforms was like the nectar of a flower to a bee. I could not take my eyes from them.

"And what is it that you do, if you don't mind me asking?"

"I work in a foundry."

"Why then you are used to the heat. Come inside and I shall buy you a pint."

"I will come into the pub with you but I shall buy my own beer."

Clapping an arm around me the sergeant said, "As sharp as a tack too. Come and I will give you reasons to become a soldier. There will be no trickery here."

The officer obviously thought he had done enough and said, "Sergeant Bourne, I shall return to the hotel. I will see you there later."

"Yes sir." As he led me into the pub he said in my ear, "Officers, eh. Now we can talk more openly."

The pub was busy but not yet full. It was too early. Men were still working and as it was Saturday many would only come to the pub when they had dined. We reached the bar and I said, "A pint of mild."

The barman had a very strong Liverpool accent, "Dark or light, we have both."

"Dark."

He looked at the two soldiers, "Are you buying?"

The sergeant, I had realised his name was Bourne, said, "We will have two halves of bitter if you please but this young man is buying his own."

The barman grinned, "Not so green as you look eh, lah?"

Sergeant Bourne spied a table with three chairs and said, "Private Cooper, be so good as to acquire that table for us, eh?"

"Yes, Sarn't."

I pointedly counted out the coins for the beer, noticing that it was half a penny dearer than in St Helen's. I sipped a mouthful and realised it was not as good either. I sat down next to the private and we waited for Sergeant Bourne. I would hear what they said and then politely decline their offer.

When he sat Sergeant Bourne held up his tankard, "Cheers."

"Cheers."

"And what is your name, young man?"

"Jack Roberts."

"A fine Welsh name. Pleased to meet you, young sir," Sergeant Bourne nodded to the private, "This is a genuine hero. See that medal ribbon on his chest?" He jabbed a finger at a purple ribbon. "That is a Victoria Cross. The highest award in the British Army. That is the calibre of the men you would be joining if you became a soldier of the Queen. Tell the young man your story, Jim."

I knew what the sergeant was doing, he was effacingly friendly and using a familiar address to the private but I knew from Trooper, that it would not be the normal form of address.

The private nodded and after swallowing half of the beer said, "Well, Jack, we were in the east, on the Andaman Islands. There they have wild men, cannibals and they captured some of our lads. We were sent in to rescue them. It was fierce hot work but we rescued every one of them and not a man among us was hurt. The Queen herself pinned the medal on my chest."

"Cannibals?" The thought sent shivers down my spine.

The sergeant hurriedly added, "Don't you worry, Jack, Africa is more civilised, as is India. All we are going to do is protect the people who are there. The missionaries who are there to bring these people to God need our help. It is our Christian duty to help them. Now if it was the West Indies then I would be worried as they are riven with disease but I don't think we will end up there again."

I drank half of the beer. That was the argument that persuaded me. I don't think the sergeant knew that but I remembered Trooper's promise to God. He wanted to be a missionary and I had the chance to do what Trooper had wanted. I felt he would approve. What else did I have? I had no friends to speak of. I liked Pritchard's but if I left, they wouldn't miss me. I had once thought of courting Marjorie, who was a bonnie girl and I knew she liked me but she was walking out with a clerk from Pilkington's. There was just my mother and while she would miss me, I knew, in my heart, that she would want me to be happy and I thought that being in the army would make me happy. After all, Trooper had been happy. I drank some beer and I saw disappointment on the sergeant's face. He had thought he had lost me. I nodded, "I will sign up then Sergeant Bourne."

The two of them looked shocked but the sergeant recovered first, "A wise decision." He shook my hand and, holding it asked, "You are eighteen, aren't you?"

"Of course," I lied. It was not a major lie as I was almost eighteen.

The sergeant frowned. I don't think he believed me but he had no other recruits and was pragmatic enough to ignore it.

"Can you write or just make your mark?"

"I can read and I can write." For some reason I wanted to use Trooper as validation, "I was taught to read by a private from the Scots Greys who fought at Balaklava."

As he took out the document from his pouch, I saw that I had impressed him, "Well, that bodes well for you. Sign here." Private Cooper took out the ink and the pen and placed them before me.

Before I dipped the nib into the ink, I read the document first. I was committing myself to years of service and I hesitated.

"It is the right decision, son. You will see the world."

I nodded and dipped the pen into the ink for a second time. The nib hovered over the paper. Private Cooper said, "This is important, Jack. You sign this and there is no going back. Once you put pen to paper and it is witnessed then you belong to the army. If you don't show up at Brecon then you can be put in jail." The sergeant grunted and the private shrugged, "Sergeant, it is only right to tell him. I am getting out next month and I wouldn't be able to sleep at night if I thought he had joined because of this piece of ribbon on my chest."

The sergeant nodded, "You are right. Well, son, it is your decision."

I smiled and as I signed, I said, "That friend of mine always wanted to join this regiment. I shall join in his honour. Thank you... Jim, I appreciate what you are trying to do for me but I am not joining because of your medal. If anything that story put me off, sorry. I am joining because I think I was sent to this pub. The spirit of Trooper Thomas told me to do it. I am content." I looked him in the eye, "But just for ten years. I am not signing on for twenty-one years or life."

Nodding, the sergeant took out a blotter and dried the ink. He turned to the man at the next table. He had been watching us. The sergeant said, "Can you write?"

"No."

"Make your mark then to witness the signature." He handed him the pen and the man scratched an x. The sergeant said, "What is your name?"

"Albert Smith."

The sergeant wrote the name underneath the mark. He carefully folded the paper and then took out another from his satchel. He handed me some coins and the paper. "Here is a travel warrant. You have to report at the home depot at Brecon in one week's time; the Monday. That will give you time to sort out your affairs." I took them. He nodded to the empty tankard. "And now I will buy you the beer."

Jim Cooper said, "And I will have a pint this time, eh Sarge?" When the sergeant went to the bar Jim said, "As Sergeant's go, he isn't bad. He is a lifer. Me? I have done my time and I want a life. The army frowns on men who are married and I have barely seen my wife these last fifteen years. My eldest is not much younger than you. Keep your nose clean and you will do alright. You seem a clever lad. Just stay away from the bad 'uns. There are plenty enough of them."

The sergeant handed me my glass and said, "Welcome to the 24th. I shall keep my eye on you. You seem like a likely lad."

I wondered if he was right but I knew that telling my mother would be harder than any battle I would have to fight.

Chapter 3

I only had two pints and I returned to the house. It is funny but my mother knew as soon as I walked into the house that I had done something. She didn't know what but her eyes widened when she saw my face. Perhaps it was guilt, I don't know but she said, "What has happened?"

I had wanted to tell her in my own time but her words took the wind from my sails and I blurted out, "I have joined the army."

Auntie Sarah shook her head, "What on earth for?"

My nan began weeping. My mother just nodded, "When I took you to Sunday School, I didn't see this as a result. I wish I hadn't."

Auntie Sarah said, "Whatever do you mean, Mary?"

"An old soldier took him under his wing. His dad was always at work and Trooper Thomas is the reason he is joining up. I have lost my dearest son and he shall die in some foreign field."

I grabbed her and put my arms around her, "No, I won't. I promise you that I will come home and see you as often as I can. I don't want to work in a foundry all my life and I certainly don't want to work in a factory." I didn't mention my father but it was there, lurking behind my words and my mother's eyes told me she understood.

All through this Billy had stood with his mouth open. I could see he was upset. Father's death had hit him harder than any and I put my left arm out and my departure was too much of a change. He came and cuddled into Mother and me.

Auntie Sarah said, "How long do we have with you?"

"I shall have to be at the depot a week on Monday."

"A week!" Mother pulled away from me. "That isn't enough time. What about Pritchard's?"

"When I go home tomorrow, I shall go and speak with Joe. I will work until Friday and then, if it is alright with you, Nan, I will stay here and get the train on Monday."

"Of course, love."

"By the way, where is Brecon?"

Auntie Sarah laughed, she was an eminently practical woman, "South Wales. You have a long train journey. I will go to the station and find the times of the trains. We will make next weekend a good one. I shall buy a leg of lamb."

We all turned to look at her. I had never eaten a leg of lamb. Only rich people did that. At best we had eaten long stewed neck of lamb. That was delicious but imagining a whole leg made my mouth water.

She looked at our surprised faces, "Well, I can't see us all being together any time soon. We shall fetch the girls, eh Mary, and give your son a good send-off. He deserves that, no matter what he has done." She shook her head in disbelief, "Joined the army!"

I could see, in her eyes, that she thought she would never see me again and I wondered if she might be right.

Mrs Sharratt was happy enough about being given just a week's notice. I had only been there for a day and that was just to move my belongings in. She was more concerned that I was going into the army and she feared the result. She went to the understairs cupboard and brought out a khaki kit bag. "I found this, it was Trooper's. It will save you buying a suitcase."

I had not even thought of that. "Thank you, Mrs Sharratt."

Surprisingly Joe was just as understanding, "Just work until Thursday. Your mam will need to see as much of you as she can. I will see you are paid up to then." He bought me a pint and said, as I took a swallow, "You were never cut out for the work. Don't get me wrong, you were a hard worker but I could see that your mind was working all the time. I don't like to speak ill of the dead but your dad should have got you an apprenticeship where you could use that brain of yours. You can read and write. You are overqualified for the Iron Gang."

At work on Monday, I found that most of the others were unconcerned about my leaving. In fact, Peter Gormley was pleased as his younger brother was looking for a job and it all worked out. The week dragged by as I was desperate to leave Pritchard's and get to nan's. On Thursday Joe gave me my pay and a present. It was a good knife. Pritchard's made such knives and I knew that they were expensive. It had a leather sheath. Joe tried to make light of it, "The hilt on this one wasn't up to scratch and we were going to melt it down again but Mr Pritchard said you can have it. You might need it where you are going."

I had told all who wanted to know that I was going to South Africa and it seemed to be a lifetime away. "Thanks, Joe, I shall think of you when I use this."

He shook his head, "I hope you won't have to use it."

I looked at the knife and saw that it was more like a dagger. Eight inches long it had a slightly curved blade and was double-edged. It was a weapon and I knew now what it meant. I would be a soldier and put in harm's way. I might have to fight for my life one day. I went to Gleave Street, which was close to Central Station to tell Joan Stretch and the girls of the plans. Joan was tearful when I told her. The whole world seemed to think that joining the army was a death sentence. I didn't. The train was not the last one to Liverpool but close to it. I had not had time to tell anyone that I would be arriving on Thursday night. I had to bang on the door and it was an angry Auntie Sarah who answered it. The scowl left her face as soon as she saw me. "Our Jack! Your mam will be pleased. We have a whole extra day with you."

I did not move from the house from the moment I arrived. I wanted to spend as much time with my family as I could. I didn't mind the uncomfortable couch upon which I slept or the crowded nature of a house used to just two people. When mother fetched my sisters on Saturday then we were all together. As children we had always got on; we had to, sharing one bedroom but my imminent departure and the death of my father had made us all much closer. Mother and my sisters sorted through the clothes I would be taking. I would not need much as the army would provide most of it but they made my father's clothes fit better. The kitbag proved a Godsend and everything fitted in perfectly.

On Sunday evening after a Sunday dinner that was the finest food I had ever eaten: leg of lamb, roast potatoes, Yorkshire pudding, carrots, peas and new potatoes, all with mint sauce, I sat before the fire in the second-best chair, feeling like a king. The tiny house could have felt crowded but it did not. It was just cosy. Already my mother was planning the food they would eat from the leftovers. It would last until Thursday.

Auntie Sarah nodded, "See, you all thought a leg of lamb was expensive. Look how many meals we can eat this week."

Billy was a wit too, "Aye, Auntie Sarah, and by Friday we shall be bleating like lambs ourselves."

She playfully cuffed him about the head and then turned to me. "I have sorted the trains out. It is not an easy journey and there are many changes." She smiled, "It will keep your mind occupied, eh? You need to get the Birkenhead ferry and get the train from Birkenhead Station. You will need to change stations in Hereford. The Great Western station is at Barrs Court and you have to get across the town to Barton to get the Midland train." She smiled, "It will keep you on your toes." She was her usual efficient self and my itinerary was detailed. She would have made a good soldier.

We sat before the fire and did as all families do at such times. Nan was the font that contained all the family history and she spoke of the family. I had never met my grandfather; he had died before I was born but she spoke of them all growing up in Ireland. Mother and Auntie Sarah spoke of coming across to England on a ship for there was no work at home. The contrast between life in the country and the crowded streets of Liverpool must have been a real shock. It made me think that I would have an equal shock for, from what I had been told, the lands to which we might be sent had few cities. Africa or India seemed the favourite. I had heard many of the stories but Billy hadn't and I saw his eyes as he took in our family history. It was strange, I knew more about my mother's family history than my father's. We were just not as close to my father's side.

When Nan became tired she rose, wearily and came to kiss me goodnight, "You take care, our Jack and you come back home. I pray to God that I shall still be alive but if not know that I shall be in heaven. If I am then I will watch over you."

The thought of Nan dying filled me with terror and I hugged her in silence. I dared not speak for if I tried then tears would flow and I was now the man of the house... and I would soon be deserting them.

Nan waited at the foot of the narrow stairs, waiting for Auntie Sarah who came to kiss me goodnight too. Monday would be a work day for Auntie Sarah and she would be away before I left.

"I don't agree with your decision but I can see that it is something you have to get out of your system. When your time is up then don't rejoin. Come home. There will always be a place for you here."

I hugged her, "It would be crowded, Auntie Sarah."

"Where family is concerned you can never be too crowded. Just come home safe."

"Come on, our Sarah, my legs are going to sleep and I would like to join them."

"Coming, Mother." She rolled her eyes, kissed her fingertips and placed them on my lips.

That left just the five of us and Mother went over to the fire to spread the coals and make it begin to die down. She went to the front door and made sure that it was locked. Night was the only time it was locked. She turned and said, "You three, say goodnight. You have an early start in the morning. I have to get you girls to Joan Stretch's in time for work. Say goodnight to your big brother."

Alice and Mary threw their arms around me, "Don't get killed, Jack."

Alice shook her head, "Our Mary, what a thing to say. We will miss you, Jack, so write home, when you can. We shall keep all your letters I promise." They stood on tiptoes and kissed me on the cheeks.

"I will write, I promise and you two be good. Help at home when you can." I realised that our home had gone. They would grow distant from our mother. I saw them both married with families. It made me sad for I knew that I would not be at their weddings. Who would give them away? Was I making a mistake?

Mother went to the back door to check it and Billy approached, "I will try to look after Mother, Jack but …" he rushed to me and buried his head in my chest, "I miss father and with you gone they will expect me to be the man of the house."

"And you will be. Don't forget you start work in a month or so. Trust me that will test you. I will write whenever I can but I am relying on you to watch out for mother."

"And I will."

She came back in and said, "Off you go, Billy, I will be up soon enough."

We were left alone with just the gaslight and glowing fire. It threw strange shadows on the walls. I took a deep breath and stood as tall as I could. I was a man and had to act like one. I reached into my waistcoat pocket and took out Trooper's guinea, "This is for you and I mean, you. Spend it on yourself."

Her eyes widened as I put the gold coin in her hand, "Where did you get this?"

"Trooper left it to me."

"I can't take this."

I folded her fingers over it, "Of course, you can. You don't think I need it, do you? The army will be paying me. Uniform, food, accommodation and pay! A shilling a day even on your days off. Rich as Croesus, am I." I laughed and watched her shake her head.

"I never thought this day would come. I mean I expected you to leave home one day but I thought that would be when you met a girl. Marjorie Allerton and you seemed made for each other."

"She is walking out with a young man, mother. That ship has sailed."

"There might have been another. I thought I would be able to visit and see your grandchildren but now..."

Her hand went to her handkerchief and her eyes and I put my arms around her, "Hey, none of that. I don't know what my future holds but when I leave the army I will come back. I only signed on for ten years. I will still be a young man when I return and then I can think about what I want to do."

"And what will that be? Do you think the Army will teach you a trade? You will have to work unskilled in a factory. I wanted more for you than that."

I said, quietly, "And what would that have been if I had stayed in St Helen's, mother? Working in the Iron Gang at Pritchard's until the strength left me and then thrown onto the street? Where is the skill in that? This way I have a pension after the army. You see, I am thinking."

"I wanted you to have a trade but..."

I knew that she and my father had argued but until then I had not known it was about me. I shrugged, "And I might have liked that but now what can I do?"

"You aren't eighteen. The paper you signed means nothing. You could work at Auntie Sarah's."

"Billy has the job that was going and, besides, I am not sure that I like the idea of being a clerk. I don't know yet what I want but I know it isn't that and it isn't working for the rest of my life in a factory."

I saw the resigned look on my mother's face and I held her in my arms. I felt her sobbing into my chest and I held her until the sobs subsided.

"Mother." Alice's voice came from the stairs.

"Coming." She shook herself clear and said, "I must look a mess. I shall keep this guinea and when you return, I shall use it to throw a party the like of which none has ever seen."

I smiled and nodded, "I would rather you spent it on you."

"And a party for my dearest son is for me." She went upstairs.

After turning off the gaslight I lay on the couch and watched the fire slowly die and thought about our lives. I don't remember closing my eyes but I must have done for the next thing I remember was being shaken awake by Billy.

"Come on our Jack. Your train isn't until later but the rest of them have to get off to work or catch the early train."

In many ways, it helped that we did not have the time for a long goodbye. Mother and the girls snatched a quick breakfast of bread and butter before rushing off to Lime Street for the train to St Helen's. Auntie Sarah soon followed and that left just me, Nan and Billy. Nan insisted on cooking me a fried breakfast of bacon, eggs and toast. I had barely finished it when I realised that I had to get to the station myself.

Billy wanted to walk to the station with me but I shook my head. Nan looked lost, "You stay with Nan. Today you really do become the man of the house and you need to look after the women, right?"

"Right, Jack."

I held my hand out and he shook it. I saw his back stiffen. He would step up to the mark.

Chapter 4

The journey south was lonely and long. The crossing of the Mersey on the ferry seemed to me to represent the great change from one life to the next; from civilian to soldier. I had no watch and relied upon the clocks in the stations as we passed to gauge the passage of time. It took two hours to reach Shrewsbury and my first change of train. I watched England and then Wales pass by from the window of the Third-Class carriage. At Shrewsbury, I had more than two hours to wait for my next train down to Hereford. I amused the two children of a mother who was also heading south too by pulling faces and doing silly tricks with my fingers. They were awaiting a train, however, to Wolverhampton and when they had gone I sat alone watching trains chug and hiss their way into and out of the station. They were a way to mark the passage of time. The travel pass did not warrant better accommodation. The hard seat on the platform was uncomfortable until I put my overcoat underneath me. I wondered when I would need my civilian clothes again. No one else was travelling as far as I was and although the people I met were friendly enough the conversations just punctuated the journey. Nan had made me plenty of food and I ate that in portions to help pass the time. The sandwiches were my favourite and as well as fruit there were homemade scones. I did not starve. I had a mile to walk when I reached Hereford and I enjoyed the walk. With Trooper's kit bag over my shoulder, I stepped out smartly. I reached Brecon at twenty past five by the station clock and after speaking to the station master found that the barracks were in the central part of the town at the Watton.

I stood across the street from the barracks and studied the two sentries. This was a momentous step. My mother was right. If I told them I was not eighteen then the contract I had signed would be invalid. I still had the chance to back out. I watched some workers as they trudged back home; they looked weary and worn down. I had no idea where they had been at work but they were dirty and had hangdog expressions. In contrast, I watched four soldiers emerge from the barrack gates in their smart red uniforms with forage caps at a jaunty angle as they stepped out of the barracks. They were laughing and they strode in the opposite direction to the workers. I think that decided me. I had seen workers in St Helen's heading for the glass and chemical works. It was dirty and dangerous work. The life of a soldier seemed cleaner and it could hardly be more dangerous. I remembered Trooper telling me that when he had been in the Battle of Balaklava less than ten men had been killed. That seemed reasonable odds to me. I stepped across the road and presented myself to the corporal.

"Yes, can I help you?" he had the lilting Welsh accent I had heard in the pub.

I stood to what I hoped was attention. "I signed on, Corporal, and was asked to report here."

The private standing with the corporal grinned and said, "It looks like we are taking on foreigners now Corp."

"1216, pipe down and fetch the duty sergeant."

I was confused about the use of a number.

"Yes, Corp."

He sped off.

"Have you come far today?"

"Liverpool, Corporal."

He nodded, "A fair journey but you don't sound like a scouser."

I shook my head and said proudly, "I am from St Helen's."

"Aah." He had no idea where that was.

It was Sergeant Bourne who came to fetch me. He nodded when he saw the kit bag next to me. "Good, you are organised. That bodes well but, Jack Roberts, when I said to get here on Monday I meant early in the morning. You will have to wait until tomorrow to get kitted out."

I said, lamely, "Sorry, sergeant, I caught the first train I could."

"Not a good start. Pick up your bag and follow me." I saw the corporal and private grinning. I guessed my discomfort brought them pleasure.

I learned the names of all the places we went to later but on that first evening, I just followed him like a lost sheep and had you asked me to retrace my steps then I would have struggled. He marched me to the battalion office where a corporal and a private went through my details. I had memorised the correct year of birth and as that was the only lie then I managed to navigate those difficult waters relatively easily. I was measured and weighed and when all was done, I had to sign what seemed like an interminable sheaf of papers. All the time Sergeant Bourne smacked his swagger stick off his palm as though he was counting out beats. It was unnerving.

That done he said, "Follow me and be smart about it."

He led me to the barrack block and a large hut with the number 2/24/1 emblazoned on it in white paint. When he opened the door, I saw that there were just three men in a room with twenty beds. At the bottom end was a bed with blankets draped around it and I guessed that there was someone in there for I could hear a conversation.

"You are a lucky lad, you get to choose your bed. Find one, dump your bag on it and then follow me."

The men, seated around a table and playing cards whilst smoking pipes just stared at me noncommittally. I saw where the made up beds were and chose one on the opposite side. It seemed to me that I would be more likely to make friends with new men rather than with ones who were already serving. Sergeant Bourne's face gave the hint of a smile. He led me to the mess hall. There were just a couple of soldiers dining there and the cooks were clearing up.

Sergeant Bourne nodded to the plates and cutlery, "Get yourself some eating irons and then see what is left." He shook his head, "If you had arrived earlier…"

As I picked up the plate, knife, fork and spoon I said, lamely, "There was no earlier train."

"You could have travelled on Sunday."

I thought about the meal I had enjoyed with my family and smiling shook my head. The problems I might endure as a result of travelling on Monday were worth it for that special time I had enjoyed.

The cooks slopped some boiled potatoes, carrots, cabbage and some thin gravy with pieces of some indeterminate meat lurking within and the cook nodded to the end where there was an empty metal tray with crumbs in it and a thin watery custard. "All the sponge has gone but you can have some custard if you like."

"No, thank you…" I did not know the man's rank and as he was not wearing a uniform I just said, "Sir."

Sergeant Bourne said, "Cook will do. Officers do not cook."

We sat at a table and I began to eat. The food was not hot and the fat was beginning to congeal but I felt obliged to eat. Sergeant Bourne sat opposite me and, taking out a pipe began to smoke. I had been the only one at Pritchard's who had not smoked a pipe and I was used to the smoke and the smell. My father had smoked one and my mother had often complained about the burns on his clothes. I saw that Sergeant Bourne ensured that any ash fell on the table and not his uniform.

"You didn't change your mind then?"

My mouth full I just shook my head and held his gaze. He just nodded and studied me. When I had finished, I put the knife, fork and spoon crossways across the plate as I had been taught by my mother. The food had not been pleasant but I knew that had I left any then I might have made enemies of the cooks. One of the orderlies came over and took my plate. I guessed it was so that they could finish their duty rather than out of some act of kindness.

"Tell me more about this cavalryman who made you want to sign up."

That was easy and I chattered like a magpie as I tried to recall all that Trooper had told me. The sergeant nodded as I went through it. "Seems like a good chap." He tapped his pipe out on his hand and leaned forward, "Listen, Roberts, you seem like a nice lad and I can see your reasons for joining up but you should know that there are all sorts in the battalion. You need to keep your wits about you."

It did not escape my notice that he had stopped using my Christian name and I was now a surname. Suddenly the corporal at the gates use of a number rather than a name made sense, I would soon be a number.

"Will we be going abroad any time soon, Sergeant Bourne?"

"They don't tell the likes of us that, Roberts. We will find out soon enough but I will say that we have more recruits arriving daily and there is a rumour, and it is only that, mind, that the regiment will be sailing soon. Why do you ask?"

"Trooper told me that the lads who were killed first were the ones who were the newest. The older hands survived."

He gave me a sad smile, "As I say he sounds like a good chap and he may be right but there is a difference between cavalry and infantry. The cavalry has the ability to run if things go badly for them and we don't. We fight shoulder to shoulder and rely on every soldier doing his duty. The first six weeks you are here we will teach you all there is to know about the rifle that you will be using and you will march until your feet are bleeding. We will all bark at you but in the end, the bleeding feet, the drills and, above all, the commands will save your life." He stood, "Anyway, it is time you went to the barracks. Five a.m. will come round soon enough and thanks to your late arrival you will stand out like a sore thumb until we get you a uniform and equipment. You will need a thick skin, Private Roberts."

I stood and stiffened standing at what I thought was attention, "I won't let you down, Sergeant Bourne."

He shook his head, "Don't let yourself down is more important at the moment and later, when you are trained, then it is the regiment you will need to think about. Never let the regiment down." He nodded towards the barracks door. "There was room in the other barrack blocks but the ones in there are good chaps and you won't be led astray." He smiled, "My father was a lay preacher and very fond of the psalms. I see you, Roberts, as a lamb that needs looking after until he finds his feet."

I entered the lamp-lit barracks alone. There were now four men in the room and they were still playing cards and the air was thick with pipe smoke. I would have to get used to that. There was a bowl of water and a jug in the corner and after taking off my jacket and shirt I washed myself. One of the card players shouted over, "Come here, young man, and don't skulk in the corner like some thief in the night."

I saw the other three grinning and I went over. The authority in the man's voice was commanding. I went over and they all examined me. The authoritative private said, "Well then, name?"

"Jack Roberts."

He pointed over to my bed, "And why, did you put your stuff over there? Frightened we would bite?"

"I didn't want to upset anyone."

A female voice came from behind the blanket, "Henry, give the boy a chance. He is new here."

The private stroked his moustache and nodded, "You are right. I am Henry Hook, and this is 716 Robert Jones, 1303 John Williams and 794, Alf Thomas. We have only been here for a few months ourselves and my wife is right."

"You are allowed wives?"

Henry Hook gestured to a seat and I sat, "You have to have special permission. My officer from the Monmouthshire militia wrote a very nice letter and the colonel allowed me to bring my wife."

716, Robert Jones said, "So, what is your story? Why has a lad who is barely old enough to shave enlisted?" He leaned back in his seat and lit his pipe. "We have time before lights out and we like to be entertained.

I took a deep breath and then realised that this was a good thing. By telling these my story I would become one of them, albeit tenuously and so I started to speak. As I did the woman, I learned her name was Ada, came and joined us. She was what we called homely but in the short time, I knew her she helped me enormously. I started with Sunday School and Trooper Thomas. I drew approving nods from both Hook and his wife. I later learned that he was also a part-time Methodist preacher and he approved. I took them up to the death of my father and the rapid decision to join up.

Private Hook smiled when I had finished, "I think, young Jack, that any dreams of glory will remain just that, dreams. We aren't the cavalry riding great white horses and carrying huge sabres. We march to war and dig trenches. We stand in line and fire our rifles but I admire your decision for it shows loyalty and that is something that every regiment needs." He looked at the others, "We will do our best with this one, eh lads? We will treat him like the little brothers we left at home." Henry Hook was a force of nature and the three nodded. He then turned to me, "But, Jack Roberts, don't let us down. Understand?"

I nodded, "Yes, Private Hook."

He smiled again, "It is Hooky to my friends."

They spent the next hour, until lights out, giving me advice. There was so much that I thought that my head would explode. Alf Thomas, who would become my best friend said, "And grow a beard."

"A beard? Why?"

"When we are …" he spread his arms, "wherever they send us then there might not be enough water to shave and a beard gives a bit more protection. It will stop you from getting sunburn, keep you warm and, in your case, actually make you look eighteen."

I nodded for he was right. I rubbed my chin and felt the stubble. I had not brought my father's razor from home as I had assumed I would be issued with one. When I lay down on the bed, that felt hard as nails after the one in Central Street, I was so weary that I was asleep before the light was extinguished. My life in the army had begun and it was not as bad as I might have expected. For that, I had Sergeant Bourne and Henry Hook to thank.

The trumpet made me jump out of bed and I looked around at my unfamiliar surroundings. Ada was already up and she smiled. She was brewing tea on the small stove I had not noticed the night before. "I have a spare mug until you get yours later on. Milk and sugar?"

I nodded.

"The lads all chip in but I don't suppose you have any money yet so we will let it go for this week eh?"

I did not want to be a burden and, having pulled up my trousers I put my hand in the pocket and brought out two sixpences. "No, Mrs Hook, I will pay my way."

She beamed, "Mrs Hook! It is Ada and just a tanner will do."

The others were all rising and dressing in their red uniforms. It meant I was dressed and ready first and I sat drinking my tea thinking that the next day I would have to do the same as they were doing. Even before they had finished the door opened and a corporal entered. He looked at me, "Are you Roberts?"

I recognised the stripes and said, "Yes Corporal."

"Well look sharp and come with me."

Ada took my mug and said, "Good luck, Jack."

She was neither my mother nor my aunt but the soft voice, and gentle smile were a good substitute and I felt better as I followed the corporal. He went at what I later learned was a quick march and we arrived at the company office. There was no Sergeant Bourne. An elderly lieutenant looked up from his desk and turned to the sergeant, "Has he been sworn in, yet, Sergeant Jones?"

"No sir."

"Well get that done and then do the paperwork. Corporal Allan. When he is sworn in then take him to the Quartermaster and get him kitted out."

I saw his eyes roll and I guessed that he would not get his breakfast until I was fully enrolled. My late arrival was still haunting me. I think that the sergeant was also waiting on his breakfast for I was sworn in with little regard for ceremony or the seriousness of the oath. Similarly, my details were taken very quickly although to be fair to the sergeant he had a very neat hand and I was able to read all that he had written easily. That I could read appeared to be a point in my favour. That done Corporal Allan propelled me out the door and we ran to the Quartermaster's Stores. I learned later that we did it in double time.

It was only much later that I realised how lucky I was. Most of the recruits that the recruiting parties were seeking were in South Wales and they had not arrived yet. The regiment was supposed to have two battalions but ours, the 2nd was seriously understrength and the 1st needed new recruits too. I was the only one being kitted out and I had the luxury of being able to choose clothes that fitted. Blue trousers, two grey shirts, two red frock coats, one undress and a dress one along with a grey overcoat, socks and hobnailed boots with leather leggings were the first pieces of equipment. They made quite a pile. Then I was given a Glengarry forage cap and a helmet. The private handed me a bag with a metal spike and a chin chain and a strange piece of metal with a small round hole in it. "Keep these safe. You only need them on special occasions but if you lose them then it comes out of your pay."

He gave me a variety of straps and belts, all of them were buff coloured. There was a black valise with braces as well as a black expense pouch that I later learned was for carrying bullets. A mess tin and mug along with a knife, fork and spoon were also issued.

The private grinned, "Right Corp, the armourer next."

Carrying the huge pile of equipment we headed to the next building. This proved to be a far shorter visit. I was given a Martini-Henry rifle, along with a sword bayonet in a black scabbard, ten bullets and a tin with the tools to service the weapon. As we left the corporal said, "You can find your own way back to the barracks, eh? When you are dressed, you can go to the mess for your breakfast." He grinned, "If there is any left by the time you reach there."

It was fortunate that Ada was at the barracks for the door was closed and I could not open it. I kicked the bottom with my boot and shouted for help. Ada had a baby feeding when she opened it and I felt embarrassed, "Sorry, Mrs Hook."

She laughed, "It is Ada and you will get used to this. When she is hungry then she eats. Put your stuff on your bed and when she is asleep, I will help you to dress." She smiled, "Start with your trousers and shirts, that will save your modesty."

I undressed and began to don the uniform. The socks were of good quality. Trooper had told me how important that was. The trousers were a little loose and so I used my braces. My father's best trousers were also a little loose and I used the ones I had fastened to them. The shirt was collarless and was also a little loose.

The bairn was asleep and Ada said, as she approached me, "They will shrink in the wash, don't worry about the fit." She took my undress jacket, I learned that they were often called the patrol jacket and she helped me into it. Like the rest, this was a little loose. She fastened the five buttons, they were a tight fit and then smoothed down the uniform. Standing back she admired me, "You suit it, Jack. When you walk out you will have all the girls admiring you."

There was no mirror and I had to take her word for it. "Will this shrink too?"

"Aye, your greatcoat will protect you from the rain but I know Henry has been caught out in a shower before now." She smiled, "A good soldier watches the weather." She put my cap on and I saw her adjust it to the same jaunty angle the others had adopted. Handing me my mess tin, mug and cutlery she said, "Now cut along and get to the mess and join your new messmates. They will keep you a seat. It will be a parade soon." She stood on tiptoe and kissed my cheek, "Good luck, Jack. Henry will keep his eye on you so mind you heed his every word. He is a good soldier."

"Thanks, Ada."

I took them and ran to the mess. I followed a couple of soldiers into the mess and there were three behind me so I was not the last. As I entered, I saw my messmates, they had saved me a seat at a table. I nervously joined the queue and saw the reason for the race to get there early. The pickings were slim but I took what was given, grateful that I had something inside me. I filled my mug from the urn that contained the tea and after taking milk and sugar went to join my new comrades. As I walked through the rows of tables and soldiers, I reflected that Sergeant Bourne had done his best for me. I could have been put with other soldiers who would not have been as kind.

They were smoking their pipes and had cleared their plates. "I hope you are a fast eater, Jack."

I nodded for my mouth was already full. It was a joke in our house that I ate so fast that everyone thought I just swallowed and didn't chew. The mess tin was cleared quickly but, even so, I saw men rising to wash out their tins and mugs and head back to their barracks. I swallowed the hot sweet tea and said, "Ready."

The four of them laughed and Hooky said, "You'll do, Jack Roberts. You are a born soldier."

If I thought it would be easy, I was wrong. Back in the barrack hut the four of them and Ada helped me to fasten the tangle of straps and belts as well as my valise. I noticed that they were not doing the same. "Why aren't you all doing the same?"

Henry Hook adjusted my belt and said, "You will be whisked away and taken through standing orders and the thousand and one other rules you have to memorise. You will have to carry your rifle with you all day, even though I doubt that you will get to use it until we are sent abroad."

He jammed my helmet on my head and hurried me out. As we raced out to the parade ground to join the rest of the regiment, I saw a sergeant approaching the next barrack block and as he entered it I heard his voice, like a human alarm clock shouting and raging at them.

"Are they in trouble, Hooky?"

He laughed, "Sergeants only have one voice and it is set to screaming pitch."

I noticed that some of the uniforms were faded and that many of the men did not have white helmets as we did but they were brown. "Why are some helmets brown, Hooky?"

Alf and Bob manoeuvred me into position in line as Hooky explained, "They are some of the older hands and served in the Andaman Islands or India. They stained them with tea. It is bad enough having a red uniform that stands out a mile without having a white target on the top of your head. Now, no more questions. You don't talk during a parade."

We stood in silence and I felt conspicuous. The other four also had bright red uniforms just like me but I was the only one with the full array of straps belts and the black valise. Sergeants prowled up and down the lines with swagger sticks ready to inflict instant punishment on any miscreants. My uniform suddenly felt itchy and I had an urge to scratch but I was mindful of Hooky's words and I resisted.

When a sergeant shouted, "Stand still that man!" And I heard the thwack of a stick then I knew I had been wise to fight the irritation.

The officers emerged, some quicker than others and they stood before us. One of them turned and nodded and a sergeant shouted, "Parade, attention!"

I was a heartbeat slower than the rest who must have seen the nod and knew what it meant. I spied Sergeant Bourne, who was standing close to the sergeant who had shouted out the command, and his eyes bored into me. I had made a mistake.

The officer I later discovered was the colonel, Lieutenant Colonel Glyn, who began to speak. He had an immaculately waxed moustache and everything about him, from his uniform to his voice was crisp and sharp. "Good morning, men of the 24th. As you can see, we have a new recruit joining us this morning and I have to tell you that he will not be the last. The regiment is being brought up to full strength for we are being sent to South

Africa sometime in the next months. There is trouble there and they need the finest regiment in Wales." I desperately wanted to ask Hooky something and I suspected others did too for you could feel the elevated sense of excitement. "We have one month before that happens and so there will be no leave and, until further notice, every member of the regiment is confined to barracks. We need to focus on the task at hand." Colour Sergeant Roberts will not be coming with us to South Africa. His enlistment will be up within six months. The new colour sergeant will be Sergeant Bourne."

Even I knew this was an important promotion. I was also intrigued by the possible connection with the retiring colour sergeant.

The colonel said, "Colour Sergeant Bourne."

"When you are dismissed, I want every man back here in undress with full equipment, including greatcoat. Colour Sergeant Roberts and I intend to whip you into some sort of shape. When we reach Cape Town, we have to be ready for anything. Parade dismiss!" As we all turned his stentorian tones barked, "Private Roberts, stand fast!"

The parade ground emptied until only Colour Sergeant Bourne and three officers remained.

The sergeant beckoned me over with his finger. I hurried over at the same pace Corporal Allan had taken me to the armourer's. I snapped to, what I assumed was attention. Trooper had taught me how to do so and it must have worked for I saw the hint of a nod from Colour Sergeant Bourne. The colonel was not as tall as me and he looked up at me, "You, Private Roberts, are joining the finest regiment in Wales, some might say the British army and we have a list of battle honours that is the envy of many regiments. You are joining B Company. This is your officer, Lieutenant Bromhead. This morning will be spent having a medical inspection by Doctor Harris and completing the paperwork necessary. You will be given a copy of the standing orders which you will memorise and return the document to the company office tomorrow."

He waited and I wondered what for. Colour Sergeant Bourne mouthed, "Answer, the colonel, Roberts."

I said, "Yes, sir."

Clearly unimpressed, the colonel and the lieutenant turned on their heels and the doctor smiled, "Come with me, Roberts. Let us see if you are fit enough to become a soldier of the Queen."

Chapter 5

That first day passed by like a blur. The doctor had me strip naked to examine my back for the marks of flogging. It would have told them that I was an old soldier trying to re-enlist and gain the bounty for signing on. My youth should have told them it was not necessary but as I came to learn the army had its own way of doing things. Once I was passed fit, I had to dress and then go with an elderly corporal to go through the standing orders and all the information I would need to avoid punishment. I was taught to salute, with my left hand. It was long way round, short way down and I was taught when to salute. It seemed to me that saluting all the time would be the best way to avoid punishment. I was taught the names for everything I had been issued. I learned that the strange piece of metal with my hat spike and chain was a button stick and was used to prevent polish from going on the uniform when the buttons and buckles were polished. The army liked things to be polished and bright.

The old soldier was kind and he smiled when he told me that. "Of course, everything changes once you leave Great Britain. On campaign, your uniform will be torn and you won't have time to polish. There are two armies, Private Roberts, the one at home and the one abroad. The one at home is all spit, polish and marching. The real army is out there and when you reach South Africa you will see it for real."

The standing orders and the various bugle commands were the most important part of the induction process and Corporal Sanders gave me some good advice, "Listen to your sergeants and NCOs," he lowered his voice, even though we were alone. "There are some good officers and others who don't know their arse from their elbow."

I smiled for that was what Trooper had told me. He had recounted the tale of a foolish Lord Lucan issuing the wrong order. We stopped for the noon break. "I could spend all afternoon telling you all that you need to know, Private Roberts, but from here on you are on your own. When the other recruits arrive, they will not have the luxury of one tired old corporal telling them the ins and outs. It will be a barking sergeant dealing with them all. Good luck."

"You won't be coming with us, will you, Corporal?"

"No, I have done my time and like Sergeant Roberts that will be when you are on the ship to Cape Town. I have saved a few bob and I will be given a pension of sixpence a day. I will just find somewhere cheap to live." He chuckled, "And bore the life out of anyone who will listen about my time in the army. Now you cut along and change into your number twos."

"Number twos?"

"Your undress uniform. This one is for special occasions. This afternoon you will be drilling until your feet bleed. Don't worry, Hooky will look after you. He knows what's what."

"But he has only recently joined."

"He did a few years in the militia and he learned well."

I hurried back to the barracks, glad to be rid of the valise and the belts. I carefully folded the jacket and placed it in the chest at the foot of the bed along with the greatcoat, helmet and other items I would not need. Ada was behind the curtain. Hooky's daughter needed feeding, it seemed, regularly.

She came from behind and I saw that the bairn was in the cot, asleep. "Do you want a brew? I will be putting the kettle on. Hooky and the lads like a cup before they have their dinner. They reckon the mess tea is only fit for sailors." I learned that the two services had a fierce rivalry and insults were frequently exchanged.

"Thanks, Ada. I have to memorise the standing orders."

"The trumpet commands are the hardest to understand. Until you have heard them you won't know if it is one thing or another. Look to the lads and see what they do."

I already knew Reveille and Dismiss as I had heard them already. I had heard a bugle the previous night and deduced that was Lights Out. I had much to learn.

The drilling was every bit as hard as the corporal had warned me. The new boots were stiff and I had not had time to apply the wax polish that would soften them. I felt the blisters as they rose and even the blood that started sloshing around in my boot. If I thought that once we were dismissed and had eaten that I would have an easy time then I was wrong. As well as learning the standing orders Alf showed me how to clean my gun. It was still packed with grease. By the time it was lights out I felt I had only learned a quarter of the standing orders and as I had to return the well-thumbed document to the company office the next day, I had no more time to learn. As Alf said, with a smile, "If you can't take a joke then you shouldn't have joined. Don't worry, Jack, we will help you all we can but we still have some way to go. Still, a job shared is a job halved, eh?"

It was two days before I needed my rifle and we were taken, in platoons, to the firing range. It was a relief not to have to march for my feet were already bloody. The instructors gave rough instructions but as I was the only one who had never fired a gun they didn't go into detail. Alf was the one who gave me the best advice, "Keep the butt pressed hard into your shoulder. You want no gap at all. This rifle has a fearful kick and you can break your collar bone." The first five rounds were fired just to allow us to become accustomed to the weapon. There were no targets placed for us to fire at. Alf was right and my shoulder, even though I had the butt held firmly, felt like I had been kicked. The next twenty were used at a target and I found that, if I listened to Corporal Allan, I was able to improve and I hit the target with the fourth bullet. I was proud of myself. It was not in the centre but hitting the target was an achievement. I learned that another fault with the gun was that it became hot and although we had only fired twenty-five bullets, touching the metal barrel meant a burn. What would it be like in the heat of battle? We marched back to the barracks for another parade and this time I was not out of step when the order was given to come to attention. I even recognised when the order to dismiss would come and raced back with my messmates to get changed, and then grab our mess tins to get to the mess. It wasn't as though you got more food by being first or even better food but it was hotter and so we ran.

The second morning found me awake before reveille and that, in itself, was a miracle for I had been exhausted the night before. It was the pain in my shoulder and my feet that woke me. Bob Jones had smeared some foul-smelling concoction on them. He had told me it wouldn't help the pain but would harden the skin. The snores of the others told me that they were still asleep and I slipped out of the barracks to go to my ablutions. I had donned my socks, trousers and boots but I had not fastened my boots. Hooky had told me how to soften them and to make them waterproof and when this next day of training was over then I would endeavour to render them more comfortable. By the time I returned, I could hear the cry of the baby and knew that the others would soon rise. I filled the kettle and put it on to boil. No one had told me to do so but I instinctively knew that it was the right thing to do. I had a new family now and the best families worked together.

When reveille sounded, I had made the pot of tea and was drinking my first mug, sitting in shirt sleeves. I looked down at my boots, dreading the time I would have to fasten them. Alf was the first awake and after he had donned his socks, trousers and boots he headed towards the door. He ruffled my hair as he passed me, "Well done, boyo. You have the makings of a soldier."

The smiles from the others as they poured themselves tea made me swell with pride. I thought back to Central Street. On the rare occasion that I had been the first awake and I had put the kettle on then my father would have just taken it for granted and there would have been no word of thanks. That was in direct contrast to Trooper who thanked me for every little thing I did for him or Caesar.

That second day was more painful than the first but I did not feel as useless especially as I was with my new comrade in arms all day. The afternoon saw us all doing something they had never done either, bayonet work. The sword bayonet, called 'the lunger' by the old hands, was over twenty inches long and made the already heavy rifle even heavier. The hour we spent lunging and fighting the sandbags made my already sore muscles burn. When we tried to fire a few rounds with the bayonet attached then few bullets struck the target. What surprised me was that some of the officers attended the session. They left before we did and Colour Sergeant Bourne gathered us around him to explain why we had just done what we had.

"When we go to South Africa it will be to bring the rebels who oppose the Queen to heel. That will involve fighting and make no mistakes bonny lads, it will mean using the bayonet.

We will have to fire our rifles and be prepared to use the sword bayonet to defend ourselves. Every day, from now on, we will practise sparring with a bayonet." A wicked smile came onto his face, "But please, gentlemen, use your scabbards, eh?"

I thanked my father for having sent me to Pritchard's. I had not wanted to go and I had not enjoyed the work but my time with the Iron Gang meant I had a muscled back and arms that were strong. I was soon able to defeat even Hooky for I had the strength to use the six feet long weapon longer than the others. I even drew a compliment from Corporal Allan. "You have a good technique, Roberts. Keep this up and in a year or so we might see a stripe on your arm."

Such praise encouraged me to try even harder and I found that I was enjoying this new life even more than I had expected.

It was Thursday when the first batch of new recruits arrived. They started to arrive not long after our parade and we saw them as we assembled for drill. They lounged around before the company office. There were just three when we began our drill but by ten-thirty when we had finished the drill and were marching to the bayonet practice area there were twelve, and by the time we headed for our lunch in the mess there were twenty of them. These, we learned, were the recruits from South Wales. The cosy world of five of us and Ada would now end as every bunk in the barracks was taken up and places around the table were hard to come by.

Although they came from South Wales there were some recruits that were not Welsh. One of them, Fred Hitch, was originally from London. His accent marked him as different even more than mine did but he became part of our little group. He was a comedian and loved to make people laugh. Ada took to him straight away and he responded in kind by amusing Hooky's daughter.

Not all the recruits fitted in as well as Fred. Some were loud and aggressive, one such was Dai Llewellyn. He did not think that the regiment, being Welsh, should be, as he put it, burdened by foreigners. As Fred and I were the only two Englishmen in the barracks then we suffered his vented anger. Henry Hook put him in his place for he was still the leader in the barracks and he did not like the raised voices. Dai Llewellyn did not like that and it fuelled his anger and he brooded. He had gathered other like-minded or perhaps, simple-minded souls and he had three friends who became a sort of gang. I could see that he might not take on Henry Hooks but Fred Hitch and Jack Roberts were fair game. He was another Henry Stanley and I knew that bullies like him never relented.

A week after they had arrived, I sat with my messmates around the table, Fred was included in that group and asked why he was the way he was. He had, once again, made very insulting comments to Fred and to me. We had ignored them and, once again, Henry had silenced him. 1303 John Williams had the answer, "The last Prince of Wales born in Wales rather than being an Englishman foisted upon us was called Llewellyn and he almost beat the English." He shrugged, "I was taught this when I was young. It is the past but in Private Llewellyn's case his name might have given him delusions of grandeur."

Hitch shook his head, "Makes no sense to me, me old cocker. If he is so against the English why has the silly bugger joined one of the Queen's regiments?"

Hooky smiled, "Probably the same reason as you and me. He wanted the security of food, a roof, clothes and money. You two lads watch out for him and his butties." I had learned that butties was the word used for friends.

It was good advice and we heeded it.

The next batch of the new recruits arrived a month after I had joined. By that time I was no longer the new boy. I had boots that were softer and waterproofed. I was used as a model for the new recruits to show them how to use a bayonet and I had mastered all the trumpet calls and knew the standing orders by heart. Life was good. I had even remembered to write home and my mother had sent me a letter to tell me how I was missed but also how Billy and my sisters were enjoying working for a living. It made me miss them but, at the same time, was reassuring. Life went on without me and that was important.

The parade held on that fateful Monday in August with the sun beating down on us was to tell us that we were leaving at the end of the week for South Africa. The whole of the 1st Battalion would be leaving and as our company was now at full strength, we would be joining them. The transports would be waiting at

Southampton for us and special trains would take us there. We had less than four days to prepare. As we were dismissed, I saw the look on Hooky's face. Wives were to be left behind. As Ada was pregnant this would be especially hard for both of them. The rest of us gave them space as Henry told her the news. Ada was a tough woman but I knew that she would find it a trial. Money would be tight.

That evening we managed to commandeer half of the table. "What will you do, Ada? Stay here?"

She laughed, "Stay here, Jack? No. I shall go home and stay with my family in Pontypool."

Hooky shook his head, "It will be terrible crowded, my love."

"We shall manage but I may have to earn money. My father believes in people paying their way."

I had not spent any of my pay and I had more than a pound in my pocket. I took out four half-crowns and pushed them over, "Here Ada, it is just ten shillings but you are welcome to it."

She tried to push it back to me, "No, Jack, I will not take charity."

I shook my head and pushed it back, "It is not charity, Ada, call it a gift for the new bairn. You and Henry were kind to me and made my life here easy. Let me do this for you, please."

She took it and the others all gave similar amounts to her.

Henry nodded, "I won't forget this, boys."

We were, unusually, given leave on Wednesday to go to Brecon. It would be our last chance to buy anything that we needed for South Africa. Alf went with Fred and me to town. We had our Glengarry caps at just the right angle and Alf had waxed his moustache. At that time I still shaved and I was acutely aware that I looked young. I knew that I would be growing a beard, especially on the voyage south but this would be my last forage with what I considered my old face.

Fred was keen for some fun, "Well boys, what is it to be? Beer or food first?"

Alf nodded to me, "First, we need to get Jack here a pipe, tobacco and a pouch."

I was the only one who did not smoke, "Why, Alf?"

"It is for practical reasons, Jack. South Africa is full of bugs and insects. You need a pipe to keep them away. You should smoke a pipe for your health." We were leaving the barracks and he waved a hand, "How many others do not smoke? Even Henry smokes a pipe and he is a staunch Methodist."

Fred nodded, "I have a pipe and baccy so I will see you boys in the Cardigan Arms." He was a cheerful and gregarious soul who loved company. In the time we had come to know him we had all warmed to him. That he did not mind us mocking his accent helped, I think.

The tobacconist's shop was full of strange smells. The tobacconist sat on a stool behind the counter smoking what I later learned was a churchwarden pipe. It had a very long stem. Alf knew him for the man nodded, "You are back quicker than I thought. Run out already?"

Alf shook his head, "We are off to South Africa soon and this young Englishman has never smoked."

The tobacconist laid his pipe down on a rack that kept it upright, "You need to smoke a pipe young man for your health. Now then, let me see…" he looked at the rows of pipes that were on the counter, each one displayed on a wooden rack. There appeared to be myriad lengths of stems and shapes of bowls. He looked from the pipes to me and finally pounced on one, "Ah, the very thing. This will suit, sir." He held it in his hands as though it was a precious object. It had a flat bottom and appeared to have a smaller bowl than most. It had a stem about four inches long, "The bowl is a good size to get you started. You will be able to fill it and if it is going well will burn for more than an hour." He looked at Alf, "You will teach him, I assume."

"Don't you worry. He will have his lessons."

"Good and heed your messmate's words, my friend, for they will stand you in good stead." He laid the pipe reverently on the counter and went to the jars of tobacco. They had exotic names like Black Cavendish, Golden Virginian, Loose Shag and more. He looked at Alf, "Never smoked, eh?" Alf shook his head. "Then Golden Brecon might do." Opening it he took out a handful and smiling at me held it under my nose. It smelled pleasant, "I make this blend myself. It is mostly Golden Virginia but I put in some Dutch tobacco that is quite fragrant. It is a cool smoke." He did not, as I had expected, take some from the jar but replaced the top of the one he had opened.

Alf pointed to a shelf just behind the tobacconist, "That looks like a serviceable pouch."

The tobacconist nodded and took a leather pouch from the shelf. "You have a good eye. This is the very chap I would have recommended." He unrolled the pouch and showed me the capacious pocket. "This will hold a couple of ounces of tobacco. You are going to South Africa?" Alf nodded, "Then when you reach the warmer climes buy an orange for they are cheap over there but keep the peel when you have eaten it. It will keep the tobacco fresher."

An orange was, like a banana, an exotic fruit. I had seen them but my mother could not afford them. I had never even eaten one. I wondered at this new world I was entering where such things were cheap.

The tobacconist opened the lid on the jar, took out tobacco and weighed it on his scales. He looked not at me but Alf, "Three ounces should suffice although I know not what muck you will have to buy when you leave the civilised world." I knew the type of man the tobacconist was. He viewed the rest of the world as a dangerous place. The Empire brought many wonderful goods and exotica to Great Britain but he regarded those places as dangerous.

"Aye, three ounces will keep him going. He will only need it when we are in those places where the insects bite."

"You are right." He turned his attention to me, "A half-pipe a day until you are used to it." He wrapped everything up and made a neat parcel. He tied it with string and said, "That will be half a crown."

My purse was diminishing at a rapid rate but I trusted Alf and besides I had plenty of coppers left for the beer. This would be the only beer I would have until we returned. I had been told that on active service we would be given a gill of spirits each day as well as beer and, when it was available, wine. Henry Hook had told me that but as he was teetotal and a Methodist, he shared his ration with his messmates. As with tobacco I had never drunk spirits before and I was not sure if I would like it. I knew that my father liked a whisky or two and he would buy a bottle each Christmas. Trooper had a nip of whisky each day and so I thought that there must be something in the taste that they liked.

We left the tobacconist and headed for the sweet shop that was just next to the pub. I had a sweet tooth and I like mints. Inside the shop, I saw that they had Mint Imperials. They were like the Scotch mints I had bought at home. They were hard and lasted a long time. I invested in half a pound and put the bag with my pipe and tobacco in the leather satchel I carried. It had been in Trooper's kitbag and was capacious enough to hold many things. We went to the pub. It fronted the main street of Brecon but, like many pubs had a small, enclosed space at the rear for those times when the pub was too crowded. In winter it was a cold and miserable place and only the most hardened of drinkers would endure it. When we forced our way into the Cardigan Arms, Alf and I knew that we would have to make our way through to the yard once we had our beer for it was heaving with others who had decided to have a last pint in Wales. I was looking forward to being given a lesson in pipe smoking. I knew, from Alf and the others, that the experience of smoking a pipe was enhanced by imbibing beer.

Alf smiled as we entered the noisy and crowded pub, "I will get this round in. You can buy the next one after we have found Fred." He had to shout to make himself heard over the noise. We had not seen Fred although there were other red uniforms to be seen. Alf turned to me when he finally reached the bar, "They have no mild, bitter alright?" I nodded.

I was used to the different beers now. I had grown up in St Helen's and that was a glass town. Glass receptacles for drinking were plentiful there but here they used the traditional pewter mugs with a handle. I could understand why. In crowded pubs, drinks could be knocked over and glass, unless you lived in St Helen's, was expensive. Alf handed me a slightly battered pewter mug and we both took a large swallow before we headed into the yard to find our friend. Inevitably beer would be spilt and drinking half made the loss less likely.

"Let's go and find Fred, eh?"

As we meandered our way through the knots of men we nodded and exchanged greetings with other men from the regiment. "Have you seen Fred Hitch?"

One of them took his pipe from his mouth and used it to point, "Out the back with some other lads from your barracks."

Alf frowned for our other messmates were back at the camp.

When we reached the yard, it was easier to breathe and we looked around for Fred. There were only a couple of red uniforms and neither of them was Fred. "He did say the Cardigan Arms, didn't he?"

I nodded, "He did. Perhaps he has gone into the alley behind the yard for a pee."

The rear alley of most pubs would also double as a toilet. There was a toilet in the pub but I could see the queue of men waiting to use it. Perhaps Fred had gone outside. Alf nodded, "And as I can't see his beer, he will be ready for one when he gets back. Down that one, young Jack."

We downed the beer in one and one of the other soldiers from the regiment said to us, "Are you looking for your mate?"

Alf said, "Aye, Fred Hitch."

He gestured with his pipe to the back gate, "He might have gone back to the barracks through yon gate. He went through there about ten minutes ago and a few of the lads from your mess followed him."

Neither Alf nor I liked that and Alf took my tankard and his and handed them to the private. "Here, friend, watch these."

We hurried to the gate and as we opened it, we heard the sound of someone being beaten. The sound of fists pounding flesh is quite distinctive. We took it all in instantly. Llewellyn and three of his cronies had Fred. Two held his arms while Llewellyn punched him. Such was their attention to their task in hand that they did not see us. I took my satchel and placed it, and my cap on the ground. Alf laid his next to mine and nodded. We were outnumbered but this was a mate and this could not be tolerated. As luck would have it, I was the closest to Llewellyn and I did not hesitate. It had been many years since I had defended Billy but I had been involved in a few fights since then. I never sought them but I was never defeated. Trooper had once told me, 'Never start a fight if you can't finish it and always finish it quickly!' It was good advice and I grabbed Llewellyn's right arm with my left and then punched him so hard in his ribs, for I was behind him, that I heard the bones crack. I whirled him round and then punched him again in the solar plexus, winding him. As he gasped for air like a stranded fish, I punched him again in the broken ribs with my left hand before delivering an uppercut that felled him.

My actions had been so rapid that the other soldier, Madog, just stood watching. Alf had punched one of those holding Fred and our numbers, at least, were even. Private Madog was short and squat. I think he had been a miner and as he recovered and came at me, I knew that he would be a different proposition to Llewellyn. I was lucky for he came at me like an angry bull. Trooper had advised me that fighting hot was dangerous, 'Be as cool as ice, Jack, and use your mind."

As he roared and ran at me, I sidestepped and punched him in the ear as he passed me. It was my left hand and the blow was not as powerful as it would have been had the punch been with my right but the Iron Gang had given me an arm like an oak sapling. It hurt and angered him. He seemed to lose sight of me and turned around like a short-sighted dog, shaking his head to clear it. I did not hesitate but closed with him and landed a flurry of blows to his middle. He had not tensed his muscles and every blow hurt. This was not the time for honour and hooking my right leg behind his left I punched once more and he fell backwards, cracking his head on the wall. He lay still.

I whirled around and saw that Fred and Alf had chased off the other two. Fred walked over to Llewellyn who was just coming to. He could not run but Fred pulled his right leg back and kicked him hard between his open legs, "You want to fight me one to one, you bastard, then I will show you what I can do. If you want to end this properly we will arrange a soldier's fight and not an ambush."

Hitch's face was a mess and Alf said, "Come on, we had better get you cleaned up. The sergeant of the guard will want to know how you got those wounds."

Picking up our belongings we headed into the yard. The two soldiers we had spoken to said, "Did his mates do this?"

Alf snorted, "Not his mates but four cowards." He nodded towards the gate, "Two of them are outside and the other two legged it."

One shook his head, "Sorry we didn't come with you."

Alf smiled, "My butty and me handled them." He looked at me and said, "Not a mark on you. You are a dark horse, Jack

Roberts." He had been caught on the nose and blood was oozing from it. He sniffed it away and wiped his face with the arm of his tunic.

We headed for the queue for the toilet. It had gone down and we did not have to wait long to get inside. It was a tiny sentry box with a cesspit beneath it. The stink turned my stomach but there was a jug of water and a cloth. Few bothered with it and so it was half full and the cloth was not as dirty as it might have been. We cleaned Fred up as best we could. The bruises would come but not for a day or so. We went through the pub and Alf and I flanked Fred. In the dark crowded pub, no one saw Fred's face.

Once in the street, we set off back to the barracks. "Slip your cap over your face and stay behind us when we reach the sergeant of the guard."

The sergeant and his detail would be watching for men coming back intoxicated and we hoped that the scrutiny would be superficial. To our horror, as we approached the gate, we saw that Colour Sergeant Bourne was inspecting the guards and speaking to his friend, Sergeant Williams. Had we turned around we would have looked suspicious and so Alf said, "Nothing for it but to face the music."

Fred said, "Sorry about this lads."

We could be punished for the fight. If the officer of the day deemed it serious enough then it could be a flogging but loss of pay was also possible.

"Not your fault. It was Llewellyn. I knew he was a bad 'un."

Alf was right. It had been clear since the first moment he had entered the barracks that Llewellyn was a bad apple.

It was not Sergeant Williams who spoke but Colour Sergeant Bourne. He took his swagger stick and lifted the cap from Fred's head so he could see his face. He then looked down and raised first my right hand and then Alf's. The knuckles were bruised, "Did you two do this to Private Hitch?"

Alf's voice was indignant as he protested, "Fred is our mate, Colour Sergeant!"

"That does not answer my question, Private Thomas. Private Hitch, who did this to you?"

Fred stood ramrod stiff at attention and said, "Sorry, Colour Sergeant, I prefer not to say."

Colour Sergeant Bourne's eyes examined our faces, "Any civilians involved?"

Fred said, "No Colour Sergeant."

"And no damage to civilian property?"

"No, Colour Sergeant."

"Then cut along and next time be more careful. If you drink too much then you will fall over. You should emulate Private Hook. Don't drink and you will live longer."

We all chorused, "Yes Colour Sergeant," relieved that we had avoided punishment.

The hut was empty apart from our messmates and Ada. When she saw Fred's face she handed the baby to 1303 Williams, "Here watch the bairn." She was a practical woman and she went to get water and ointment for Fred's face.

Henry said, "What happened?"

Fred put his hand to his mouth and pulled out a tooth. John Williams was fast enough to put a handkerchief to his mouth to stop the blood from adding to the mess on Fred's tunic. "I had drunk my first pint and Jack and Alf hadn't come so I went outside for a pee. The next thing I know I was pinioned by two of Llewellyn's cronies and he was laying into me like I was a piece of meat."

Alf nodded, "Jack and I came out and managed to extricate Fred."

Ada sat Fred on the bench and began to clean him up, "This witch hazel will make the bruising less obvious." Fred winced as she applied it.

Henry said, "And Llewellyn?"

Alf nodded to me with a huge grin on his face, "Babyface here is not a man to mess with. He felled Llewellyn with a punch that John Morrissey would have been proud of and then Madog. The others ran off."

I wanted to deflect the attention from me for the others all stared at me, "Colour Sergeant Bourne saw us come in. He knows that there was a fight."

Henry nodded, "This is my barracks and I will have to deal with Llewellyn when he comes back." I saw Ada flash a worried look at her husband and he smiled, "Don't worry, there will be no violence but we can't have him here. There would be bad blood and I do not trust him. He has always seemed to me a sneak who might use a knife. No, I will confront him if and when he returns."

I looked at him, "If?"

"Do you think that anyone in the regiment will want anything to do with him after that? It is one thing to have a fight with someone but quite another to gang up and beat one of your comrades up."

Our one day of leave had been cut short and the camp was largely deserted. After Fred had been tended to Alf and 716 gave me lessons in smoking a pipe, "You could soak the bowl in vinegar; some men favour that but not me. You have a good pipe and walnut wood smokes well."

I nodded as I held the stubby pipe in my hand.

He unrolled my tobacco pouch carefully and took out a small amount of tobacco. He placed it in my hand and said, "Now rub it together and when you are happy with how it feels then put it into the pipe's bowl but be careful not to pack it yet. You need it loose. This is your first pipe so make it just three quarters full."

I did as he suggested and then he said, "Now put the stem in your mouth. Hold it with your teeth but not too tightly." He went to the stove and took one of the spills that were in the jar there and after lighting it from the stove, brought it over. He held it over the bowl. I could see that the flame did not touch the tobacco. "Now suck but don't swallow." I sucked but nothing happened. He smiled, "Suck and puff. Picture yourself as a human bellows."

I did as he said and suddenly there was smoke and then I tasted the smoke in my mouth. Ada said, "Don't swallow."

When Alf took the spill away and snuffed it out, I knew the pipe was going. If I thought I was done I was wrong. "Now keep puffing and take the end of your finger and tamp down the tobacco a little,"

I tried but it burned and I pulled the finger out.

716 said, encouragingly, "Your finger end will get hard and be used to it. Keep going. You are doing well."

I did as they said and just when I thought I had cracked it I felt myself becoming dizzy. Ada saw it too, "That is enough for your first attempt, Jack. Take the pipe out of your mouth and sit down."

I obeyed and laid the pipe on the table. I saw that the bowl and stem had a flat bottom and so the pipe remained horizontal. Alf said, "The pipe will go out naturally. You have another smoke there for later."

Men began to return from their day's leave. Many had packages. The old hands had been buying the things they thought that they might not be able to get abroad. I recognised the wrappings from the tobacconist's. He had done a good trade. I felt I needed some air and so I went outside and breathed deeply. I wondered if I would ever be able to smoke a pipe with the ease of the others. Was I soft? I walked around the barracks and then headed to the ablutions. I needed to make water and the water I splashed on my face when I had finished refreshed me. I went back to the barracks. As I entered every head swivelled. Most of the men had returned and a couple came over to me and patted me on the back, "Well done, Jack. That bully needed to be put in his place. More to you than meets the eye."

"Thanks 616." I guessed that Henry had told them what had taken place.

It was just then that the door to the barracks opened and Llewellyn, Madog and their two lickspittles entered. The faces of the men showed the effect of my fists and both men glowered and glared at me. I wondered if this was to be round two. I bunched my fists, ready to do battle again if I had to. There was no need for Henry took charge, "Llewellyn we all know what you did to Fred here and no one in this hut wants to share the same air as you. I suggest you find Sergeant Jones and ask him to move the four of you."

I saw the bully's fists clench but before anything else happened Colour Sergeant Bourne strode in and, using his swagger stick, moved the four to one side, "Right boys, I have had a word with Colonel Glyn and he has decided that you four will be moved to D Company in the 1st Battalion. It is for the benefit of everyone. Let us put this afternoon down to high spirits before departure. There will be no punishments but any future infractions of military discipline will result in flogging. Do I make myself clear?"

We all snapped a, "Yes Colour Sergeant!" Although it was noticeable that Llewellyn's was a fraction later than the rest and was more of a growl. I saw his eyes murderously fixed on me. Whilst the beating of Fred had been the cause of this it was clear that I was the one who would bear the brunt of the blame in the bully's mind. I was going to face enemies in South Africa with one in our ranks.

Chapter 6

In the event, the fact that the four were now in not only a different company but also a different battalion meant I did not see Llewellyn or the others again for some time. It was clear that the senior officers in the regiment did not blame us for the incident in the pub alley. It seems the other soldiers who had been in the yard had told the tale to their messmates and the whole regiment now knew what had really gone on. We had not informed on them but I knew that Llewellyn would add it to his list of imagined grievances. He and the others involved were shunned and sat alone in the mess.

Our training was over and the last couple of days saw us simply preparing to depart. There were debts to pay and letters to be written. I sent another letter home telling them that I would be in South Africa and that they would be unable to write to me. I knew that I was unusual. Few men could write. I could thanks to Trooper and all my family were able to write. We had one goodbye the day before we left. Henry said goodbye to Ada. The five of us were given permission to take her and her baby to the station. Ada only had a short train ride on a local train and she would be in her family's home before we had lunch. After putting all that she needed in the Third-Class compartment we said our goodbyes and she hugged each of us. We stepped away so that Henry could say his goodbyes and as she turned, she said to us, "And you look after Jack! He is the baby and needs your protection."

I blushed. I knew she meant well but the last thing I needed was my youth to be mentioned. My beard was growing but slowly.

Henry and Ada held each other tightly and we looked away to give them privacy. We waved them off as the train chugged out of the station and we headed back to the camp. It was a clear marker that we were leaving. As we headed back to the barracks Henry said, "Perhaps it was a mistake to get married so young."

716 said, "Perhaps it was the joining of the army that was wrong, Hooky. I have no plans to marry until my enlistment is up. A man has time to sire children and the time will pass."

Henry shook his head, "I always wanted to join the army, either that or become a missionary and preach God's word to those who are not blessed to be born Christians."

Alf said, "You are too good a soldier to be a missionary, Hooky."

"I confess that I like being a soldier. You know that I was a sergeant in the militia?"

I was surprised, "No, I did not. Then why did you not keep the rank?"

"That is the militia and this is the British Army. We are senior to the militia. It is for the best. When we leave for South Africa we will be doing God's work. In the valley, I was just drilling and drawing admiring glances from the girls."

Fred chuckled, "And when I get a leave and manage to return to London then I will take full advantage of the red uniform and the row of medals that shall be on my chest."

We all laughed and Henry said, "Medals?"

"Of course. There will be fighting and I do not doubt that we will be awarded medals. Who knows there may even be a promotion? I might be a corporal."

716 said, "I am glad you are in our section, Fred."

"Why is that, 716?"

"You make me laugh and a resident comedian is always handy."

We were marched to the station the next day where a troop train awaited us. There were only two carriages and they were for officers and senior warrant officers. We were herded into cattle trucks. All the equipment was also with us and we made ourselves as comfortable as we could for the journey south, to Southampton. Packs, blankets and greatcoats made cushions and we were better off than we would have been seated on the hard seats of the Third Class. It was more fun than we anticipated for it did not rain and we entertained ourselves by singing songs on the journey south. This was a Welsh regiment that prided itself on its choir. Trooper had told me that I had a good voice when we had sung hymns at Sunday School and I was not ashamed of my voice. I joined in with gusto. Many of the songs were in Welsh but I picked up the words through the tune and although I understood not a word I sang along with the others. Some of the songs that were in English I already knew and many of them were hymns. Fred performed for us when we tired of singing and kept the sections in our cattle truck well entertained.

It was getting on to dark when we pulled into the docks at Southampton where a veritable fleet of ships awaited us. I saw the blue uniforms of the Army Commissariat and the artillery as they boarded their steamer. The days of sail were in the past although I noticed that a couple of the steamships that awaited us had a couple of masts. I did not know if they were for show or if they were necessary. We had a long voyage ahead of us and I confess that I was nervous. Although we had a regimental doctor there would be doctors and attendants from the Army Medical service too. We watched, while we awaited our order to disembark, the guns of the Artillery hoisted aboard the ship, RMS Andean.

Alf turned to me, "Ever been to sea?" I shook my head, "Me neither. I am not relishing the prospect." We had all heard of disasters at sea where huge waves had taken passenger ships. We lived on an island but none of us had ever crossed such an ocean before.

All the ships looked to be built to a similar design and I saw the smoke rising from their funnels. Their boilers were lit and they could take to sea at any time.

I turned to Henry, "How many men do you think they can get aboard each one, Hooky?"

The normally knowledgeable Hooky shook his head, "Not a clue but there are plenty of ships."

We soon had our answer when Colour Sergeant Bourne's voice boomed out, "Right my lucky lads, time to embark. Form up in company order and please ensure that you have left nothing on the train. Losses will be taken from your pay."

Once we had all stepped onto the dockside Hooky went back into our wagon to confirm that it was empty. Although not at attention we still stood in regimented lines. The difference was that we were encumbered by greatcoats and kit bags as well as rifles. I had emulated my fellows by fastening the greatcoat diagonally across my body. It was too hot to wear. I saw the colonel conferring with the ageing adjutant who, we discovered, would be staying in Brecon and organising the training of the rest of the 2nd Battalion who would be joining us in due course. Sergeant Major Pugh and Colour Sergeant Bourne hovered nearby. There would be a new adjutant when we were in South Africa, Lieutenant Melvill would perform that task.

Eventually, Colour Sergeant Bourne strode over and said, "2nd Battalion company B and 1st Battalion Company A, pick up your bags and follow me." I saw our officers already ascending the stairs to our ship, RMS Danube. Their bags were carried by their servants. Even Colour Sergeant Bourne had to carry his own bags. I marched behind Alf and in front of Fred. The good news was that Llewellyn would be on a different ship. Even as our companies headed for the Danube, I saw another pair of companies march towards the RMS Florence.

There were cabins but they were for the officers, warrant officers and NCOs. There were mattresses laid out in the hold and we went with our messmates to find our own nests for the duration. The rest of B Company headed with us and then 1st Platoon found a place we liked. Within that Number 1 Section, my section took over a corner of the hold. The metal ribs of the ship were handily placed so that we could use the rivets to hang equipment from them. Soldiers are organised and Henry ensured that everything was neatly laid out and to hand. Donning our forage caps we went back to the main deck for below decks felt claustrophobic and we wanted to set sail watching the land. Darkness had fallen but the docks were lit by gas and we watched the lines of red and blue uniforms as they boarded all the ships. It was clear that we would be travelling as a fleet and that gave me some comfort as there seemed to be safety in numbers.

The crew of the ship were scurrying around like busy ants and they shooed soldiers out of the way when we became an encumbrance. As one coiled a rope Henry asked him, "When do we leave, my friend?"

He grinned, "When the tide is right. You are at sea now and she is the mistress of this ship and the others. It doesn't matter what you chaps want to happen, the sea will decide."

I wondered how Colonel Glyn would take that. In the short time I had been with the regiment I had learned that he liked order and timetables. The men of the 24th Foot would be spread out on ten ships and it would be Captain Spalding who was in command of our ship. He was not from our regiment but attached to the headquarters company. The rumour was that he was already a brevet major. There were many such appointments. Even Colonel Glyn was a major and the rank of colonel was a temporary one. The army still allowed the purchase of ranks. It was different for us. Corporal Allan, who was our section corporal had been a lance corporal and Sergeant Windridge had been a corporal before his promotion. We all sought such promotion for it meant more pay and better conditions but rank had to be earned. As Hooky said, there was more chance of that showing courage under fire than being able to march better than anyone else.

We knew when we were leaving as the stevedores on the docks began to unfasten ropes which were thrown to the ships where sailors deftly caught them and began to coil them neatly. The colonel would approve of the neat nature of the ships where everything had a place: ship shape and Bristol fashion. It would appeal to his organised mind. The leading ship was RMS Asiatic and she led us, like a mother duck with her ducklings, down the Solent towards the sea. The handful of dock workers was the only audience to our departure and they raised their hats and cheered as we left England and began the journey that would, according to the sailor we asked, be almost six thousand miles and would take us up to a month to make the journey. He had delighted in telling us of the storms that might await us in the Bay of Biscay and off the African coast. 716 Jones was already a little green as we headed down the Solent and when we cleared the Isle of Wight and struck the larger waves of the English Channel, he was sick over the side. He was not going to enjoy this voyage.

I found myself quite happy to be at sea and I did not feel any discomfort. I wondered if the times I had ridden Caesar had prepared me in some way. Certainly, I had an appetite. The food was no worse than at Brecon. It was cooked by the crew of the steamship who seemed to know what they were doing. We had less drilling and the weather became much warmer as we headed south. The equator would prove to be unbearably hot but that was in the future. As we passed France I thought about the alternative. I could be working in the foundry in St Helen's and I was well prepared for the heat of an equatorial sun. So far the life of a soldier seemed much easier than the more dangerous life as a factory worker. In the time I had been in the regiment there had been no deaths and the fight apart the only injury I had witnessed was when one of D Company was cut on the arm by a sword bayonet. In the first three months at Pritchard's one man had been killed, two had lost limbs and half a dozen had minor injuries and burns. Life in the army was safer. I knew, however, from Trooper, that the most likely killer would be disease. He told me that more men had died in the Crimea due to disease than had been killed in the Charge of the Light Brigade. There was also the flora and fauna. South Africa, we had been warned, had snakes, scorpions, spiders and even insects that could bite and kill. That was not to mention such creatures I had read about like lions, tigers, hippos and crocodiles. I was not sure if they lived in South Africa but I did not relish meeting one.

We had a routine established by the second day and we would gather on the starboard side of the ship to watch the sunset. The others would smoke their pipes but I was uncertain if the motion of the ship might combine with the smoke to make me ill. I declined the offer to join them for a smoke but it didn't matter because the sunsets at sea were always spectacular. Even when there were clouds the sun dipping in the west made everything flare with colours. They were not always reds, yellows and orange but the blues, vivid pinks and purples were equally delightful. While we watched we would discuss the food. The prospect of war and fighting was assiduously avoided as it was considered bad luck. The food was a safer topic. There was little in the way of fresh food. We seemed to be eating tinned goods and they were of German origin. We knew this from the cans that were hurled overboard each night. Our viewpoint on the stern starboard rail facilitated this. The company was called Kopf Erbwurst. We liked the sausages but the sauerkraut was not to our liking. Best of all was the pea soup. Although not as good as my mother's which was made with a ham shank and was wonderfully glutinous, it was still a good soup and we looked forward to the days when that was served.

It was when we neared the equator that life became more unpleasant. It was good that we heeded Colour Sergeant Bourne's advice and stayed out of the sun whenever possible as the ones who did not became the same colour as their uniforms. "You will find, my lucky lads, that it will be just as hot where we are going. Not all the time, mind, but more often than we will like."

I knew what he meant for the woollen uniforms we wore were ill-suited for such tropical climes. Our headgear, too, afforded little protection. We all determined to get some other kind of headgear once we landed in Cape Town. Had we thought about it we could have bought something in Brecon. A neck cloth tied to our helmets seemed the best option.

We kept together as a unit and we were able to watch the others who seemed to spend every spare moment gambling. Hooky was a Methodist and did not approve of gambling. We played cards but it was whist that we played or dominoes and no gambling was involved. Others did gamble. Money was lost and there were fights. We were on a ship and there was something called a brig. It was like a nautical prison. The first ones found guilty were put there for three days but when that failed to curb the violence then the cat was brought out and there were floggings. Thus far I had not seen a flogging and the first one turned my stomach. Sergeant Williams wielded the whip and the two men who were flogged, 818 Jones and 1323 Williams were given twenty strokes. Henry told me that the sergeant dared not show leniency and after twelve strokes the backs were a bloody mess. Sea water was poured over their backs once the punishment was over. It was partly to keep the wounds clean but, as far as the ship's captain was concerned, to keep the deck clean. The men were then put in the brig for a week. The two floggings had the desired effect and the fights ceased although the gambling continued unabated and there were the raised voices of dispute.

All other aspects of army life continued. We had a daily parade and a weekly Church parade where our voices rang over the sea as we sang hymns. We even had a daily drill. Henry told us why we continued to drill for we could not see how it would help us to fight for we knew that we were being sent to South Africa to fight.

"The thing is, see, that drill makes you do something without thinking and, in the heat of battle, that is important."

"Have you been in a war, Hooky?"

"No, but it makes sense, doesn't it? My uncle was a carpenter and he could hit a nail every time on the head without even looking. When I was a child, I thought it was magic but now I can strip and put back together a Martini-Henry without even looking. And there is natural talent like you when you use a lunger. I find it quite remarkable that you seem to be able to flick away an opponent's sword bayonet without looking at the end of your own weapon. That is a talent, boyo, that may save your life. From what I have heard these natives are quite handy with a spear and I am betting that they don't look at the tip of their own weapon when they are stabbing. No, I am happy to drill as often as they like."

Corporal Allan had been listening and he said, "Assegai."

We all looked at him and Henry asked, "Assegai, Corp?"

He nodded, "It is what they call their spears. They carry two of them and they are about the same length as our rifles. They also have a club that they call a knobkerrie." We stared at him. "We had a talk from Captain Spalding. He has served over there and knows what we can expect. He is a good chap."

"Do they have guns?"

He laughed, "Oh, aye. Some of them even have breech loaders but they can't get the ammunition, see. They make their own bullets and they don't fire true. Still, if you are hit by one then you will know and it will not be a clean wound. Most of the guns they have are muzzle loaders." He saw the fear on our faces. "I wouldn't worry. You would have to be very unlucky to be hit by one."

Alf nodded, "But if we are standing in close order then the odds of being hit increases, doesn't it Corporal?"

He nodded and Hooky did too. It was Henry who answered, "As with all things, Thomas, we are in the hands of God. Say your prayers and he will watch over you."

The storm we had was off the coast of German South West Africa and the ships took a real pounding. It was so bad that we were confined below decks and, if truth be told, many of us feared that we would die. The ship tossed and turned. It bucked and seemed to rise into the air before crashing down. Of course, we saw none of this. We were in the blackhole that was the hold. There were lamps but only four of them and the dim glow they gave out merely helped us avoid others. Some men were sick but the crew had anticipated that and there were plenty of pails. Men began to cry out and weep. They were unmanned and none thought to mock them for, in truth, we all thought that we might die. Henry led our section in prayers. I found it helped. I thought about my family at home and prayed for them as well as myself. What helped me was that Trooper had told me of storms he had endured heading to the Crimea and he had survived. I doubted that his experience had been worse than ours but, even so, it gave me some comfort.

We were put to work and it helped to clear my mind. The phrase, 'all hands to the pumps' was a familiar one but we experienced it first hand when Colour Sergeant Bourne set us to relieving the crew on the pumps. The hard physical labour of operating the pumps that sucked water from the bilges and sent it overboard drove all thoughts from our minds. We worked in teams until our shoulders and arms burned and then enjoyed hot sweet tea. The Colour Sergeant was a clever man and he made sure that everyone was busy. 716 was too preoccupied to be sick. When our shift was done we collapsed in our beds and slept the sleep of the dead. Even the violent motion of the sea did not disturb us.

When the motion of the ship became easier we were allowed out on deck again and the blue skies we had enjoyed for most of the voyage had gone to be replaced by thick black clouds filled with rain, but the winds had abated. We were alone on the ocean and I wondered if any of our consorts had been lost. Of course, the visibility was poor and with larger than usual waves it made visibility without a telescope difficult.

The crew seemed unworried. When questioned one laughed, "That wasn't a proper storm. Now on the Australia run, you can get typhoons as can lift a whole ship out of the water." The twinkle in his eye told me that he was making fun of us but he left us with the news that the lookout had seen another two of the ships and we would all make our own way to Cape Town. He seemed quite pleased that we would be the first to arrive. "We shall have the best berth and there is always a bonus to the fastest ship. Thanks to the storm that will be us."

Before he left us, I said, "Are there Germans over there then? Is that why they call it German South West Africa?"

"It is not officially German; I mean they have neither soldiers nor ships there but they have merchants and the place is filled with missionaries. It is not like the land the Dutch took and we have now appropriated. Most of it is a huge desert. We were here first and we have the best land. Still, I think that the Germans have designs on it. One day they may have a colony like Cape Colony."

"I thought you said the Dutch landed here first."

He shrugged, "The Dutch had America first, my friend, New York was originally called New Amsterdam. The Dutch settlers need you boys. Why do you think we have brought you? The natives have been attacking the settlers and they have bleated to the Governor." He leaned in, "You lads want to be careful, they have wicked spears and a club called a knobkerrie. Shoot 'em before they can get close."

I shook my head, "Then why do people want this land?"

He looked surprised, "Haven't you heard? They have found diamonds. They say they have one the size of my fist. This whole land, it seems, is filled with jewels and gold."

"Really?"

He nodded, "All I will say is that there are more ships travelling this route and rich men are returning to England."

I remembered the sailor's advice long after we had landed for it proved to be sage. I suppose travelling the world gave you a greater knowledge than the rest of us. Until I had joined the army the furthest I had travelled was to Liverpool. I remembered crossing the Mersey on the ferry to Birkenhead and thinking that I was further south than I ever had been in my life. Now we were in waters that were as far south as anyone could travel. What a change in my life.

He was in a chatty mood and he pointed to the waves breaking to the east, "That piece of coast is called the Skeleton Coast."

Alf looked fearful, "Skeletons? You mean it is haunted by ghosts and dead people?"

"Aye," he laughed, "The skeletons of wrecked ships. Even now steamships can get blown onto the rocks but in the days of sail…" The bosun shouted to him to stop lollygagging and we stared at the rocky coast.

When we turned to sail due east then we knew we were getting close to Cape Town. We spied ships heading west towards us. They had to have come from Durban or Cape Town. During the voyage, we learned that many ships now used the Suez Canal. Sailing to Australia or India a captain could save ten days by taking the recently built canal. I should have liked to see that. It was supposed to be a wonder and had only been open for ten years. We did not see any of our consorts ahead and our chatty friend seemed inordinately pleased that we had won the race. He told us that we would be landing within the next day. I saw Henry sitting at one of the tables we had been given to use. He was writing.

"What are you doing, Hooky?"

"Writing a letter home. The odds are this will be the last chance for some time. I have had a word with one of the sailors and he will post it when he returns to England." He gave me a strange look, "When was the last time you wrote to your mam?"

I suddenly felt guilty. I had only sent two letters; one the day after I had arrived at the barracks and the second, a hurried note when we had learned we were leaving. My mother had sent three letters to me. There was probably one at the barracks now. I would write one and then she would know that I had survived the voyage south.

He smiled and handed me a sheet of paper, "Here."

I took my pencil and began to write.

RMS Danube,
Off the South African coast
20ᵗʰ November 1877
Dear Mother, Nan, Auntie Sarah, Alice, Mary
and Billy,
I am sorry that I have not written much before but life as a soldier is busier than I expected. I have made

some good friends and they help to look after me. I do not know when you will get this letter, as you can see, I am on a troopship heading for South Africa. The things I shall see!

I know that I will be with a large army but what you should all know is that a soldier only sees the men who are around him. My world is a small and cosy one and, if it gives you a better picture, then think of it as a temporary family. I hope that gives you comfort. I don't know why we are here except to say that we are protecting the families who live here. Not all are English, there are Dutchmen too but I know that you would want me to do my best and protect women and children. Henry, one of the soldiers, says we are here to do God's work and I hope that pleases you.

The food we eat is wholesome but I miss home cooking and when I come home, I shall want all my favourites. That day may be some time off, years probably. It has taken us almost a month to reach South Africa but I will return.

We crossed the equator and, strange though it may seem, although it is November, it is summer here! The world seems topsy turvy. I hope this letter reaches you.

All my love to everyone and I say my prayers each night so that God will protect us all.

Jack Roberts, (Private)

I had wanted to say more but I had filled the page and knew that I had to fold and seal the letter so that I could write the address. I determined to buy some paper when time allowed. I could have bought it in England and much cheaper. The fight with Llewellyn had upset all of my plans. I folded the letter and wrote on it Auntie Sarah's address and then waited while Henry finished his letter. His was two pages long and he had written on the reverse of one of the pages. He had much to say. When he finished, he took out the small stub of red sealing wax. I knew he would have one for that was Hooky all over. He was prepared and I was not. He carefully creased the letter and then melted a blob of sealing wax to seal it.

"Could I borrow some, Hooky?"

He gave me a wry smile, "What say I give you a blob eh? I can't see either of us getting the wax back."

The letter sealed I blew on the wax and then Henry rose, "Let us go and find a postman, eh?"

I suppose we could have gone to one of the sergeants and asked it to be sent home with the regimental paperwork but we both knew that it might well be delayed by days or even weeks at Brecon. We found our chatty friend and we both gave him sixpence to post the letters. He nodded, "I would be glad to." He was normally light-hearted but he looked serious, "You lads need to do a good job here. I have a brother who lives up Natal way and I would not like to think of him being attacked. Your red coats will tell those who wish harm upon the settlers that this is now part of the Empire and that means peace for everyone. You are here to bring God and civilisation and that is no bad thing."

I had not thought of it like that. Trooper had gone to war because of holy places in Palestine. There had been no real need for the Crimean War. This was different. We were going there to protect families and that was a much more worthy cause.

Chapter 7

Cape Town had a mixture of fine buildings and ramshackle shanties. The former structures were all the Government buildings and, as we watched from the deck the town appear, I wondered if we would have time to explore this exotic place. We had been ordered onto the deck in full uniform and with our greatcoats wrapped around us, we sweltered in the early summer heat. Captain Spalding and Lieutenants Bromhead and Carlton, along with the senior warrant officers, prowled the deck ensuring that we were all in perfect order. All collar buttons were to be fastened and we would have to endure the stiff collar that bit into our throats. We would be the first ashore as the other ships were still at sea and Captain Spalding wanted us to set a good example. We were not his regiment but whatever he did while in temporary command could only help his career.

As the sailors and stevedores fastened us to the bollards, Captain Spalding shouted, "We will march in perfect order when we land. I want us to be in perfect step and our faces will be forward. You will not respond to cheers and shouts. I want Colonel Glyn to be proud of us!"

We stood to attention and after the gangplank had been lowered Captain Spalding led us from the ship. We marched ramrod straight down the gangplank but it was not easy to keep the step. We were lucky in that the gangplank we used was the shortest of the three. As soon as we reached the dockside Sergeant Windridge and Corporal Allan began to chivvy us into a straight line. The fact that we were already in a straight line did not appear to matter. I was learning that all non-commissioned officers loved the sound of their own voice. Once we were all assembled then the order was given to right turn and we were marched out of the port and up the slight slope to the town. I think Captain Spalding would have quite enjoyed having the band playing as we marched in perfect step with sloped arms but we made a magnificent sight and there were cheers and applause as we marched. We kept impassively straight faces. The whole town was dominated by the imposing Table Mountain and we seemed to be heading to it. Once we reached the flatter ground and passed the white colonial buildings, I saw that there appeared to be, in the distance, a camp. As we marched down the street women and children waved and cheered. I did as I had been ordered and looked ahead but I could not help but notice that the clothes they wore were different to those at home. I don't know why but I had expected them to be the same. It was later that I learned that more than half of the population had Dutch ancestry and the clothes they wore, along with the African lifestyle determined the clothes they wore.

There were sentries guarding the camp. It was brand new and it was clear that it had been built for a large regiment. The huts were raised from the ground and neatly laid out. The sentries wore blue uniforms that I did not recognise and their tanned skin told me that they were locals. Captain Spalding gave them a cursory glance before he strode in. He wasted no time in handing over to Colour Sergeant Bourne and he had the officers' call sounded. One of the blue-uniformed guards took them to what I assumed was the officer's mess. The march up the slope, the heat and my greatcoat had me sweating as though I was standing next to a roaring coal fire. I wanted to disrobe as soon as I could.

Captain Spalding was a stickler for rules and even though there were just two companies of soldiers it took as long as I would have expected for a battalion. Officers first, senior warrant officers next, then the NCOs and finally the other ranks were assigned barracks. We were allocated our huts and each one held twenty men. Although they were new, they were not as clean as we would have wished. Wind and loosely fitted doors and windows allowed dust and dirt to cover every surface. We took off our tunics, helmets, greatcoats and belts. After placing them on our beds we procured brooms and swept the hut clean. As in Wales, it was Hooky who was the unofficial leader of our hut and he examined it all to see its shortcomings. We each had our own blanket and if the day was anything to go by, we would not need more than one. I did not know if there would be sheets and neither did Hooky. After giving us orders to clean the barracks he went off to find Sergeant Windridge to clarify the issue. When he returned it was with the news that there were sheets but they were with the Quartermaster and his ship had yet to dock.

There were cooks and a mess who were part of the skeletal garrison. When we heard the trumpet sound we grabbed our mess tins, mugs and cutlery and raced. It would be the first meal not cooked from a tin and we hoped for a feast. We were disappointed. It was corn beef hash and it was served not with the potatoes we recognised and vegetables that we knew but a sweet, yellowy one and unrecognisable vegetables. We were soldiers and we made the best of it but when we left, we were not happy.

As we had expected we were all confined to barracks but the hut we had been allocated afforded a fine view of Cape Town and its harbour. There was a veranda that ran along one side and we sat there taking in the fine view. I had only been sitting there for a few moments when the first of the insects arrived. There were little insects like the midges from home, bluebottles the size of small birds and a large number of other insects in between those sizes. I splattered two and then realised that the others were laughing at me.

Alf said, "Have you noticed, Jack, that they are only bothering you?" I looked and saw that he was right. Then it dawned on. Alf nodded, "Aye, now is the time for your pipe."

I went into the hut which felt stiflingly hot and retrieved them. The pouch had been unopened for a month but, even so, the tobacco was a little drier than it should have been. The advantage of that was that it lit quickly but it also burned hotter. The tobacconist's advice about orange peel came to me. I had to refill the pipe but it worked and kept away the insects. It also made me feel slightly nauseous but Henry told me I would get used to the pipe and that would cease. With my newly grown, month-old beard and pipe, I felt like a real grown-up. I was a man. I worked out that when we had crossed the equator it had been my birthday. I suppose I should have mentioned it but I did not want attention drawn to me. I wanted to fade into the background. Llewellyn's singling out of Fred and me had been a warning. We chatted about the strange smells in this land as well as the sights. It was totally unlike anything we knew. When my pipe went out, I did not relight it for by then there was enough smoke from the others to keep me safe from insect hell.

I soon discovered that British soldiers were expected to march at a moment's notice. At parade, the next morning, we had not even eaten when we realised that something was up. There were blue uniforms and civilians at the regimental office and horses tied outside. We stood, at ease while we waited. The warrant officers had the luxury that they could talk but we had had to stand and sweat in the heat which, even at that hour, was hotter than any English summer I had could remember. I was lucky that I had worked in a foundry for a year or two for I found that I could bear it slightly better than many of my comrades.

The doors of the office opened and disgorged the red and blue uniforms. Captain Spalding and Lieutenant Bromhead came over and spoke to Colour Sergeant Bourne who saluted and then shouted, "All sergeants and non-commissioned officers to me."

Captain Spalding was an imposing officer and he had a voice like a sergeant. He turned to Lieutenant Bromhead who shouted, "Attention!" He elongated the word so that it echoed. Even so, his voice was thin and a little reedy.

Captain Spalding, in contrast, boomed his words out, "There is trouble further east in Gcalekaland. B Company will collect their gear and be prepared to march down to the port where they will embark on a steamship. Lieutenant Bromhead will command. B Company, dismiss!"

It was a far from satisfactory command and posed more questions than it answered. Trouble could mean anything from a minor disturbance to a complete rebellion. We were, however, soldiers, and we obeyed. We raced back to the hut. We had occupied it for less than twenty-four hours.

"What is going on, Hooky?"

"You heard the same as I did, Fred. I would suggest you leave your number 1s here. I can't see us needing to parade."

I packed my spare socks and shirts, along with my pipe and tobacco in my valise. We rarely used it but I knew it would come in handy. I made sure the knife, given to me by Joe when I left Pritchard's was also packed. The greatcoat and blanket we would definitely need for we knew now where we would be sleeping.

Sergeant Windridge poked his head in the door and shouted, "Get a move on you slovenly shower. Outside, now!"

I rolled my blanket and greatcoat together and fastened them en banderole. If we had to sail on a steamship, I would soon be able to take them off. Grabbing my rifle and my helmet I ran outside and joined the others as we formed up in fours. I saw a wagon being loaded with supplies and even before we had begun to march back down the hill to the port it had set off. I was close to the front of the column and I saw some new ships approaching the port. I had a good eye for such things and recognised three of them as our consorts. The rest of the regiment was arriving. It begged the question of why they did not simply carry on east but that would have to wait until we could question Sergeant Windridge. I watched as Lieutenant Bromhead mounted the horse held by his servant. I did not know my company commander. I had saluted him and seen him when we paraded and he had been present when I had been in the pub in Liverpool, but when he had ordered the attention that had been the first order, I had heard him give. As the last of the company arrived, I was relieved to see Colour Sergeant Bourne, complete with greatcoat and blanket join us. I felt safer.

It was he who roared, "Attention! Slope arms! Quick march!"

Hooky had been right; all the drills we had done now paid off. I didn't need to think. Everything seemed to fall into place without me thinking about it. Fred and Alf flanked me and my feet were in step immediately. We marched down the slope following Lieutenant Bromhead who seemed to have acquired a fly whisk which he used to flick away the flies from his horse. Captain Spalding mounted a horse and caught up with the Lieutenant. Their heads were together as they headed for the ship.

A Company were heading for breakfast but some shouted comments, "Good luck, B Company."

"Save some for us."

"Don't drink the water."

They were silenced by Sergeant Jones who bellowed, "Silence and get a move on!"

Our consorts had yet to dock by the time we reached the much smaller coastal steamship. It was an old ship. I knew which one we were to board for the supplies were being unloaded. I saw tents, ammunition boxes and metal tins that I knew would contain food. There were no other steamships with smoke coming from their funnels so we would be the only one sailing. Perhaps that was why just one company was being sent. I saw that the ship had sails as well as a funnel and that told me she was an older vessel than the RMS Danube. The SS Baronda would be cosy by comparison with the ship that had brought us from Southampton.

As we waited, I said to Hooky who was before me, "Why us, Hooky?"

"A Company has fewer men but I am guessing they will be following."

"Silence in the ranks there!"

We had not moved our heads and so Sergeant Windridge could not identify us.

We tramped up the short gangplanks and were ordered by one of the ship's officers to keep moving until we found an empty part of the deck. With just one hundred of us, we soon managed to board. It took longer to get Lieutenant Bromhead's horse aboard. It did not want to board and we found the efforts of the sailors and Mr Bromhead's servant quite amusing. Taylor was not a popular soldier as he had an easy life and thought himself better than the rest of us. He managed to avoid most of the drills and I had never seen him on the range. I dreaded to think how he would cope under fire.

By the time we were all boarded and our bags, blankets and greatcoats neatly piled where we would sleep, the first of the other ships with the regiment aboard had docked and Captain Spalding rode down to greet them for one of them was the ship with Colonel Glyn and the headquarters staff. Our captain was keen to go and I do not know if the captain wished to speak with us again but he was denied the opportunity in any case as the ship was released from the shore and headed out to sea.

As with our previous ship, we found sailors who were quite happy to speak to us. Henry asked, "Where are we off to then, chum?"

The man had a Geordie accent and said, "Why, man, we are off to Port Elizabeth. There is an uprising of sorts there and you fellows are going to sort it out."

Henry nodded, "And how long to get there?"

The Geordie rubbed his chin, "Steaming at nine or ten knots we should cover the five hundred miles in a couple of days. It is why the captain was so keen to leave. He wants to get there in daylight if he can."

The bosun shouted over to the sailor who, grumbling, wandered off.

If we thought that we were in for an easy two days at sea we were mistaken. The trumpet sounded for assembly and we ran to its sound. Colour Sergeant Bourne had found the only piece of the deck where we could all stand and not encumber the crew. It was close to the bows before the foremast. The spray from the bows constantly splattered over us. I noticed that Mr Bromhead and his servant were not with us.

"Right, my lucky lads, you will be wondering why you have merited another ocean cruise and I am here to tell you. There has been a little trouble to the north of the Buffalo River. The militia cavalry regiments are there now trying to deal with it but it has been decided that the 24th Foot are handily placed to sort it out and as we were available our task is to be the advance party and set up a camp. Between Fort Murray and King William's Town." The names meant nothing to any of us but a fort sounded like somewhere we could defend and I liked that thought. "Until the rest of the regiment arrives, we will be responsible for patrols and assisting the cavalry." He pointed with his swagger stick to an open hatchway, "You will have to make do with the floor for a bed. Go below and sort yourselves out then return with your valise and expense pouch. I will signal assembly when I want you to return."

We obeyed because it was Colour Sergeant Bourne but we were all wondering why we needed our valise. There was plenty of room below deck and the six of us made our own neat little camp. We used our greatcoats as beds. By folding them then the buttons would be on the outside and would not irritate us at the night. We folded our blankets on them and placed our bags as pillows. We even had time to unpack the items we would need over the next two days and then the trumpet sounded. When we reached the deck, we saw that there were members of the Commissariat there with ammunition boxes. One of them was chatting to Colour Sergeant Bourne.

Sergeant Windridge shouted, "Attention!"

We snapped to attention.

Colour Sergeant Bourne nodded, seemingly satisfied, "I am not sure if there will be enough wagons and oxen for us and so we will carry most of our own ammunition and tents. There are eight men in a tent. Sergeant Windridge will allocate the tents. This officer is acting Assistant Commissary, Mr Dalton." The blue-uniformed officer stood and acknowledged us. I saw the hint of a smile on the Colour Sergeant's face. "If I tell you that Acting Assistant Commissary, Mr Dalton, was a staff sergeant in the 85th Foot then you will know to treat both him and his men with respect. I believe he still knows how to use his voice." It was a warning and we all heeded it. "Sergeant Windridge?"

"Right, line up in your sections. Smartly does it."

We were allocated to our tent and, as we had hoped we were together along with Shadrack Owen and Harry Cole who were also in our section. Shadrack was the unofficial choirmaster. We got on with both of them and as Harry Cole was also a northerner, a paperhanger from Manchester, then it seemed to be a good mix. We were called up in tent groups and issued ammunition. We placed twenty rounds in each of the two ammunition pouches on the valise and then another thirty in the expenses pouch. Colour Sergeant Bourne said, "Hook, who is going to carry the tent?"

Without a moment of hesitation, Henry turned to me and said, "Roberts. He is a strong lad."

The others grinned but it was wiped off their faces when Colour Sergeant Bourne added, "Then the rest of you can share the other eight hundred rounds that you will carry."

It was my turn to grin.

It was noon by the time we had all the ammunition stored and I had been given the tent. It was big and it was heavy. I dreaded any rain. If it did rain then the weight would be doubled. I laid it next to the bulwark where I was to sleep. It would provide support for my back. If I had to carry it then I would, at least, have some benefit while I was on the ship. The trumpet sounded 'mess' and we grabbed our mess tins and hurried for the hot food. I noticed that Lieutenant Bromhead was not eating with us but the sergeants and corporals were.

Corporal Allan ate with us and I ventured a question. The answer seemed important to me, "What is Lieutenant Bromhead like, Corp?"

He had finished his food and was lighting his pipe. He glanced at me to determine the nature of the question. Was I trying to be funny? What was the reason behind the question?

The hesitation prompted Fred to ask, "Yeah, Corp, I mean we have seen little of him and if we have to fight then he will be the one giving the orders."

Alf added his two pennorth, "If it was the Colour Sergeant giving the orders then we wouldn't be asking Corp but…"

He had the pipe going nicely and he nodded, "I can see your reasons for the questions are honest ones but to tell the truth, I don't know. I might have served a lot longer than any of you but that doesn't mean I know Mr Bromhead." He took a screw that had been taken from the ammunition boxes and used it to increase the flow of air into his pipe by rootling around the tobacco, "The man is deaf. I mean not totally but orders have to be repeated. That is all I know except…" he looked around as though he was expecting to be spied upon, "and this is just a rumour mind, but I have heard that the other officers think he is a bit, well dull."

I was not sure what he meant by that and I was not going to show my ignorance by asking but thankfully 716 Jones came to my aid, "That is a good thing though, isn't it? It means he will be more likely to be cautious. We will be safer."

We all nodded for that made sense but Henry shook his head, "We are on our own and heading into danger. It might be that if there is fighting then we might need an officer with ideas." The others had finished their food and had lit their pipes too. I was saving mine for the land and the insects. I did not seem to get as much pleasure from the simple art of smoking as they did. Henry asked, "Were you in the Andaman's, Corporal?"

"No, I joined while they were over there."

I remembered Private Cooper who had won a medal there.

"And the Lieutenant?"

Shaking his head, Corporal Allan said, "He was in Brecon when I arrived, so no, he wasn't there and I know what you are getting at, Private Hook. Has he had any battle experience? The answer is no but the only ones who have are Colour Sergeant Bourne and Sergeant Windridge."

Henry nodded and pointed his pipe to the two sergeants who unlike the corporals were sitting apart and eating their food with acting Assistant Commissary Dalton, "Then I shall listen for their voices when the fighting starts."

Chapter 8

We made good time and it was just before dawn when we saw lights in the dark that told us we were nearing our destination. Port Elizabeth was a small port and was empty. There were no ships there but I spied some horses and cavalrymen wearing brown uniforms sitting around a brazier. By the time we had reached them and tied up dawn had broken and we needed no orders to tell us that we would be disembarking soon. Lieutenant Bromhead appeared, perfectly attired and with Taylor festooned with his rifle and the lieutenant's. His discomfort made us smile.

"Colour Sergeant Bourne, I shall go ashore and find out what we are to do. I believe that those fellows on the dock are our guides and I assume they have instructions." I noticed that he spoke loudly, Harry Carter who had worked at Pritchard's had been deaf and he had always spoken loudly. The corporal had been right.

"Yes sir."

"Get my horse landed and have the men ready to march. Acting Assistant Commissary Dalton I leave the supplies to you," He waved a hand at the buildings, "I have no idea where you will get wagons."

Assistant Commissary Dalton's voice sounded unflustered as he said, "Not to worry, Lieutenant Bromhead, I have lived in this land for the last six years. I am certain that I can acquire at least one."

I came to know James Dalton quite well over the next two years and a more dependable man you could not wish to meet. He reminded me in many ways of Trooper. He was always calm and knew his way around the army.

The lieutenant and his servant marched down the gangplank towards the four horsemen.

"Hook, take your tentmates and see if you can get the lieutenant's horse ashore." He pointed his swagger stick at us, "Wait until the rest of the company has disembarked."

Inwardly we groaned for we had seen how hard it had been to get the animal aboard the ship but Henry said, "Yes Colour Sergeant."

The horse had been tethered at the stern. I had no idea who had been looking after the animal but it seemed that all they had done was to feed and water it. The deck was covered in horse dung and stank of piss. We put our bags, helmets, rifles and coats well away from the beast and walked carefully towards it. I could see that the others were fearful of the animal but I had been brought up with regular visits to Caesar. I was not afraid of animals and I saw the fear in the horse's eye. It was a shame I did not know his name. I put my hand into the pocket of my trousers. I always kept a mint there and I took out a Mint Imperial. Holding it before me I stepped carefully towards it. I kept my voice calm. Trooper had taught me that a sing song sort of voice worked well and I used that, "There's a good boy. Left alone. eh? Well don't worry, Jack is here to look after you." Trooper had said to speak to horses as though they were children. I could see from the expressions of the others that they thought it daft but the horse, smelling the mint, did not seem to mind. His rough tongue lapped the mint from my hand and I took hold of his halter whilst stroking his head. "There's a good boy." Without taking my eyes from him I gave my orders. "Fred, get his saddle blanket and saddle."

I kept stroking the horse and I put my forehead next to his. Trooper had told me that calmed an upset animal and it worked.

"What do I do, Jack?"

"Put the saddle blanket on the horse and then the saddle."

Henry said, "Alf, give him a hand. You are doing well, Jack. Another talent, eh?"

I put my hand in my pocket and found a second mint. I would save that for the gangplank. I tried to remember how many I had left. I doubted that I would find any more here in South Africa. I would have to husband my supplies. I saw that they had fitted the saddle and tightened the girth. Trooper had told me how you needed the girth very tight.

"Alf, tighten the girth another couple of notches."

"It seems tight enough to me, Jack."

Henry said, "Listen to the lad, Alf, he seems to know what he is doing."

When that was done and the reins and bridle fitted, I said, "Well, let's take him to the gangplank."

Henry said, "Fred, get the tent, Alf and 716 pick up Jack's gear. He has done our work for us."

"Come on, boy, let's get you on solid ground, eh?" I remembered the trouble they had to get the horse on board and I kept talking all the way along the deck. The last of the company were still disembarking and the horse was becoming anxious. I recalled that Trooper had said songs often calmed horses and so I sang the only one I could remember.

I am a broken-hearted milkman, in grief I'm arrayed
Through keeping of the company of a young servant maid
Who lived on board and wages, the house to keep clean
In a gentleman's family near Paddington Green

She was as beautiful as a butterfly and proud as a Queen
Was pretty little Polly Perkins of Paddington Green

The horse calmed immediately and waited patiently while the last of the company disembarked. I saw Colour Sergeant Bourne glance down the deck and begin to smack those at the rear with his swagger stick, "Get a move on you slovenly soldiers." As the last ones hurried away, he nodded to me and I led the horse, whilst still singing, to the gangplank.

Despite the song, I felt the animal begin to baulk and so I took a second mint from my pocket and held it before the horse so that he had to step onto the gangplank to eat it. I led it down the gangplank and he walked calmly.

As I reached the land and the waiting company they all spontaneously cheered. "Quiet in the ranks!" There was no venom in Colour Sergeant Bourne's voice and as I passed him, heading to the Lieutenant, he said quietly, "Well done, Roberts."

I felt ten feet tall at praise from the colour sergeant. Lieutenant Bromhead stopped talking to the troopers as I arrived. He looked, first at me and then the horse, "Did you saddle him?"

"Yes, sir." I made sure that my voice was loud.

102

He gave me a thin smile, "Then be so good as to mount him."

"Sir?"

"If anyone is going to fall on his arse because the girth was not tight enough then I would prefer it to be you rather than me. Mount."

I had never mounted a saddled horse, I had ridden Caesar bareback, but I had seen it done. Luckily, I was unencumbered and I lifted my leg to put it in the stirrup. Still holding the reins I grabbed hold of the saddle and swung my leg over the back. The saddle remained in place.

"Taylor, take the reins." He nodded to me, "You may return to the company." That, it appeared was the only thanks I would get.

I swung my leg over the saddle and, after patting the horse's neck I went back to the others. They were all grinning. By the time I had donned my helmet and fastened my greatcoat and blanket en banderole, we were ready to march. We stood at ease while we awaited the arrival of Acting Assistant Commissary Dalton. I felt my stomach rumble. We had enjoyed a brew on the ship but such had been the urgency of the landing that food had been forgotten. As though someone had read our minds a line of sailors marched down the gangplank with trays of corned beef sandwiches.

As they approached Colour Sergeant Bourne shouted, "Permission for the lads to eat, sir?"

The laconic lieutenant turned and drawled, "Just so long as they don't move."

The Third Mate, who led the sailors, said, "The bread is a little stale but was intended for you and the corned beef was also for you. The captain thought you might need it."

We were all grateful for the sandwiches. True, there was neither butter nor mustard but there was plenty of corned beef that would keep us going. We had barely finished when we heard the rumble of a wagon and saw Acting Assistant Commissary Dalton marching alongside a pair of oxen and a large high sided wagon. One of his men was driving the wagon and the others were running to the ammunition and other supplies piled next to the ship.

He strode up to Colour Sergeant Bourne and Sergeant Windridge rather than Lieutenant Bromhead who was still talking with the colonial cavalry. "Sorry, I could only get one wagon, Colour Sergeant and that was because Franz owed me a favour. We won't be able to carry the men's valises but we should be able to take the tents."

"That is better than we hoped, Mr Dalton."

"I managed to get two water barrels too. That is the main reason it took so much time." He turned to his men, "Come you shower, get the wagon loaded!" I smiled as I heard the former sergeant's voice. He had not forgotten how to command.

Lieutenant Bromhead came over to speak to the three of them. Due to his deafness, we heard every word, not that what was said was a secret.

"We have thirty odd miles to march to Fort Murray, Colour Sergeant. I do not want to camp out in the open so we will push on, eh?"

"Of course, sir." He turned to Acting Assistant Commissary Dalton, "Are we packed yet, Mr Dalton?"

The blue-coated officer nodded, "Ready for the tents to be loaded."

Colour Sergeant Bourne commanded us, "In sections put the tents on top of the wagon and do so neatly."

I was the closest and I threw my tent up and then pulled myself onto the wagon. It was higher than I had expected. I pulled the tent around so that it lay across the boxes and barrels and was close behind the driver's seat. I jumped down and picked up my rifle. Others emulated me. It did not take long and then we began to march. All the drills and the practice came to our aid as we trudged through the heat of a November day along a dusty, stone-covered road. Shadrack Owen began a song and soon we were all singing as we marched.

After two songs the Lieutenant turned around and said, "Colour Sergeant, must they sing?"

"It helps them march, Lieutenant Bromhead, and keeps their mind off food."

The officer said nothing. He and the four troopers of the Natal Native Police were the only ones riding. Even Private Taylor was having to march and it gave us all great pleasure that he was suffering more than the rest of us. He had managed to avoid marching at Brecon and now it would come to haunt him. It was not only the heat that was unbearable but the burning of the sun. The high collars we wore, whilst uncomfortable, afforded some protection but our faces and necks, not to mention our hands began to redden in the sun. When we stopped for water and to relieve ourselves, then shade was sought by everyone. The first place we used was a farm run by a Dutchman. A small stream ran by the side of the road and there were some trees. I suppose he was grateful that Imperial troops were close to his farm for we were greeted well.

Lieutenant Bromhead must have been told how I had managed to get his horse from the ship and he called me over, "You there, Roberts isn't it?"

"Yes sir."

"Take my horse and water him. You seem to have a way with horses."

"What is his name, sir?"

"Blackie, I believe."

I took the reins and spoke to the horse, "Blackie, that suits you but with the white blaze I might have named you Badger." The horse neighed and nuzzled my head, "Sorry, Blackie, I have not enough mints to give you one every five minutes but you need a nice drink and I will keep my eye out for an apple or two. I suppose they must grow here."

I found where feet had muddied the water and I led Blackie upstream. Trooper had told me that horses were greedy and would take too much at once. When I deemed he had taken enough I pulled up his head and walked him into the water. It would cool his hooves. He swished his tail at the flies and then I led him back to drink a little more. Eventually, he was satiated and I returned to the column. The lieutenant merely nodded.

I went back to Fred and the others. Fred handed me a mug of tea and nodded towards the farmhouse, "The woman there saw you with the horse and said that anyone who watered a horse before he had a drink was a good man." I drank the hot sweetened tea. From behind his back, Fred flourished a sweet fruit bun. He was like a conjurer. "She gave you this as well."

I wanted to eat it myself but that was not right and I broke it in two and handed half to him. "Thanks, Fred." There was no butter on it and so I dunked it into the hot sweet tea. That first break was like a feast and put a spring in my step for the next ten miles.

None of us had any idea where we were going. Such information was kept from us. We were all intrigued by the landscape. Most of the company had never been abroad and everything from the houses to the trees, the animals to the mountains, were all new and the march was not as hard as it might have been. Everything was a wonder. Cape Town looked like a metropolis in comparison. There were enough trees to give us some shade and it was the distraction of trees that almost spelt disaster. We knew that the Buffalo River was to the north of us. We had seen its estuary in Port London and could see the other side of the valley. The valley had many farms and we noticed that, as we passed them heading west, they all had ditches for drainage and defence and looked like little forts. The last one had been passed five miles earlier when there was a flurry of gunshots from the trees to the north of us.

Henry had been right about the training for even as the trumpet sounded, we grabbed our Martin-Henry's and slipped a bullet into the chamber as Sergeant Windridge shouted, "Right face. Front rank kneel."

As I turned, I saw a Natal Native Policeman struck in the shoulder but he managed to keep his saddle. All that we could see were the puffs of smoke. Blackie was not happy at the firing and I saw that the lieutenant was struggling to control him. Colour Sergeant Bourne shouted, "Fire at the smoke. Front rank, fire."

Sergeant Windridge shouted, "Rear rank fire." I was used to the kick now but the smoke from almost fifty rifles made it seem like a fog had descended. I had reloaded by the time I heard the command for the front rank to fire and when our order came, I squeezed the trigger. It was a blind volley from all of us and I had no idea what effect we were having.

The Lieutenant's voice sounded out before Colour Sergeant Bourne could order us to fire again, "Fix bayonets."

Even as I pulled the long sword bayonet from its scabbard I heard from our left the voice of the officer of the Natal Native Police, "You don't need a bayonet, Lieutenant."

"I do if we are to go in there and winkle them out."

"Front rank fire."

I slipped another bullet into the chamber and heard the trooper say, "I wouldn't do that, Lieutenant. It might well be an ambush and besides, they have stopped firing."

I suddenly realised that he was right. The only smoke I could see was from our guns.

The Lieutenant said, "Colour Sergeant, send a section in to see if there are any of them left."

"Sir! Corporal Allan, take your section. No further than two hundred yards and take no chances."

"Sir. Right you lot, let us go, skirmish order."

Dropping our valise, greatcoats and blankets we followed Corporal Allan in a loose line. As usual, I was between Fred and Alf. There were trees ahead and bushes. As we neared the tree line the officer of the Native Police shouted, "And watch out for snakes! Stamp the ground as you move and they will shift."

I had a fear of such creatures and I stamped as hard as I could. The grass and shrubs suddenly appeared dangerous. My rifle was ready to fire and I swung it from side to side as we moved into the trees. This was not like an English wood. The trees here were widely spaced and we saw our first body fifty yards in. It was Henry who found it and he approached it gingerly. Old hands, like the soldier who had spoken to me in the stores, had told us that sometimes enemies played dead. Using his lunger Hooky turned over the body and saw a large hole in his chest. The Martini-Henry fired a .45 round and from the look of the dead Xhosa made a mess when it hit. We found another two dead men and blood trails showing where they had taken their wounded away. There were no weapons to be found and the dead men had just a loincloth around their lower regions and feathers in their hair.

Corporal Allan reported to the Lieutenant, "Three dead Xhosa, sir, and no weapons. We must have hit others for we saw where their bodies had been dragged away."

We were close enough to the Natal Native Police for me to see their ranks and the officer was a captain. He nodded to Lieutenant Bromhead, "As I thought, they were hoping to lure you into the woods to try to smoke them out. Had your men gone in then the dozen or so who had guns would have been supported by a hundred or more with spears and clubs. They want your rifles."

"Damned cheek." He turned us, "Thank you, Corporal Allan. Colour Sergeant, let us resume our journey. We have wasted enough time here."

Having been ambushed once the thought had been planted that it could be repeated and the last ten miles to Fort Murray were the most tiring as we were all in a state of nervous tension. Every noise filled us with fear. We saw the flag and the palisade of the fort and there was relief but we had the Buffalo River to cross and the bridge itself was a wooden pontoon. It did not look particularly sound and when we had crossed it and we saw the men on the ramparts, we almost cheered. We would be safe, for the night, at least.

We were expected and a section of the fort, built more than twenty years earlier, had been left for us to erect our tents. We had practised in Wales but there the ground had been grassy and soft. The pegs had slid in effortlessly. Here we had to hammer them into the bone hard ground of a hot summer. Even worse was the sight of the ants and insects we disturbed. I knew that they would return, especially after dark and I wondered how many of them might bite. The camp commandant, also a militiaman, had organised our food. Lieutenant Bromhead would have the luxury of a roof and a bed as well as servants to bring his food as he ate in the officer's mess. We would eat in the open and sleep in tents. The food was a stew but I did not recognise the meat. That did not matter for it was filling and as the fort had bread ovens, we had the joy of freshly baked bread. Washed down with copious mugs of tea we felt as though we had dined like kings and, as there were natives to wash the dixies and cooking pots once we had rinsed our mess tins, we were able to sit and enjoy a smoke. We lit our own campfire and took the advice of one of the garrison to put the leaves of a citrusy smelling plant onto the fire. It had a strong smell and we were assured that the flying insects would stay away. I took no chances and kept my pipe going. I had learned that it burned faster if you kept puffing too much and a more regular regime resulted in a pipe lasting longer and burning less tobacco. I was learning to be a pipe smoker.

One of the militia contingent came over from his barracks to chat to us, "We hear you boys had a little trouble down the road with the Xhosa." His English was accented. You could understand every word he said but the Dutch had been here a long time and even the English settlers had an accent.

Hooky nodded, "We found three bodies."

He confirmed what the officer had said, "They would regard that as a fair rate of exchange had they managed to get a rifle. The Xhosa have no weapons that are effective at range. When they throw their spears, you can see them coming. When they get hold of a rifle then they are a nuisance. Of course, they don't know how to look after them and have no means of getting hold of bullets but when they do then watch out."

We chatted about nonmilitary matters and we asked about the food, the beer, and the pubs; we discovered the latter were few and far between. The women, we learned, were even rarer than the pubs and jealously guarded by their men.

I tapped my pipe out for I was down to ash and as I refilled it, I asked, "Are there tobacconists out here?"

He laughed, "What do you need them for? Every farmer grows his own. They are happy to sell it to you. It might not be the stuff you are smoking but it is not bad."

I brightened. That meant I could replenish my supply, "Do you know where we can get oranges?"

He looked at me strangely, "Oranges?"

"I need the peel to keep my baccy dry."

He smiled, "A good trick and one I use. I will bring you some in the morning. I am on duty serving the officers their breakfast and they have freshly squeezed orange juice. We usually throw the peel out. You are more than welcome to it."

"Thanks."

Henry said, "Everyone has been really pleasant to us. Why?"

"Because, my friends, your arrival means that we don't have to patrol and keep the farmers and their families safe. You and your red uniforms, not to mention your rifles will draw the Xhosa to you like moths to a flame. It is a sad fact of life but your arrival means fewer of our men will die." He shrugged, "It is the truth and there is no denying it. Your white helmets and red tunics, not to mention your rifles make you a more attractive and easier target. You lads stand in lines to fight. We hide!"

Henry nodded, "So what you are saying is that we are like the Judas Goat and will attract the spears." He nodded, "Well at least we know where we stand."

We were silent for a while and then Fred said, "Of course, after our last stand we don't know where we will be buried."

Chapter 9

When we left Fort Murray, the next morning, we had an escort of a troop of the Natal Native Police. We were heading closer to the Xhosa rebels and the cavalry acted as a screen. We marched just fifteen miles north under a baking sun until we reached a small plateau above Yellowwood's River. When the riders all dismounted then we knew we had reached our new, albeit temporary home. We sank to the ground for we were all exhausted. The last climb had been a hard one. As there was a river close by, I drank half of the water from my canteen. We had husbanded the water thus far but now there was no need for we had river water. Of course, it would have to be boiled before we could use it but there appeared, even though it was summer, to be plenty in it.

Lieutenant Bromhead and Colour Sergeant Bourne walked the proposed site for the camp. There could be more than two thousand men here eventually. It would not just be the two battalions but the cooks, commissary, medical staff and militia. We just sat and waited. The horsemen had carried on to patrol the ground around us although we had a good view of it.

Alf had found a stick and he was using a penknife to whittle it. He pointed in the distance, "You can barely see those boys on their horses." I nodded. He continued, "The point I am making, Jack, is that they are wearing brown colours and they disappear. If just one of us was a mile away from here then he would be easily spotted." He tapped the stick against his tunic, "Proper daft it is wearing red."

Henry had been listening and said, "Tradition."

Fred laughed, "Aye, and it doesn't show the blood."

I remembered something Trooper had told me, "The longer we are out here the more faded it will become."

Alf had taken his helmet off to scratch his head and he said, "And now I see why some of the older hands have stained their helmets with tea. I shall do that with mine."

"Attention!" We all jumped to our feet, Alf jamming his helmet on the wrong way around. As Corporal Allan glared at him, he quickly remedied the situation. "Right, my lucky lads,

Sergeant Windridge is marking the ground out. First, we put Mr Bromhead's tent up, then the sergeants' and lastly, yours. Then I want Number 1 platoon to gather as much of the thorny bushes as they can and use that as a temporary perimeter. Number 2 platoon will clear the few trees that are here and then help Mr Dalton to erect the kitchen and the rest will be on water detail."

The only ones who would have a relatively easy task would be Number 2 platoon. There were just a dozen or so thin and straggly trees. I was sure that they could just pull them out by the roots. They would be used for firewood. I did not relish our task. The thorny bushes had long deadly spikes and made the brambles and roses we had at home seem like nothing. We had taken off our packs and greatcoats when we had reached the top and now, we took off our helmets. It exposed our heads to the hot sun which, even in the afternoon, still burned hotter than an English sun at noon. I had an idea and I took out my spare shirt and tied it around my head; the tail hung down over my neck and I felt the relief as soon as I did it.

The ground was rock hard and we had to use rocks to hammer in the wooden pegs. As the whole company erected the first tents then the camp took shape quickly. Our next task was our own tent. Sergeant Windridge had put markers where the tents were to be placed and ours was at the end of one line. We carefully removed every stone we could find and then made sure that the pegs were in at an angle and would withstand any winds. Being at the end we would be exposed to the full force of any storm. The stones we would use to pack around the pegs and help to hold them down. That done we placed our gear neatly inside each tent. The rifles were stacked together outside each tent. Colour Sergeant Bourne had assigned men as sentries.

Corporal Allan shouted, "Number one platoon, bring your lungers and come with me."

I saw that a couple of others had emulated me and their heads were now protected from the sun. I looked at the thorns and took off my tunic. If my shirt was torn then I could use a needle and thread to repair it. It would not be seen beneath my tunic. I was not certain what the punishment would be for damaging my tunic and would not take the risk of stoppage of pay.

Henry took charge of our section and organised us. "You two," he pointed to Shadrack and Harry, "Go and fetch your weapons. Fit your bayonets to your rifles and lift the bushes as high as they will go." As they hurried off to fetch their guns he said, "When they lift it the rest of us will crawl underneath and use our lungers to cut off the plants as close to the base as we can. Then we can use our rifles to lift it and move it as one."

It seemed a good idea but Fred refined it, "If we wear our helmets then it will prevent us from getting our heads torn."

While we were the last to get started Henry's method paid dividends and we suffered far less than the rest of the platoon who shouted and cursed as heads and arms were slashed by the wicked thorns. We were also the first to finish for we were able to lift the whole section of thorny bushes in one and we had it in place, secured by stakes driven into the ground, while the rest of the platoon was still labouring. We eked out the last part of the job for Hooky was no fool and realised that if we finished too early, we would be asked to help the others.

"Corp, we will take the bits left over to the fires. They are dry enough."

He nodded absentmindedly as the other sections struggled to make a barrier as effective as ours. We were not exactly skiving but we managed to get away from the rest of the platoon and help Number 2 platoon. The huge pots were placed on fires so that water could be boiled for drinking and for cooking. The cooks would remember who had helped them and might just reward us with more food. As we had learned already, a soldier can never have enough food.

By the time the food was ready the camp was surrounded by a barrier of thorns. It was a primitive sort of defence but having endured the thorns I knew that a scantily clad warrior would suffer even more than we had. Corporal Allan explained as we ate that the next day would see us add a ditch and then place ammunition boxes behind the thorns to provide some protection. As they had enjoyed the easier task Number 2 Platoon was given the night watch. The sections would each take one-third of the night and watch for enemies. The attack on the road had been a warning that we were in a war zone. We knew we would have a night watch. It meant every soldier had one night in six where they would lose four hours of sleep. We accepted it philosophically. It was better than being attacked in our sleep.

Of course, the corollary of having a whole night of sleep was that we were the ones selected for the first patrol. Sergeant Windridge and Lieutenant Bromhead would lead our platoon on a patrol to the north and west while the rest of the company dug ditches and latrines. The troopers had ridden back to Fort Murray at dawn but they had pointed to the north and explained that the rebels were attacking King William's Town and the borderlands between the colony and Gcalekaland. The governor of the colony, Sir Bartle Frere, was at King William's Town and we now knew that it was he who had summoned the regiment. Once Colonel Glyn and the rest of the regiment arrived, we would be used to suppress the rebellion. Our patrol was so that the lieutenant had a better picture of the land. He would be able to impress the colonel with his diligence. Perhaps he was not as dull as Corporal Allan had been led to believe.

He continued to ride Blackie even though it made him an easier target. The militia trooper who had been shot in the ambush was a warning of the dangers to men on horses. We went where there there we no roads and Blackie had to pick his way through thorn bushes and stony ground. There was plenty of cover for an ambush as the grass was often so high that even Henry Hook could hide there. Even when birds took flight it was hard to work out the cause. There were far more animals here than there would be in England. We knew that there were lions and leopards and although we had never seen one the thought of their teeth and claws was terrifying. The previous night Fred had found a spider the size of a baby's hand and we watched out for those too. Fred had killed it but we had heard of spiders that, like the snakes in this land, had a deadly bite.

When we heard firing, just before noon, the lieutenant had us double-time to get to it. Even before we started to run my shirt and tunic were soaked with sweat. The gunshots were irregular but as we had no idea who was firing against whom it made little difference. As we drew closer, we could hear shouts and the sound of banging. I could not work out what was causing the banging. Ahead of us was a ridge and we could see, beyond it, smoke rising in the air. Lieutenant Bromhead showed that he was not as dull as some men thought. He dismounted and handed Blackie's reins to a dishevelled and exhausted Taylor. The man could barely get his breath.

"Skirmish line, Sergeant Windridge, and have the men fix bayonets."

"You heard the officer!"

I attached the sword bayonet to the end of my rifle and slipped a bullet into the chamber. Sergeant Windridge had a pistol, as did the Lieutenant but he held a rifle as we did. Holding his pistol in his left hand he raised his sword and shouted, "Forward!"

We made our way up the steep slope passing between more of the thorny bushes and the trees that covered it. As we neared the top, we could hear the banging more loudly and it was punctuated by the sound of rifles and muskets.

When we reached the ridgeline, we saw a line of wagons. They were being attacked by warriors with shields, short stabbing spears, clubs and firearms. I saw that the banging was caused by the warriors hitting the shield with the butt of a spear. The wagons had women and children as well as a couple of men in uniforms. I saw that even the women were helping, reloading the guns for the men.

Lieutenant Bromhead shouted, "B Company, open fire."

This was not like the other ambush. I could see the backs of the warriors who were less than one hundred yards from us and I aimed at one who had what looked like monkey tails hanging from the back of his loincloth and they also adorned his head. They were relatively close to us and, even with the lunger on the end of my barrel, were easy targets. Even though smoke from the barrel clouded my vision slightly I saw the warrior slammed in the back and red poured from the gaping wound. He pitched forward and I reloaded whilst moving forward. Fred was screaming but I couldn't make out the words. I fired at a warrior who ran at me with his shield held before him. My bullet hit his shield when he was just twenty paces from me and spun him around. I saw men falling to our .45 bullets but they seemed intent on getting to us. I wondered if the lieutenant's order had been the correct one. I had no time to debate as a spear-wielding warrior ran at me before I had managed to slip another bullet into the chamber.

When we had practised with a bayonet it had been against a similarly armed opponent. The shield of the warrior who came at me gave him an advantage. He held it invitingly before him and I feinted towards it. He chose that moment to stab with his short spear. I flicked the head aside with my lunger and then whipped the sword bayonet back across the unprotected stomach. When we had finished clearing the thorns the night before I had honed my bayonet so that, if I had wished I could have shaved with it. It seemed to tear open the flesh effortlessly. His hands went to his middle as he attempted to stem the flood of guts and blood that poured from it. As he fell, I loaded my rifle again and raising it, fired at the nearest warrior but we had ripped the heart from the attackers and they fled. The man at whom I had aimed turned and my bullet caught him on the arm. He kept running. When the defenders of the wagons saw them in flight they cheered.

"Sound recall."

As the bugle sounded, I looked and saw that a couple of soldiers from another section were chasing after the fleeing attackers. We wandered through the bleeding bodies towards the road on which the wagons stood. Although some of them still moved it was clear that they were dying. I kicked the weapons away from their hands for I was wary of them. When we reached the wagons a young tanned woman, she was no more than twenty, threw her arms around me and planted a kiss on my cheek. To say I was taken aback was an understatement.

Fred laughed, "You could fall in a pigsty, Jack Roberts, and still come up smelling of roses."

The woman was Afrikaans and her voice was heavily accented, "Thank you. You have saved my mother, my sisters and me."

I waved a hand at the others, "I was not the only one."

Any further conversation was ended by Sergeant Windridge's voice, "Number 1 section check the bodies on the other side of the road."

I went with Hooky and the others. I had chambered another round and was ready to open fire at the first sign of any danger.

There were fewer bodies on that side and I saw some of the warriors halfway up the slope. They waved their shields and spears at us. Henry slowly raised his rifle, took aim and fired. The warrior in the middle was punched backwards and the rest all ran.

"That will teach the cheeky blighters."

The Lieutenant's overly loud voice rang out, "Secure the perimeter. You there tell me what happened."

He did not dismount but rode over to speak to the leader of the wagon train who was having his side bandaged. I made my way up to a rock so that I could see further. Alf and Fred took positions ten yards from me. Fred waved his rifle at the dead, "They don't lack courage, I will say that for them."

Alf shook his head, "Proper daft, if you ask me. How is a bit of cowhide going to stop a bullet?"

I had no answer to that but I had been terrified when they had run at us. I was grateful for the drills. They meant I did not think about what to do. My body seemed to know instinctively.

After a short conversation, Lieutenant Bromhead said, "Sergeant Windridge, Corporal Allan, take Number 1 section and escort these people to King William's Town. We will head back to the camp."

"Sir!"

Fred rolled his eyes. Who knew if there would be a bed and how we would get back to the camp? The same warriors we had chased away could be watching and waiting their moment to descend upon a thin line of red-coated soldiers. I took some pleasure from the exhausted look on Taylor's face. The servant had not, as far as I knew, even fired his rifle and he now had a long march back to the camp. We knew our march would be the shorter one.

Sergeant Windridge left us in no doubt that he did not care about beds or food. We had to obey every order. As the rest of the platoon marched south, he shouted. "Form two lines parallel to the wagons. One form on me and one on Corporal Allan."

Alf followed Corporal Allan as the wagon drivers, eager to reach the walls of King William's Town, used their whips to get the wagons rolling. Despite the heat and our previous march, the colonists did not go slowly and it was nearer to a quick march than our regular gait. I felt the sweat pouring off my back and was desperate for a drink of the tepid water in my canteen. I learned a lesson that day. From then on whenever we stopped, however briefly, I took a drink.

We had about four miles to cover and the walls of King's William Town were well made. The gates were just wide enough to grant us entry and no more. Once inside the walls, I bent over double just to catch my breath. I saw that the others, even the mighty Sergeant Windridge did the same. A Natal cavalry officer, a major, strode over. "Thank you for your intervention, Sergeant." He pointed to a hut that was raised off the ground. "You can spend the night there. We will sound the bugle when it's time to eat. Until then if you could confine yourself to the hut, we would appreciate it. There are women here, you know." It seemed that while they welcomed our intervention, Imperial troops had a dubious reputation.

With that, he turned on his heel and strode off. As we entered the rather dirty hut, I could see that it had not been used for some time and was covered in both dust and the detritus that had blown in. Hooky spotted some brooms that were in the corner. "Here, you four, get this place swept out." Fred, Alf, 716 and I took the brooms and walked to one end to begin sweeping the hut.

Fred shook his head, "Well I wasn't expecting the kiss that came Jack's way but I expected something better than this."

There were some palliasses in the hut and the others began to beat them. Sergeant Windridge said as he did so, "The thing is, Hitch, that these people don't want us here. They don't want the soldiers of the Queen marching up and down their country. They need us to get rid of the danger to their families but as soon as these amaGcaleka rebels are sorted out then they will want to be rid of us."

Fred shook his head, "Ungrateful blighters."

"It has always been this way. The Dutch who settled this land did pretty much as they pleased. When they invited us to help them, they didn't know we would stay. Just do your job, Hitch, and when it is over you can go back to England and moan all you like. While you are here you say, yes sir, no sir, three bags full sir. Is that clear?"

"Yes Sergeant." I saw the twinkle in his eye that told me he was going to add 'three bags full, Sergeant' and I shook my head.

Sergeant Windridge had sensed it too and said, "Very wise, Hitch. Listen to Roberts he has some sense in his head."

Sergeant Windridge had not even been looking in our direction. How had he known?

Despite our rescue and the unexpected kiss, we were treated more like convicts labouring on a road rather than rescuers. Any thoughts that we would be regarded as chivalrous knights saving damsels in distress were shattered. We were workmen doing a necessary job. The food was wholesome enough and the rough beer had a better taste than I expected. When the regiment arrived at the camp we would have wine, spirits and beer. This would do for now.

We sat on the veranda as night fell to smoke our pipes. The fug of smoke we put up was effective against the insects. It also drew the farmer who had led the wagon train. He was a large Dutchman and he came over with a package. "Thank you for what you did. Take this with my thanks. It is good tobacco." He unwrapped the package and the most amazing smell drifted up. "How you divide it is up to you but take it with our thanks. Defeat these rebels and then go home." He turned on his heel and left.

Hooky gave a sad smile, "The Lord giveth and the Lord taketh away. I can see that you are right, Sergeant Windridge. Will you do the honours, sarge?"

"No, Hooky, we all trust you to be fair." He was scrupulously fair and in the absence of scales gave us all what looked like an identical portion.

My drying pouch of tobacco was improved by adding the damper, fresher leaf and I did as the others did and mixed it all together. True we would not get the full effect of the taste but the tobacco we had would eke the new supplies out further.

We were awoken the next morning by the bugle awakening the garrison. This was a town but a frontier town. The militia ruled it. We breakfasted and were given dried meat called, biltong, as well as a loaf of bread each. We filled our canteens and then prepared to head south. Before we had taken our first patrol, I would not have been worried but now I knew that just stepping from your doorstep was a dangerous act.

"Roberts, you and Hitch lead off. You are both young and have young eyes."

"Yes, Sarn't Windridge."

Slipping a bullet in the chamber of my rifle, we left the gates and headed along the road south. Rutted during the winter rains it would not have rated the name road in England but here it was considered a well-made and serviceable road and Fred and I took our places on either side of the road, avoiding the ditch where we knew all kinds of slippery, biting, scratching and generally evil creatures lurked. I had to force myself to look beyond the ditch to the scrubby tree line. I knew that any warriors who were there to attack us would hide as best that they could. We had found leaves and feathers on the dead warriors we had killed. I deduced they were to disguise the warriors. I decided to look for movement reasoning that any animal or bird would take flight or run well before a man approached them. If I saw anything move it would be more likely to be a warrior who was tired of remaining still. I knew that when I had done sentry duty in Brecon, I had learned to move just slightly when under the eagle eye of Colour Sergeant Bourne. I assumed a warrior would do the same. It was easy to mistake the slight breeze that moved the leaves slightly as a threat but I managed to control my fearful heart.

We stopped after two miles and drank water. "Anything?"

We both chorused, "No, Sarn't Windridge."

We continued and the water had helped. I felt more alert and perhaps it was that two miles later, which made me see the warrior standing behind the tree just forty paces from me. He was almost invisible and I might have mistaken the white feather as having fallen from some bird but he made the mistake of looking too soon and I saw his hair and his head.

What was I to do? I just raised my rifle and shouted, "Stand to!"

Even as I raised it the panicked warrior broke from cover and ran at us. I was aware of more movement but I aimed at the warrior for he was a clear target. He was a moving target and I squeezed off my round too soon. It spun him around and I saw the spatter of blood but he was not dead even though he disappeared from view. Reloading my rifle I heard the others firing.

"Close up!"

It was the right command for there were so few of us that we were vulnerable and could be isolated. From what we had seen so far, the warriors we faced either used old rifles or tried to close and use their spears. We needed a wall of lead to deter them. More of them appeared and I raised my rifle and fired before moving back to join the others. I seemed to have no control over my actions. My hands just fed bullets into the chamber, I raised my rifle and I fired. I felt Alf join me on my right as I stepped back to the centre of the road. Sergeant Windridge was using his pistol and that gave us an advantage. He could empty the six bullets and then fire his rifle knowing he had a bullet in the chamber. The attack lasted moments but it felt like a lot longer. The smoke hid the warriors from us and we only stopped when Sergeant Windridge shouted, "Cease fire!" We saw no bodies but I, for one, had no intention, unless ordered to do so to seek them.

Henry shouted, "We are getting low on ammo, Sergeant."

As the sergeant reloaded his pistol he muttered, "And you get the prize for stating the bleeding obvious, Private Hook." I smiled. It was rare for Henry to be reprimanded. "Anyone hurt?"

We all shouted in the negative.

"Good. We keep on in the same formation. Well done, Roberts. You have sharp eyes." I took a drink of water. I desperately needed to pee but I wasn't going to risk laying my rifle down to do so. "Head off, boys."

I grinned at Fred Hitch and moved off again. I knew that the sergeant would allow us to get twenty paces ahead. We were live bait and having been attacked once I was nervous. It was the sound of horses that brought relief. From what we had been told the warriors we faced were no horsemen and that could only mean one thing, cavalry.

The Durban Light Horse reined in when they spied our red tunics. The young lieutenant grinned, "You must be the lost souls we were sent to find. Keep marching south, Sergeant Windridge. A company of your chaps are following us."

Pointing to the north the sergeant said, "We were ambushed a mile or so north of here sir."

"Right, Sergeant, we will take a look."

We rounded the next bend and, thanks to the slope saw C Company marching along the road behind Captain Spalding. The rest of the regiment had arrived and we were no longer alone. They cheered us as they passed until Captain Spalding barked at them to be silent. Their looks were ones of admiration. We had endured fire and, thus far they had not. In this little colonial war, we passed, at the moment, for veterans.

Chapter 10

Already most of the recently arrived regiment and ancillary soldiers were busy erecting tents, digging deeper ditches and building a blockhouse. Pails of water were being drawn from the river and emptied into barrels. Fires were heating cauldrons of water for food and for washing. The only ones wearing their tunics were the sentries and the officers. Lieutenant Bromhead and Colonel Glyn strode over with Colour Sergeant Bourne in close attendance.

"Attention!" Our heels all snapped together and our rifles were brought up almost as one. Our training showed through because I was so tired that I could barely lift my rifle.

"Report, Sergeant Windridge." The Lieutenant's loud laconic voice drawled out.

"Yes sir. We escorted the wagons safely to the town and left this morning to return here. A few miles up the road we were ambushed by unknown warriors. We fought them off, sir, and were relieved by the Durban Light Horse and Captain Spalding."

The colonel asked, "Any casualties?"

"No sir."

"And how many of the enemy did you manage to hit?"

"Hard to say, sir. There were no bodies when it was over."

The colonel frowned and the lieutenant said, "It is a damned difficult country, colonel, and it is not as if they stand in straight lines. They take away the bodies of their dead."

"Then how do we know if we are winning, Bromhead? Damned unsatisfactory. Come with me and we will try to make sense of those maps we have. If we can find their village then we can do something about them, eh?"

We were forgotten. Colour Sergeant Bourne strode up, "At ease, lads." He smiled, "You have not let yourselves down. Now go and get cleaned up. You have earned a rest."

"Colour Sergeant, we are low on ammunition."

Nodding he answered, "The Commissary is all set up as well as the quartermasters' stores. "He pointed his swagger stick at some wagons which formed a laager inside the fort.

When we reached the Commissary, we saw it was well organised and acting Assistant Commissary Dalton smiled when he saw us, "You survived, well done. A small band of men such as you would be an easy target." He turned to his assistants, "Give them as much as they need."

Henry said, "Acting Assistant Commissary Dalton, you have lived here. Can we beat these people? I mean they hide in plain sight and then disappear."

"Just call me Mr Dalton, eh, laddie? Otherwise, we will get nowhere." His Scottish burr was still there. "Oh, aye, they can be beaten but you need horsemen to confine their means of escape. They won't face a line of redcoats, that is for sure. They have learned that we don't move and they aren't good enough with rifles to be effective. Their success will come in catching small groups of men alone and attacking them. That is why I am impressed. We heard the firing and I knew what was happening. I expected the horsemen to be bringing back mutilated bodies on the backs of horses."

"Mutilated?" There was horror in Fred's voice.

"When they kill an enemy they like to take a trophy. To them, it is a sign of honour to both men."

"Well, I can do without such honour Mr Dalton."

When we had loaded our valises and expenses pouches with the ammunition we headed for the quartermaster and his supplies. Sergeant Wilson was the Quarter Master and, in the past, he had been parsimonious at best but as we approached, he greeted Sergeant Windridge with a smile, "Well done, lads. I hear you drew enemy blood. What can I do for you?"

We had left Brecon ill-equipped and we now knew it. There were items we could have claimed but had not. Henry said, "Neck cloths sergeant, we forgot to get them at Brecon."

He took a box down and handed one to Henry who said, cheekily, "A second one would be handy, sergeant."

He hesitated until Sergeant Windridge said, "They have done well, sergeant, and this is not cheek. Whatever they ask for they will need."

"But if others all ask for the same then I will have none left."

Sergeant Windridge grinned, "And less to carry around too. Between you and me I don't think we will be staying here for very long. Do you?"

He nodded and we all took two cloths. Fred managed to get three. We also picked up other bits and pieces, none of which would win the war but they would make our lives better and more comfortable. I was learning that was what a campaign was about. A soldier did the best he could and made his life as comfortable as possible.

Back at our tents, the first thing we did was to fit a cloth to the rear of our helmets for protection from the sun. We had been lucky and had enjoyed more shade than we might have expected but as we had marched in the camp, we had seen the red burned necks and cheeks of the sentries. Standing in a hot sun would do that to a man. That done we set to cleaning our guns. Corporal Allan came over as we were doing so. Our three skirmishes had made us closer, "An old hand's tip is to pee down the barrel," he grinned, "wait until it is cold though and don't let the officers see it. Your pee is acid and breaks down the carbon. It makes it easier to clean."

He left us and Alf was the first to try it. We laughed as he managed to spray his hand but when his ramrod pulled out more carbon and soot than we had, we emulated him. We were learning to be soldiers. We sharpened our sword bayonets realising that they would be as important as the bullets we fired. The rest of the platoon joined us around our fire after we had eaten. We generously gave each of them a fill of their pipes with the free tobacco. After all, they had earned it every bit as much as we and it made us closer. We learned that the colonel had sent Captain Spalding with C Company on a ship to follow us as soon as he had landed in Cape Town while the rest of the regiment had not even disembarked from their steamships but continued to sail on to Port Elizabeth. Captain Spalding had made better time and had been at the camp when the lieutenant returned. The regiment had been marched through the night to reach the camp and I knew that those toiling would be exhausted. A rota for duty had been established and we would have the night watch the next night. We had the luxury of a whole night of sleep. It was not uninterrupted sleep however and 163 Williams was killed in a night attack. To Colonel Glyn's chagrin, there were no enemy bodies despite the fusillade the sentries had fired. He was frustrated by the lack of evidence. I just thought that the Xhosa were showing that they were clever warriors and would take some beating.

He sent out D Company and E Company the next morning to scout out the places held by the rebels. It meant we spent all day working on the camp's defences. The night attack had shown us some weaknesses. It was much easier working with a forage cap and a cloth to keep our heads cooler and with plenty of water we were able to keep drinking. Our early adventure had prepared us better for the campaign than some of the others. Sick call had an increasing number of patients. Some were sun-related, either dehydration or sunburn while at least half were either insect bites or snake bites. One man in F Company died and it was a warning for all of us.

When the two companies returned it was with our first casualties of war. Four men had been wounded in ambushes and the colonel was furious. At parade the next morning he castigated the men of the two companies pointing out that in three actions Number 1 Section of Number 1 platoon B Company had suffered no casualties and, thus far, inflicted the only reported losses on the enemy. None of us liked the accolade especially as it was that it had been Llewellyn's company that had suffered two casualties and he would resent the praise heaped upon us. We wanted anonymity. Had we been lucky or were we simply better soldiers? I knew that we were closer than most sections and that was down to Henry Hook who seemed to me to be a non commissioned officer rather than a private.

That night was our first duty. There had been another attack the previous night but we had suffered no casualties. Sergeant Windridge prowled around our section of the perimeter, it led to the water and growled, "The whole regiment expects good things of us, my lads, so stay sharp and keep one loaded. They went away empty-handed last night and I think that increases the odds of them coming tonight."

Henry asked, "Should we fix bayonets, sarge?"

"There are no orders to do so but if you are happy with the extra weight then by all means. Eyes peeled!" We fixed bayonets. If the extra weight could save my life then I was happy to bear it.

Fred was twenty paces to my left and Alf twenty to my right. We had been allocated the weakest section of the defences as there was a zig-zag path down to the river. The hurdle gate at the top was no barrier and whoever had put the thorn bushes there had not done as good a job as we had on our side of the fort. My experience at the point of our patrol had taught me two things. Move your eyes and not your head and watch for movement, any movement. We had the duty, we called it stag, I don't know why, for the middle watch until two a.m. Number 2 platoon would relieve us. I couldn't work out the time by looking at the moon and so I just focussed on the ground. The first movements I saw were small animals and, in many ways, there were reassuring for I could ignore them once I had worked out they there the local rats, foxes and other vermin. The insidious slithering of snakes sent shivers down my spine but they were relatively easy to spot as they hunted the smaller animals.

It was a cloaked warrior, trying to emulate the movement of a snake that drew my attention. At first, I thought it was a reptile but I realised that it had to be an enormous snake if it was. I hissed, "Movement down the slope. Closer to you. Alf."

Fred had heard and hissed back, "Snake?"

Alf said, "Too big."

I looked again and saw that the warrior had rested against a rock some forty paces from us. If there was one there had to be others. Alf said, "I will pass the word for Corporal Allen."

It was the right decision for gunshots in the night deprived the whole camp of sleep and we all needed sleep. Even so, I aimed my rifle at the figure and watched as it slithered once more. The movement was almost imperceptible but it was movement. When he was twenty paces from us, he rose and Alf fired. I also fired. I don't know which one hit him but he fell and his body began to roll down the slope to the river. There was a shout and ten more warriors rose from the dirt and rocks. Even as Fred fired at a warrior close to him another ran towards him with his spear ready to strike at his unprotected side. I took two steps and bayonetted the surprised warrior in the ribs; he tumbled down the slope towards the river. The bugle sounded 'stand to'.

"Watch out, Jack!"

Another warrior had crept closer to me and even as I turned to Alf's warning cry, I saw the amaGcaleka warrior just six feet away. I still had the next bullet in my hand and my gun was empty. I had to use my lunger. I flicked it at his thrusting spear. It deflected it but the edge tore through my trouser leg and scraped along my calf. The weapons they were using might be primitive but they were sharp. I brought my bayonet back and it sliced across his cheek and nose. Undeterred he came up the slope and I was aware that I had stepped too far beyond the safety of my comrades. I stepped back and that saved my life for he had a second spear in his other hand and that sliced the air I had just occupied. Meeting no opposition he fell on his face and I just reacted. I planted the bayonet between his shoulder blades.

Suddenly the line of sentries was doubled as more of our company joined us. Rifles fired at the now fleeing amaGcaleka. I looked down the line and saw the smiling, relieved faces of my section. We had survived. I was about to pull my bayonet from the body of the last warrior I had slain when Colour Sergeant Bourne's voice halted me, "Leave it there lad so that the colonel can see that they can be killed."

I suddenly realised that he was the only body that remained.

"Over here, Colonel Glyn."

The Colonel, Captain Spalding and Lieutenant Bromhead all arrived with pistols in their hands.

"The other bodies rolled down the slope or were taken away, Colonel, I told Roberts to leave his lunger where it was so that you could see the enemy."

Someone had brought a lighted brand from the fire and by its light, we saw the two stabbing spears. The heads were slightly shorter than our sword bayonets and crudely made but I could attest to their sharpness. In the warrior's belt was a curved knife. His face was scarred with tribal tattoos and he had ostrich feathers in his hair. There were other markings too but, at the time we did not know what they meant."

"Good work Roberts. You may remove your bayonet now." As I did so he said, "Have the body brought to Headquarters, maybe some of the militia can enlighten us about the man."

Colour Sergeant Bourne said, "And you get yourself to Surgeon Reynolds, Roberts. We don't want that wound turning bad."

As soon as the bugle had sounded 'stand to' then the medical staff had prepared the hospital. An orderly looked at my leg and said, "Spear wound, Surgeon Reynolds."

"Put your helmet and rifle down and hop onto the bed."

I had not felt the pain until that moment but hopping was not an option. After obeying the first two orders I scrambled somewhat untidily onto the hospital bed.

"The trousers are ruined. Hopkins, have we still got those trousers from the man who was killed yesterday?"

"Yes, Surgeon Reynolds." I heard the disappointment in his voice. I suspect he had plans to sell them on.

With my torn trousers removed and an inspection light fetched forward the surgeon peered at the wound. "Looks clean enough but it will need stitches. I don't want to waste morphine. That is for serious cases." He handed me a mug, "Drink this." It was neat brandy and the surgeon laughed at my gasp. "Good, you are not a drinker. Who knows you may even last a year or two. Now lie back and try not to shout, there's a good fellow."

I don't know if it was the brandy or the surgeon's skill but it was relatively pain-free. He numbed the wound with alcohol and then sewed it shut.

"Restricted duties for a week, and then return here for me to take out the stitches. You are a lucky boy. Another inch or two and he would have struck an artery and then Lieutenant Bromhead would have to write a letter to your mother." That thought chilled me. I do not know why but I had not expected to die in any of the four encounters in which I had been involved. The surgeon's words told me I was wrong.

The section was still on duty and so I went to the campfire near our tent and put on a dixie of water. They would want a brew when they came off duty and I felt guilty that I had been relieved. The stitches and the wound ached but I had borne worse as a child. The rest came back an hour before dawn and were grateful for the tea.

"You should have your head down, boyo. That was a nasty wound." Alf seemed to have a morbid fascination with wounds for he had examined closely the cuts and scrapes we had suffered in our first skirmishes.

"It will stiffen up when I stop. I thought we could all do with a brew." He nodded. "I am on restricted duties, Hooky, what does that mean?"

"You stay in the camp and do nothing to aggravate the wound. Alf is right that spear thrust cut you badly. We saw the blood. You will be helping the surgeon and the cooks. No heavy lifting and no sentry duty."

Fred shook his head, "I shall miss you at my side, Jack. You saved my bacon this morning."

I shrugged, "I just reacted."

Henry said, "Aye, and got yourself a wound as a result. That shows guts, boy."

I hadn't thought of it that way.

The next seven days were interesting for me as I got to see other parts of the regiment and how they worked. There was a hospital and while I hadn't needed a bed others had. There were wounds and the inevitable illnesses. I helped there, taking food and the like to the patients. I peeled potatoes for the cooks and helped to make the soup. Mother had already taught me how to cook and I was pleased that I seemed to have some skill. The only bad moments were when I came across Llewellyn. It had been some time since the incident in Brecon and I hoped that he would have forgotten it but he had brooded and the wound had festered. It was ironic that the real wound I had suffered was healing well and itching while the imagined wound he had suffered was eating his insides out.

I was carrying some papers for Colonel Glyn when he saw me and he sneered, "Proper little brown nose you are, Englishman. You only have so much luck and one day yours will run out. I just hope that I am there to see it."

I had decided that silence was the best policy and so I returned the insult with a smile. There were warrant officers nearby and the brooding Welshman could not do anything more than sneer at me. I did not mind for it did not hurt.

Two days after restricted duties ended and my stitches were removed, we were told that the next day the two battalions would be taking the field against an amaGcaleka village eight miles away. The colonel had finally discovered it was the home of the man I had slain and we were being sent to punish them. It did not sit well with me for I knew there would be women and children close by. The hurts their warriors had caused would not excuse, in my mind, innocents being put in danger. Trooper had said that a good soldier did not make war on women and children.

Some local light horsemen arrived at the camp. They were farmers who were called to their colours in time of need. They bore the name of the man who paid for their uniforms. Tom Nicholson owned the largest farm in the area. It was to the north of Port Elizabeth and his one hundred men were armed, clothed and trained by him. I heard he had been in the 11th Regiment of Hussars at Balaklava. Had I met him I would have liked to ask him about the battle. I never got the chance but, like Trooper, as a survivor of the battle he had learned well and his men were well trained and knew their business. Wearing slouch hats and a khaki-coloured tunic and breeches, they were armed with a variety of short carbines. As with all the native regiments or militia they wore a red scarf around their hats to identify them as British. Two riders were allocated to each company. They were to help scout and to give us information about the land through which we passed.

When Lieutenant Bromhead saw the two men leading their hardy ponies towards us, I saw his imperious nose sniff. He waved them over to Sergeant Windridge who gave them a much warmer welcome. He brought them to our tent which, being the first one in the row had room for the men to tether their horses. They were both young men and very friendly. We got on well.

"I am Peter Brent and this is my cousin Ralph Brent. Pleased to serve with you chaps."

We had heard how they had been raised and bombarded them with questions. For the first time, we felt like we might find out why we were actually here. Peter was the chattier of the two and he did most of the speaking.

"Where are we heading then?"

Peter pointed to the north and west, "There is a large village there filled with troublemakers. They are the ones responsible for attacking your camp and your wagons. There are others who are more dangerous, towards Ibika but if your Colonel Glyn can destroy the warband at the village then he can move on to Ibika and this war can be ended quickly."

Henry asked, "What started this war?"

Peter laughed and filled his short stubby pipe, "Believe it or not a bar fight. You see these tribes around here, the Xhosa, all lived many miles north of here and had fine lands. Then, generations ago I guess, a stronger tribe, the Zulus came and were so fierce and successful that they took over all the Xhosa land. The Xhosa came south and settled closer to Cape Colony and that is when the Xhosa wars started. We have had to fight them regularly for the last hundred years or more." He pointed to the distant Fort Murray. "That one was built after the last uprising. We hoped it would control them but it did not."

I asked, "A barfight?"

He nodded, "You see there are two main tribes of Xhosa, the amaFengu and the amaGcaleka. Now the Fengu quite like the British and even the Dutch. They cooperate with us. Most of them form the police. If you see any native horsemen then they will be Fengu. The Gcaleka keep to themselves and live in what they call Gcalekaland. The Fengu live close to British and Dutch farms. Gcalekaland had a drought a year or two back. We all suffered but they suffered the most. Anyway, resentment has been simmering and a few months back they attacked a police station where a wedding feast was being held. That's when the bloodshed started. That's when the Gcaleka started slaughtering the Fengu and then the Dutch and British farmers."

Fred was a clever lad and he said, "Hang on, a couple of months ago. We had already left Brecon by then."

Peter grinned, "Governor Frere is a clever man and he knew what was coming. The powder keg was there already, we could all see it. All it needed was a spark."

The men joined us for food and we sat outside our tent to eat. Alf asked, his mouth full as usual, "So you think we can beat these Xhosa?"

"Easily," he laughed. "You threaten their village and they will have to fight. Your rifles will decimate them and on to Ibika and end the war."

Alf swallowed and grinned, "And then back home, eh boys?"

Ralph had not said much but he added, "I am afraid not."

Peter smiled, "My cousin is the clever one in the family. He reads books and takes an interest in politics. By the time he has finished, we will have a farm to rival Colonel Nicholson's."

Ralph gave a shy shake of his head, "Books tell what others have done. We can learn from their mistakes. No, I do not think you will be going home. The Dutch want the Zulu lands. The Zulus have been pushed back each year and, thus far they have not reacted. It will not take much to spark a fight."

Alf nodded, "And like your cousin says, our rifles will defeat them, eh?"

Peter said, "Not so simple, my friend. The Zulus are more like you. They are a military machine. They are organised into regiments. No man may marry until he has fought in a battle. That was the cause of some of the wars many years ago when the Zulus needed to blood their warriors. They even tried a couple of wars against the Dutch and acquitted themselves well. If you have to fight Zulus then you will be facing an army of thirty or forty thousand, perhaps more. They will be as organised as you are. I am just glad that we won't have to face them."

I asked, "Why not?"

"Too far from here means we don't have to and the fact that they can run over the land as fast as my horse for another. You try to outrun a Zulu and you are a dead man. You keep facing him and fighting because he won't stop until you are dead or he is." I took out my pipe and began to fill it. "And remember, my friend, you will be outnumbered by at least ten to one. How fast can you reload?"

We learned a great deal from the two cousins in the days before we left. They taught us which snakes were poisonous and which were not. They showed us how to find the nests of insects and the other creatures which bit and how to destroy them. "The creatures you avoid above all others are the bees and the wasps. I have never been to England but our father told us there that a bee sting or a wasp sting is mild. The bees and wasps here are deadly. You do well to smoke pipes. They hate smoke."

From that day on, whenever I could I had my pipe going. They also showed us a plant whose fruit could be used, not to eat but to smear on the skin to stop it from burning. The arrival of the Brent boys saved us much hardship and prepared us well for the battle to come.

Chapter 11

We set off before dawn and it was already warmer than an English summer's day in August. Ralph and Peter Brent walked their horses while Lieutenant Bromhead insisted upon riding Blackie. Whenever I could I gave the horse mints or fruit. I had bought some mints in King William's Town. They were not as good as my mint imperials but Blackie enjoyed them. I envied the Brent boys for their uniforms were light and did not attract the heat. With an open collar, the two men were much cooler than we were in our woollen tunics.

Our company had enjoyed the greatest success thus far and so we marched ahead of the command party. It meant we were under the eagle eye of both the colonel and Colour Sergeant Bourne. We did not have the opportunity to talk as much as we would have liked for there were strange new trees and animals we had not seen before and we would have asked the brothers about them. For their part, with pipes stuck permanently in their mouths, their eyes scoured the land for danger. We were the head of one column while a recently promoted Major Spalding marched at the head of the other column. The plan was to march in a single column but form a line of companies if danger threatened. In that event, Nicholson's Horse would form up on our left flank while the Durban Light Horse on our right. I liked that formation for we would be close to Nicholson's Horse and we had faith in them.

The Durban Light Horse had scouts out and they reported the Xhosa warriors forming up ahead of us. We were close enough to the colonel to hear the numbers. There would be more than two and a half thousand warriors ready to meet us in battle.

Fred shook his head, "I don't like those odds."

Peter said, spitting into the brush, "Don't worry about numbers Fred. Just keep firing."

Sergeant Windridge said, "The young trooper is right, Hitch. Look to your front, obey orders and, as unlikely as it might sound, you will survive."

I knew what Fred feared for he had confided in me, "You were lucky with that wound Jack, I know that for I saw the spear that did it. Six inches the other way and it would have been your groin and not your leg."

I had tried to tell him that our sword bayonets were longer and sharper but the fear was in his head and that was never a good thing. Trooper had often told me that fear was the biggest killer on the battlefield. He and the Scots Greys believed that they would win and, against all the odds they had. Until Trooper was proved wrong, I would keep that axiom in my head.

It was just before noon that the scouts rode in again and this time it was with the news that the Xhosa were just half a mile ahead. We could see nothing. The land undulated and there were blind crests and dead ground. We knew that the village was on high ground and had a palisade but that was all. From Peter and Ralph, we knew that the Xhosa could run as fast as horses over rough ground and so when the bugle sounded for us to form a line we did so with precision and alacrity that made Colour Sergeant Bourne smile. Number 1 Platoon was proving, once again, that we were the best in the regiment.

It was always easier to march in a column than in line and when the order came to march in an extended line, we had to ensure that none of us got ahead of Sergeant Windridge or Corporal Allen. Peter and Ralph Brent had mounted and were now riding just behind Lieutenant Bromhead. I was not sure he was happy about the close company. I was in the front rank with the rest of Number 1 Platoon. We marched steadily forward. There was just one line of men behind us. All the time the Xhosa warriors were banging their shields and chanting. The brothers had told us this was a strategy of both the Xhosa and Zulu warriors. The chanting helped them be braver and intimidated their enemies. We remained stoically silent as our sergeants barked out the commands necessary to keep us in a straight line. I wished we had artillery with us. There was something reassuring about cannons belching shells at an enemy. Trooper had told me of the effect of canister or grapeshot on an enemy. He had said it was like firing a giant shotgun. That concept appealed to me when I saw the mass of warriors waving their black and white shields with spears and knobkerrie held aloft. They had appeared as though by magic and yet I knew it was not magic. We had just crested a rise and saw them on the ridge ahead of us but they seemed far closer than was comfortable. We kept marching and I wondered if the colonel was going to order a charge. As we had not yet fixed bayonets that seemed unlikely. Eventually, when we were three hundred yards from the enemy, he ordered the halt.

Perhaps the Xhosa were waiting for that command because before we had even presented our rifles they charged. It was so sudden that it took us all by surprise. It was terrifying and it was as though a black and white wind was hurtling toward us. The officers and militia took their horses behind us where they would be able to fire over our heads.

Colour Sergeant Bourne took command, of our battalion at least. "Company present!"

The colonel echoed the command a moment later for the regiment but it meant that our battalion was ready to fire first. The Xhosa were astonishingly fast. Even as I levelled my rifle, I saw that they were just one hundred and fifty yards from us.

Colour Sergeant Bourne shouted, "At one hundred yards, volley fire! Fire!" It was all too quick for the colonel and Lieutenant Bromhead. The Brent boys had their carbines levelled and using their saddles for stability were already firing. As four hundred rifles fired, I was deafened by the rifles just behind my ear and my view was masked by the fog of smoke before me. Drill took over and I had a cartridge chambered and present before I even knew. The rest of the regiment fired and it was almost like an echo to our volley.

"Independent fire at will!"

It was terrifying for I knew there was a wall of warriors hastening towards us and I had no idea how many, if any, we had felled for there was a wall of smoke before us but I fired and reloaded, fired and reloaded. I could see shadows and those shadows appeared to move like lightning. A spear and a face manifested themselves before my face and my bullet took off the warrior's head. We had not been given the order but common sense told me that I needed my bayonet and even before I had loaded another bullet, I fixed it. The platoon behind us could keep firing for if any men were going to be gutted it would be us. I chambered the bullet and fired.

"Fix bayonets!" Someone higher up had realised that we needed bayonets and our ranks bristled with steel.

The hiatus allowed the smoke to clear a little as most of the rifles stopped firing. I saw that the Xhosa had been halted but they were less than twenty yards from us and with fewer bullets coming their way they were emboldened enough to race once again. Peter Brent had told us how to identify a leader, a war chief. They wore ostrich feathers in their hair. It made them taller and easier to spot and was a little like our guards and their bearskins. I saw a chief open his mouth to shout an order and I squeezed the trigger, taking great delight when it hit him squarely in the chest, throwing him back.

The next regimental volley was erratic; some had fitted their bayonets more slowly than others and the result was that the Xhosa hit our line. I had a bullet in the chamber but I remembered the other fights and used my bayonet. I flicked the spearhead that came for my chest away from me and then backslashed with my lunger. It tore across the chin and throat of the warrior. Spurting bright blood he fell. With no immediate foe to my front and a body before me, I lunged at the warrior fighting Alf. I drove the bayonet up under his ribs and into his chest. Turning I saw more warriors heading for us, a second wave and I raised my rifle and fired. Even as the warrior fell, I was chambering another bullet into my rifle. I did not fire but I drove the bayonet into the surprised warrior who thought I was still busy reloading. I did not have the luxury of aiming my bayonet and it caught his breastbone but his speed and my strong arms made the blade break the bone and hit his heart. He fell at my feet.

All along the line our regiment was firing the deadly bullets and slashing with a sword bayonet that was better made than the spears the warriors used. The Xhosa broke. Some men tried to chase after them but Colour Sergeant Bourne's voice halted them, "Stand fast and keep firing until ordered not to."

I fired three more bullets before the order came, "Cease fire."

The next order was greeted by a cheer, "The regiment will advance."

The two militia regiments mounted their horses and hurried ahead of us and I was able to watch the devastating effect of cavalry chasing fleeing men. Peter Brent had been correct, the Xhosa were fast but they were also tired after the battle and the fresher horses soon caught them. Nicholson's Horse used their carbines while the Durban Light Horse slashed and hacked backs with impunity as they had swords.

By the time we reached the village it was over. The warriors laid down their shields and weapons and abased themselves. Wailing women tended those with wounds while the children stood open-mouthed mesmerized by what they had seen. The unwounded warriors were herded together and placed in the village animal kraal. F Company were given the duty of guarding them. We collected and burned all the shields, spears and knobkerrie that we could find. That done we were ordered to form a ring of rifles around the village while the officers held a conference. I saw that our platoon had not lost a single man although Sergeant Maxwell had a slight wound to the upper arm and was being tended to.

Some of the others, Henry included, took some of the necklaces from the dead warriors. They were for their wives, sweethearts and mothers back at home. I did not see any of my family wearing them and besides, I could not bring myself to take them from their bloody bodies. I saw our wounded taken to the rear where Surgeon Reynolds and the other doctors would tend to them and then I saw the horsemen coming back. Surprisingly they had prisoners. Seeing them approach the colonel sounded the bugle for non commissioned officers and it was just the rank and file left guarding the prisoners. We were still in plain view and there was no way any man would risk punishment to light a pipe but we could talk.

"Fearsome fellows aren't they, 716?" Shadrack had been shaken by the attack. His tunic was badly torn and while the spearhead had not torn through flesh it had been a warning of what these warriors could do."

Henry nodded, "They are that but a good job the Colour Sergeant gave the order when he did." He pointed to the other side of the circle of red-coated sentries. "The other battalion did not fire when we did and, see, they have more wounded."

716 plunged his bayonet into the soil to clean the worst of the blood from it, "Aye, Hooky, and I have taken this much from the battle. Shoot first and apologise later."

A sergeant ran to D Company while other sergeants returned to their companies. "Right boys, D Company are going to burn a few bodies. When they move we shuffle around and tighten the line."

Fred said, "What about food Sarge? I could eat a horse with the skin on."

"Ah, you poor thing. The Commissary is setting up kitchens in the rear and yon horsemen will guard it. Food will be fetched but not for a while. The colonel wants assurances that the enemy as a force is finished."

The resultant fire and smell of burning bodies took the edge from our appetites. While the officers returned to our wagons and tents for their food and rest, we were fed where we stood and built fires so that we had a circle around the village. Without even our greatcoats or blankets it was a hard and cold bed we endured. I was glad when, the next day, we were told we would head north to join the rest of the army at Ibika. There, we were told, was the rest of the Imperial Army as well as the Lieutenant-General Sir Arthur Cunynghame. He led a mishmash of units. We learned this from Peter Brent as we trudged under the hot summer sun. The Dutch colonists were led by Commander Veldman Bikitsha and the British by Chief Magistrate Charles Griffith. The latter two leaders had, Peter told us, acquitted themselves well in the early part of the rebellion by defeating an enemy army in the field. We marched confidently, expecting the war to be over soon. We had first marched back to our camp and spent the day dismantling the tents and loading them in Mr Dalton's wagons. With fresh ammunition, we had marched north knowing that the threat to King William's Town was over.

We talked as we marched. None of us was impressed, as yet, by our officers. Trooper's view of his regiment and officers appeared to be different from my experience thus far. He had thought the officers in his regiment were fine officers. Major Spalding appeared to know his business but not the others. Most of the hard work and orders were done by the sergeants and corporals. The officers had been behind us in the battle and it had been the sergeants who had braved the enemy with us. I suspected that the three men we had lost at the battle might have lived had the officers been quicker thinking.

Ibika was the largest settlement in Gcalekaland and was a sprawling town rather than a village. Set on a piece of higher ground it had ditches and a palisade but as we had a battery of guns, I did not think that would be a problem. I knew that artillery could easily pound even stone to dust and the palisade was just made of wood. This was my first war but already I was learning and even I, a lowly private, saw that this enemy could not stand up to Imperial troops. We were the only red coats. I saw the uniforms of a regular cavalry regiment; there looked to be a couple of troops rather than squadrons. The militia were largely horsemen and they, like the rest of the army, were camped discretely with fellow units. The only other infantry I could see were the two regiments of amaFengu. I saw rifles and muskets stacked and knew that they would be fighting alongside us. They were larger regiments than we were. Each had some red about them to identify them as allies.

With such a large army we had the luxury of only guarding our camp and that was a relatively easy duty. The first day was spent erecting tents and digging toilets. The mood was ebullient for we had won a victory and lost not a single soldier. A soldier looks to his own and not only had our section been unscathed, but also our platoon and our company. The tiny 2nd Battalion had suffered wounds but what we thought of as the heart of the battalion was intact. It sounds insular I know but the section was my family and we were as close as any family. With Henry as the head, we bickered, bantered and rubbed along the same as any family in England with ten of them living in a house with two bedrooms but we were as close as any family. We endured the same hardships and the same trials. Trooper had been right; the army was a new family and I began to understand why his life had been empty after the Crimea. He had lost his sweetheart and with wounds to make life hard he had to eke out a living. I thought about how he had taken me under his wing. Had it been to have a family of his own? I found that when I smoked my pipe such thoughts came easily into my head. I was able to have conversations with myself and it was then I realised how much I had meant to Trooper. It made the fact that he had died alone harder to bear. I should have been there; it would not have been to help but just to hold his hands and share his last moments on this earth. Sometimes words were unnecessary and just a human touch was needed.

We were the last major unit to arrive and the most important for we were soldiers of the Queen, redcoats. We all expected a battle but it did not happen; not immediately anyway and we wondered about that. The senior officers were summoned to the general's tent each day and it soon became clear that Lieutenant-General Sir Arthur Cunynghame was not a confident general. It was four days before he issued his orders and we formed up to fight the battle of Ibika.

We were placed in a block, four companies wide in the centre of the line and Lieutenant-General Sir Arthur Cunynghame placed himself and his headquarters behind us along with a troop of Hussars. To our right and left were the amaFengu regiments. They each outnumbered ours. On the flanks were the horsemen and before us were the six batteries of seven pounders. To me, at least, it seemed a sound plan and we awaited the attack of the enemy. The amaGcaleka were arrayed before their homes about a mile away.

"Fix bayonets." The colonel had learned his lesson and this time we would be prepared.

In this battle, we had the advantage of artillery and when the bugle sounded for them to fire, we watched in eager anticipation. The guns belched forth and there was so much smoke that both the enemy and guns disappeared from view. Their rate of fire was steady so that when they reloaded, we were able to see the effect of their shots as the smoke dissipated somewhat. The effect of their shells was erratic. Some had hit short while other shells had sailed overhead to hit the wooden palisade. Only two shells exploded where they were meant to and we saw bodies. After five rounds from each gun were fired, they had become more accurate and it stung the amaGcaleka into action. They charged. This time our officers were ready. Stones had been placed before us to mark the range and we had a better idea of the progress of the amaGcaleka. The gunners fired one last round each, canister, I think from the effect and then ran back to hurl themselves at our feet.

Alf said out of the side of his mouth, "If the guns had been in line with us then they could have kept firing." He was right and I wondered why they had not been.

"Quiet in the ranks there!"

"Present arms!"

With a chambered round and fixed bayonets we levelled our rifles and aimed at the enemy. It seemed to me that it was impossible for us to miss as the slope meant that even a high shot would find flesh. The effective range for the rifle was four hundred yards but we knew that the bullets could travel for up to nineteen hundred yards and still cause a wound.

"At two hundred yards volley fire! Fire!"

The voices of our sergeants were like metronomes as they barked out 'fire' and we continued to fire into a foggy haze through which the black and white shields of the enemy melded into one. The barrel of my rifle was becoming too hot to touch when the order came to cease fire. I saw why immediately. Our rifles had cut a swathe through the enemy regiments and there was no one left for us to hit. Instead of attacking the red-coated devils who belched fire and death, they had turned to fall upon their deadlier enemies, the amaFengu. We could not help our allies as it was hard to discriminate friend from foe and so the two sets of Xhosa fought each other with a bloody ferocity that was nothing like war. It was more of a bloody feud with neither side asking for or giving quarter. It was horrifying to watch for this was what we might expect if they ever closed with us. While we watched I took one of my neck cloths and tied it around the barrel of my rifle so that my hands would not be burned.

I was a relative novice but even I could see that action was needed and that action had to come from the general. He seemed incapable of doing anything. 716 said to me, from the side of his mouth, "Now is the time to order the cavalry to attack their flanks and for us to march and attack them."

I nodded. If even two privates could see that then it was the obvious thing to do. Our artillery remained inactive for had the gunners returned to their weapons they would have been attacked and probably killed immediately.

When our attack came it was not ordered by the general but Commander Veldman Bikitsha had clearly had enough of the inactivity and he led his horsemen to attack the flank of one of the amaGcaleka regiments. It had an immediate effect, the enemy began to flee and seeing it, the order to advance was finally given. The other amaGcaleka regiments broke and fled back to Ibika. The war could have been ended there and then but General Cunynghame's poor decision making meant that thousands of warriors survived and fled into the Amatola mountains for we advanced too slowly and the horsemen, who could have pursued the enemy, kept pace with us such was the general's fear. By the time we reached the village they were beyond even our best horsemen up in the rocky vastness of the mountains. Until that day I had thought a victory was a victory but I learned differently. This victory felt like a loss. With just women and children as trophies of war, General Cunynghame divided his army up and used them to act as garrisons to prevent the amaGcaleka from leaving Gcalekaland. We were marched with A Company, C Company and D Company from the 1st Battalion to guard a village and a river crossing five miles from Ibika. Once more we built a camp, albeit smaller this time.

If I thought that we were unhappy then that was nothing compared with the resentment from the militia. They had farms and families. With better leadership, the war would have been ended and we would be back in Cape Town in what passed for civilisation while the militia would be able to work their farms. Peter and Ralph did not hold back in their condemnation of the general who was summoned back to England. That did not help us for we were still stuck there. We had to make the best of it. The general's incompetence spread an air of depression amongst the whole army. We should have been ebullient but we were not. Peter told us that until the survivors who were up in the mountains were caught then the whole of the area was in danger. "There are many farms here in the borderlands and the Xhosa will attack wherever they like. You and your redcoats can do little to contain them and so we have to stay here when we could be at home with our families making their lives comfortable. We do not blame you for we saw how bravely you fought but your general... he should be sent home. Let a real soldier lead."

Each company had a village close by and each day we would send a patrol beyond the village to see if the rebels were close by. Of course, they were not or if they were when the boots marched and they saw the red coats then they disappeared. They were like the flies we had to fight. You swatted but never caught anything and the flies danced away. They were raiding isolated farms and the lands of the amaFengu. Wherever we were not they were. It was like the shell game, now you see it, now you don't.

One good side to it was that we got to know the villagers and as we did not mistreat them were greeted with smiles. We even shared some of our rations with the children. Some of the men of the village had been killed in the battle and we were not hard-hearted men. We did not wish to see the widows and children suffer. What little we had to spare we gave to them. As duties go it was not unpleasant but it was hard. We used our kit to make our tent as comfortable as we could and we made the best of it. We had regular duties, sometimes at night and we became quite proficient at it. We did not look like the smartly dressed army that had marched ashore at Port Elizabeth all those months ago. The sun had bleached our tunics and trousers. Thorns and spears had meant they were stitched and patched. However, our guns were well maintained and we were well fed. Even though the battle had not been properly won we might have enjoyed our winter in Gcalekaland if it were not for the actions of a pair of soldiers in D Company who got drunk one night and attacked a couple of villagers. That was when our war changed. Even before we were told the identity of the perpetrators, we knew who one would be, Llewellyn.

Chapter 12

In theory, it should not have affected us at all but it did and the bullying Welshman continued to be our Nemesis. As with all such matters we heard the rumours long before we were summoned to witness the punishment meted out to the two men. The two men, it seems, had managed to get hold of a bottle of spirits. The rumour was that they had forced their section to give them their rations over the period of a week so that they had two bottles each to drink. That, in light of what we knew about Llewellyn and Madog, seemed likely. They had then left their camp, a second punishable offence after the first of hoarding strong liquor and gone to the village they were supposed to be guarding. They had abducted a girl in her teens and taken her in to the rocks to have their way with her. Her screams alerted the sentries and the two men were apprehended before they could do anything more than terrify the girl. The men had compounded their offences by fighting their captors and assaulting the duty sergeant sent to arrest them. Each crime on its own was a serious one but together they were unprecedented. Certainly, even Sergeant Windridge and Colour Sergeant Bourne seemed shocked.

In our tents, we debated the crimes and the punishments.

"They will be flogged."

"They could be shot. This is war."

There were dozens of opinions but until we witnessed it we would be in the dark. Such was the way of the army.

While that was the general consensus some thought a dishonourable discharge was possible. We debated the matter long and hard. The court-martial was not held in public and that confirmed what we knew about Colonel Glyn. He did not want the name of his regiment besmirched and it was held in private. The sentence was also unsurprising. The colonel had, so we heard, demanded one hundred lashes each but the adjutant, Lieutenant Melvill, had pointed out that since the Cardwell reforms of 1868 the maximum number was restricted to twenty-five.

Despite the trial being held in private, the punishment was in public as we knew it would be. The colonel was making a point to the rest of us. The flogging would be a warning for the regiment to obey every rule or suffer the consequence. The whip would be wielded by the sergeant from D Company, Sergeant Griffiths, and as the culprits had shamed the whole company he would not hold back. Both men were brought in and Llewellyn fought and kicked all the way to the wheel.

"By God, sir! I am tempted to order a second flogging for your disgraceful behaviour."

"Ah, you stupid little man you can shove your regiment up your…"

He got no further as Colour Sergeant Bourne smacked him so hard in the stomach that he could say nothing, "Sorry about that, Colonel Glyn."

The colonel was so angry that he was speechless. If he had not already been given a dishonourable discharge then as soon as his wounds healed, he would be.

Lieutenant Melvill said, "Carry on with the punishment, Sergeant Griffiths."

"Sir."

Llewellyn would not be done any favours. He would be awake when he was whipped and so Madog endured his punishment first. After ten strokes his cries had died to a whimper and his back had no flesh left that was not red. He slumped to unconsciousness after twenty and had to be revived by water to continue. By that time Llewellyn was awake and shouting once more. Sergeant Griffiths put even more effort into the whip and by the fifth stroke, Llewellyn was crying like a baby for it to stop. He did not pass out but he did become sinisterly silent. It was as he and Madog were being taken away that he raised his head and, passing the officers, tried to spit at them. He missed and before he could be struck for his actions said, "I will have my revenge on you and this regiment, I swear."

That night, sitting around our campfire we debated the flogging. "Barbaric."

Henry nodded, as he sucked on his pipe, "But justified, Fred. You suffered at Llewellyn's hands. The man is an animal. That poor girl will have nightmares for the rest of her life. He deserved the punishment and I think I agree with the colonel; it should have been more severe."

"Aye, but there is a limit, eh? And that is no bad thing. My da was in the army before the changes and he heard of men being flogged for minor misdeeds. It is not right. Would an officer be flogged?"

716 made a good point but I did not know as much about army life. I had learned of the army through Trooper and I now saw that he had given me a slightly sanitised version or he may just have been lucky. However, I agreed with Henry about this particular punishment and thought of my sisters. I thought myself a law-abiding citizen but if a man had tried to do to either of them what Llewellyn and Madog had done then I would kill them and to hell with the consequences. The two men had stepped over the line. The crime was heinous. The more I thought about it the worse it became. We had little crime in St Helen's and certainly, no woman or girl had ever been attacked. A few fights when the pubs closed were the worst that I had heard of. I knew of no one who had been robbed and never heard of the heinous crime of murder.

D Company's camp was more than a mile away from us and we heard nothing that night but two days after the punishment we heard that the two men had escaped. That was bad enough but they had murdered the medical orderly who was tending to their wounds as well as the young private guarding them. They had taken weapons and horses and fled. The horses were officer's horses and that, in the eyes of the colonel would make it a more serious crime. There would be no way back now for Llewellyn and Madog. For once the whole tent and section were of the same opinion. The two men should be executed and the only debate we held was the form. Hanging was seen as a better punishment but a firing squad seemed the more likely outcome. If we thought that the colonel was angry the first time then after this outrage the opinion was that his head would explode. I was the one to witness his anger for, at noon that day, I was summoned to headquarters by Colour Sergeant Bourne and I saw the colonel's purple face close up.

I had been on patrol when the command came and the Colour Sergeant was impatiently smacking his swagger stick against his hand when I returned to our camp. We double-timed across the camp to Headquarters.

The colonel was seated behind his desk and lieutenants Bromhead and Melvill were with him. The colonel's angry eye sought out Colour Sergeant Bourne's who said, "Private Roberts was on patrol, sir. No disrespect intended, sir."

Seemingly mollified the colonel sniffed and then looked me in the eye. I had never seen a live hawk but I had seen a stuffed one in the taxidermist on Church Street. That was the colonel's expression. It was unblinking and bore into me. I felt as though I was having my soul examined. I squirmed in my boots and wished to be anywhere but there.

Colour Sergeant Bourne said, quietly, "Stand easy, Roberts. You are not in any trouble."

The colonel nodded, "Quite the reverse, Roberts. I have heard nothing but good things about you. Even Colour Sergeant Bourne seems impressed by you." I did not know what to say and so I gave a weak nod. I saw Colour Sergeant Bourne roll his eyes. "That is in direct contrast to the two miscreants who have killed a private of this company and a medical orderly as well as stealing two fine mounts. Lieutenant Bromhead and Lieutenant Melvill are going after the two men. They need a soldier who can ride to act as their servant and they have selected you." His face became still and he almost hissed out the next words, "You can, of course, refuse for this is a volunteer mission." Trooper had told me that soldiers never volunteered but I knew that would be a mistake in this case.

"Of course, sir, I would like to go."

"Good." He pointed to a khaki uniform on the chair next to the tent entrance. "Take that and return to your camp. Change into it and take anything you might need. You may be in the hills for some time."

"Yes sir."

"You are dismissed."

I picked up the tunic, trousers and slouch hat and hurried outside. Colour Sergeant Bourne followed me. "Next time an officer asks you a question don't nod like you are some doxy at a dance hall accepting an offer to dance. Say, 'yes sir' firmly when you answer."

"Sorry Colour Sergeant." I looked up at him, "What are we supposed to do?"

"Catch the blighters and bring them back so that they can be shot."

I pointed at the hills, "But aren't those hills full of rebels, Colour Sergeant?"

"They are that and with any luck, they will do the job for us but we need proof that they are dead."

"Why Lieutenant Bromhead, though? I mean, he is not D Company's officer."

"Quite right Roberts he is not but Lieutenant Colville has a slight wound and the doctor does not wish it to become infected. Lieutenant Bromhead is keen to go, as is the adjutant." He added, "They are, I believe, friends."

We were approaching our camp and I saw my tent mates looking anxiously in my direction. "Just the three of us then, Colour Sergeant?"

"No, there will be a couple of native trackers and a trooper from the militia."

"Will I need my rifle?"

For the first time, I had stumped the Colour Sergeant. He stopped mid-stride and looked up at the hills and then back at the Headquarter's tent, "No, I will get you a carbine. Good thinking, Roberts. You are a smart lad. Use your brain and you might just survive. Now get changed, tell your butties where you are going and then return to the Headquarter's tent. Don't hang around. Every moment wasted gives them a better chance of escape."

As soon as he had gone, I was surrounded by my friends who bombarded me with questions. I answered them but did so whilst first undressing and then dressing.

"You in bother then, Jack?"

"No, I am being sent after Llewelyn and Madog with Mr Bromhead and Mr Melvill."

Fred looked towards the distant mountains, "Up there?"

Nodding I said, "We are supposed to bring them back for trial and execution."

716 said, "Shoot the buggers if you can. That is all that they deserve."

"Why you?" Fred, like others, was curious about my inclusion in the hunting group.

I began to fasten the tunic. It did not smell clean and I wondered if it had been taken from a dead man. "I can ride and I am supposed to act as a servant to the two officers."

Henry began to fill his pipe, "And do you know what that means, Jack?"

I shook my head, "Not really but I am guessing it means looking after the horses, cooking their food, cleaning their boots…"

Henry laughed, "I doubt they will want you to clean their boots but you be careful. Fred is quite right, you are going to a very dangerous place."

There had been a small haversack with the uniform. It was empty and I began to put in what I thought I might need. My pipe, tobacco and flint were obvious choices as were the mints I had bought. I laid it on the ground while I rolled my blanket up. I would most definitely need that.

Alf handed me some biltong, "Here, Jack, you might need this."

"Thanks, Alf," I remembered my canteen and I fastened my webbing belt around my waist. I took out the cartridges from the expenses pouch. I doubted that they would be of the same calibre. "Keep these for me." The knife Joe had given me when I had left Pritchard's now seemed the most valuable item I possessed and I fastened the scabbard to my belt. "Well, I had better go now." I did not know what to say and felt embarrassed and I did not know why.

I was even more embarrassed when Henry said, "Attention" and my tent mates all saluted me.

I gave a weak smile and ran back to Headquarters. I saw that in addition to the two officers' horses there were four of the local, hardier horses. I stood outside the tent and the sentry. 812 Williams said, "I was told to admit you. In you go."

I stepped in and saw that the tent looked to be even more crowded. The two native trackers were there and, to my delight, Peter Brent.

The colonel said, "Trooper Brent volunteered for this mission when he heard it was you who was going, Roberts. You are a popular chap, it seems. Do not let that go to your head. The four of you head to Mr Dalton. He has your supplies and ammunition."

As soon as we were outside, I said, "Peter, you need not have volunteered."

He grinned, "It is a dangerous country, Jack, and you might need me. These are two of the best trackers I know. Their names will be unpronounceable to you but they are happy to be called Chappy and Koppy which is a close approximation of their names."

The two trackers cheerily grinned. As I came to learn, they spoke a form of English but were happier speaking their own language and their words were translated by Peter. I suppose using their nicknames was no different to referring to my tent mates by numbers.

We headed over to the Commissary. I saw that my three companions carried their carbines. The trackers' weapons looked to be old and I wondered if they were muzzleloaders. Mr Dalton said to me, as he handed me a brand new carbine, "You are a lucky lad and no mistake. These are prized items and only a couple of regiments have them." He handed me a carbine that was about three feet long and had a curious looking hammer arrangement. It was still greased. "You will need to clean the grease off before you can use it but you will be familiar with the ammunition. It is the same as your rifle." I need not have emptied my expenses pouch. He held the carbine out to demonstrate. "This is the Westley Richards carbine. The breech is activated by pulling on this lever. As you can see it is peculiarly shaped and gives the gun its nickname, Monkey Tail Carbine. The range is much less effective than your rifle. Between a hundred and two hundred yards is all that you can hope, if you wish to be accurate." It had a leather strap but there was no sheath. It would have to be tied to my horse. He handed me a box of ammunition. "Here are a hundred rounds. It is more than you will need but…" he left unsaid the rest but I knew what he meant. More bullets meant that in the last stand I had a better chance of survival. "Fill up your expenses pouch first and put the rest in your satchel. You three come with me and I will give you the dixies and your supplies."

After they had finished, I did as he had suggested. The majority of the bullets fitted in my expenses pouch but I slipped three into each of the pockets on the tunic I would wear. They had not returned and so I took the cloth that Mr Dalton had left and began to clean off the packing grease from the gun. I began to become more familiar with the weapon and by the time they had returned I felt confident that I could load effectively enough. The three were laden and so I slipped my carbine over my shoulder and carried some of the supplies. We would be eating mainly corned beef.

As we reached the horses and the other three began to attach the supplies to their horses Peter said, pointing to the horse I would use, "This is one of our remounts. He is called Copper." The horse was a golden colour with an almost blond mane. "He is a gelding and a good horse. They said you could ride but I was not certain how well. He is not the fastest horse but he is a good one and is sure-footed." He began to tie dixies onto the leather straps attached to the saddlebags. He took the blanket that was wrapped around my body and tied it behind the saddle. "If I were you, I would tie my carbine to the blanket." He shrugged, "Your choice." I followed his advice. "That is a fine-looking weapon and far better than my old one. You are, indeed, lucky."

I slipped a mint from my satchel and offer it to Copper. He was suspicious at first and I do not think he had ever had one but, as with Blackie, he loved it and we became firm friends immediately. As Peter finished fastening his equipment, I saw that he now had a pistol in a holster and criss-crossed across his chest were bandoliers of ammunition. The two scouts had wicked looked knives and each had a single bandolier of ammunition. We were going well-armed but I wondered if six of us would be enough.

The two officers strode over leading their horses. Neither was wearing red and had wisely chosen their blue forage tunics and caps. I saw that both had scabbards attached to their saddles for their rifles. They had hunting rifles, I guessed as I did not recognise the stock as the Martini-Henry.

It was the adjutant, Lieutenant Melvill who took charge, "Brent, you will be in charge of the trackers. Find us the trail, eh?" He seemed to be friendlier than Lieutenant Bromhead. With a neatly trimmed moustache, he looked far younger than Lieutenant Bromhead. Turning to me he smiled, "We will try to impose upon you as little as possible eh, Roberts."

"It is not a problem, sir. I am honoured to have been chosen."

Nodding he urged his horse on and I kicked Copper in the flanks. He seemed to be an affable sort of horse. To Lieutenant Bromhead's obvious annoyance Blackie insisted, for the first mile or so, on turning his head to look for me. He was obviously seeking more of the mints. The lieutenant knew how to ride and Blackie soon gave up his attempts as Mr Bromhead wrested control of the horse. Whilst I had ridden there was a world of difference between that and knowing how to ride. My experience had been on Caesar's back when Trooper had let him run on the common ground close to North Road. There had been no saddle and Caesar had not galloped. More importantly, I had only spent half an hour at most upon his back. An hour into the ride, through Gcalekaland highlighted all the differences between being a rider and knowing how to ride. My thighs were rubbed red raw by the saddle and the gait, as the smaller horse tried to keep up with the cavalry mounts, was uncomfortable, and I was grateful whenever Peter stopped to show the officers evidence that we were on the right trail.

I confess that even I, with a totally untrained eye, could have spotted the evidence. Llewellyn and Madog had made no attempt to hide their tracks. Discarded bottles and pieces of army equipment they deemed to be useless were scattered along a trail.

Lieutenant Bromhead was an irritable man and he could not disguise his annoyance with the slow progress we were making. "Teignmouth, why do we not move much more quickly than this? They already have a three-hour start on us."

"Gonville, my dear fellow, it is better that we know the direction they take before we rush." I saw Peter smile as the adjutant swept his arm around the huts that dotted the hillside. "They could hide in any one of those. That they have not thus far gives me hope but we keep this steady pace until all civilisation is left behind us. Don't forget that they have weapons and we trained them how to shoot. If they chose an ambush site well they could pick three or four of us off easily. Now we will continue to be cautious." He waved at Peter, "Carry on, Brent. You and these chaps are doing sterling work. Carry on."

I liked Lieutenant Melvill. He was clearly a good officer and more like the ones Trooper had admired from the Greys. I never, in all the time I knew him, doubted Lieutenant Bromhead's courage but I never liked him as I did Lieutenant Melvill.

"I cannot understand why these two creatures would take such a risk as riding through a land we do not control."

I heard Lieutenant Melvill sigh. Thanks to Lieutenant Bromhead's deafness the adjutant could not keep his voice down and while Peter and the scouts might not be able to hear I could. "Gonville, do you wonder why you have not had advancement yet?"

"I cannot afford a captaincy."

Lieutenant Melvill laughed, "And neither can I yet I am adjutant and hopeful that this campaign will afford the colonel the opportunity to make a battlefield promotion."

"He likes you."

"Because I work hard and offer positive suggestions. You wonder at their route and I say it shows cunning. From their actions, the two men are clearly animals but like all such animals, they have natural instincts and abilities. Perhaps, better led they might have become good soldiers. There are no warriors within twenty miles of this part of Gcalekaland. We know that from our cavalry patrols. They are in the hills and making forays to attack isolated farms and slaughter colonists. The two of them are getting as far away from the regiment and the rebels as they can. Now I do not doubt for an instant that once they think they are beyond pursuit they will halt and then cause mischief."

"Mischief?"

Another sigh. "The general, in his wisdom, has concentrated all his efforts on containing these rebels. There are farms to the west of us that, as yet are untouched. There are farmers who have happy homes. Llewellyn and Madog may seek to approach these farmers under the pretence of having been attacked. I shudder to think of what they might wreak upon such people. No, we shall continue with our present course of action." He turned in his saddle, "What say you, Roberts? Being privy to our conversation, do you have an opinion?"

I smiled, "I agree, sir, with your assessment of the two men. They are cunning. In Brecon, they lured Private Hitch into a position where he could not defend himself and gave him a savage beating. They are nasty men. As for the other? I do not know this country but I could see how they might well use such subterfuge."

"You see Gonville, you are in a minority of one. And tell me, Roberts," he did not look over his shoulder, "what would you do with these former messmates of yours."

"Simple, sir, shoot them for the mad dogs that they are."

He laughed, "A wit too. You see, Gonville, that is a sharp wit." He dug his heels into his horse, "Come, Brent has found another clue."

This time I might have missed the clue but Chappy had good eyes and he had spotted where the two men had left the main trail we had been following and headed along the slope, across stones to hide their trail. The trail we had been following headed up into the hills while the rocky stone strewn ground they had taken headed north and west and, more importantly, began to descend into a valley. A valley, as I had come to realise meant farms and farmland.

"Sir, Chappy found one hoofprint here where the horse slipped from the stone. He and Koppy picked up their trail heading that way."

"Good work. There you are Gonville, animal cunning. They are no longer heading into Gcalekaland but northwest, towards the Fengu controlled land. How they know that there are fewer patrols here I know not but their escape was well planned and they must have worked this out. They know where they are going and that worries me." He looked at the sky. The sun was already much lower in the sky. "Brent, we need somewhere to camp but I would make as much progress as we can whilst it is safe. This track is a tricky one and I would not have Private Roberts tumble from his horse."

Lieutenant Bromhead snorted, "He is a soldier in B Company and he will keep his saddle until otherwise ordered."

The three of us smiled and I saw that Lieutenant Bromhead had not seen the ridiculousness of the statement.

It was almost dark when we stopped. Since we had left the main trail, we had seen no sign of human habitation. Chappy had found us a dell with enough grazing, rough though it was, for the horses and there was a stream that bubbled down the valley. I tethered and watered the horses grateful for the help the other three gave to me and then I set to building a fire. First, we had to gather kindling and there was precious little to be had. I had seen some before we left the main trail and now, I regretted not collecting it. Chappy and Koppy helped me by bringing dried animal dung which Peter assured me, whilst being pungent, would burn well. I found enough dead wood to make a serviceable fire and after using my flint soon had a blaze going. With a dixie of water, I began to make a stew using corned beef, some potatoes and a couple of chopped up carrots. I wanted speed and so I cut them finely. Koppy found some wild onions and chopped them up, they would add to the flavour. I put a second dixie next to the fire to heat up so that I could make a brew when I took off the stew.

I was not sure of the protocol and so I just stirred the pot. Peter and the trackers sat and chatted on one side of the fire while the two officers smoked cigars and spoke of the regiment. Glancing around I saw that while this was a good campsite there was nothing to be seen. Cloud cover stopped us from seeing the moon and the stars and the mountains made everything so black that beyond the fire I saw nothing. I wondered what creatures lived here. The fire might deter them but what of the snakes, insects and other biting creatures? I also wondered if the rebels might be close enough to do us harm.

"Peter, what if someone comes to attack us while we sleep?"

He pointed back along the trail we had just followed. It had been a narrow one that necessitated single file and had been hard to navigate, "The rocks on the trail will give us a warning if anyone comes along it. Chappy here found the only place we could camp for five miles. You can sleep soundly tonight and besides, even if the cavalry horses don't smell danger our four will." He seemed confident and he allayed my fears.

When we had eaten, we cleaned out the dixies and washed the officers' mess tins. Lieutenant Melvill thanked me for the food. It had not been an unpleasant concoction but I knew that officers ate better than we did. The nod from Lieutenant Bromhead seemed like high praise. I was desperate to smoke my pipe as, despite the fire, insects were still annoyingly around my face. The adjutant noticed me flicking at the flying insects and said, "You should smoke a pipe, Roberts. It seems to discourage these flying wee beasties."

I smiled and took out my pouch, "I have one sir, only…"

"Only what, Roberts?"

"I didn't know if I was allowed."

Shaking his head and smiling he said, "We are not on the parade ground, Roberts. If you need to smoke a pipe, relieve yourself, or even take a sip from your canteen then pray do so. What you have been asked to do is not in Queen's Regulations. We go to save the honour of the regiment."

I knew that Lieutenant Bromhead would not see it that way but I was happy that the adjutant led us. The pipe, that night, drew like a dream and was the sweetest pipe I had enjoyed thus far. With just one light from the fire it smoked down to the ash and the insects kept away from us all. Despite the hard ground I slept reasonably well but when we rose and I relieved myself my thighs and buttocks complained. I did not look forward to mounting Copper. The camp, however, was a cheerful one. The two native trackers were cheerful chaps and Peter bantered with me. Lieutenant Melvill seemed happy and confident and I wondered if we might soon catch up with the deserters.

The good feelings I had felt when we left our first camp lasted just seven miles. We came upon a farmhouse.

"Sir, there is no smoke and that is the Huys farmstead, The trackers know them."

With no smoke coming from the chimney and no sign of anyone moving around the farm we were wary and we tethered our horses to what looked to be a struggling orchard half a mile from the farmhouse. With a bullet chambered in my new carbine, we moved in a skirmish line towards the farmhouse. There was not a sound emanating from the farm and that had the hairs on the back of my neck prickling for every farm that I knew kept chickens and none were clucking. Waving Chappy and Koppy to the left and right to go around the farmhouse the four of us entered the yard through the open gate. Any animals that had been kept within would now have fled and explained the silence. There was a stable but the gate was open and it was deserted. The door to the farmhouse was ajar and it was Lieutenant Melvill who entered first with a cocked pistol in his hand.

I smelled the bodies as soon as I entered the door. Death lay within these walls. We found the farmer first. He had been shot at close range and his facial features were almost obliterated. He lay in the kitchen and, lying out of the back was what I presumed was his wife. She had been shot in the back and lay spread-eagled on the cobbles that lay there.

"Roberts, check the rest of the rooms. Brent, have the scouts find the trail. I think we know who is responsible for this." His voice was grim and tight. I think he had feared something like this. It was more dishonour for the regiment.

I kept my carbine levelled although it was clear that the rats had fled. The house had been ransacked. The two killers had obviously searched for whatever could be found and when I found the floorboards opened then I knew that whatever safe place the farmer had used for his valuables had been breached. There was a wooden staircase and an upstairs. I went up with my back to the wall and my carbine ready to fire. The large room upstairs was the bedroom and, like downstairs had been ransacked. On the floor lay the two uniforms of Llewellyn and Madog and the chests that had contained clothes had been ransacked and what they had not wanted was strewn about the floor. They now had a disguise. Slipping my carbine over my shoulder I took the uniforms downstairs. Brent was helping to drag the farmer's body outside for burial. I put my carbine and the uniforms on the kitchen table and helped carry him.

Lieutenant Melvill saw the uniforms and nodded. "Sir, I found their uniforms upstairs. It proves who did this but also tells us that they are in disguise. Save for the signs of the flogging none would take them for soldiers."

The adjutant nodded, "Good thinking, Roberts, thank you. You have a good man there Gonville. He is corporal material and perhaps more." He knew what my words meant. The two men would no longer be identified as soldiers and therefore deserters. They would appear as two farmers. "I know that it is much to ask but would you two dig graves and bury these two? Shout for me when you have done and I will say words over them."

"Yes sir."

I grew six inches at the praise and knew that Trooper would be proud of me.

Peter knew the ground better than I did. We fetched spades and picks and found a flattish piece of ground that Peter assured me would be easier to dig. "This was once a vegetable garden and has been turned."

We set to work and did so as a team. I hacked at the hard soil with the pick while Peter used his spade to shift the soil.

"We had better make it deep and if we pile the stones you uncover to one side then we can give the poor souls some protection from the wild animals." I had not thought of that. Parish Church cemetery did not have animals that would dig to uncover a corpse.

When we deemed it deep enough, we stopped and sorted out the stones. As we did so Chappy and Koppy returned. They could speak English but they used their own language to talk to Peter who nodded. He spoke to Chappy who hurried off inside while Koppy led the horses to join ours in the shade of the stables where there was forage and grain for them. They, at least, had some benefit from this tragedy.

"What did they say?"

He shook his head, "I will wait until the officers return. It will save telling it twice."

It was only a few moments we had to wait and by that time we had begun to pile the earth back in the graves. "Good job, men. We will bury these good people and say our words before you tell me what the scouts had to say."

With four of us toiling it did not take long to bury them and lay the soil and stones on the top. The lieutenant's words were eloquent and touching. He paused towards the end and said, "Do we know their names, Trooper?"

"Yes sir. The scouts know them and say that they are Piet and Bertha Huys."

"Thank you. So, Almighty God, we commend the souls of Piet and Bertha Huys to your charge. They died as innocents and deserve all your tender care. Amen."

We each said, "Amen" and I took a handful of soil and threw it on the grave. I had done so when Trooper and then my father had died. I saw a nod from Lieutenant Melvill who emulated me. The others followed.

"Let us go inside and have a brew while we hear the scouts report."

The kitchen stove still had embers and it did not take much for me to rekindle them and then put on a kettle. It was good to have something to occupy me and take my mind from the stain on the kitchen floor and stop my imagination from reliving what the last moments might have been like for this family.

"The two soldiers took off due west, sir, where the road eventually heads south and I believe that they are heading back towards Cape Colony. There were horses in the stable and they have taken them. They have remounts." That was not good news for we did not.

"And I presume they still have a head start on us."

"Yes sir. The scouts think that they left after dawn."

I put the tea in the pot and calculated that their lead was the length of time it had taken us to reach the farm, about an hour, plus the time it had taken to bury the bodies and now drink our tea. It would be a three-hour lead. Not as much as before but with remounts that lead could lengthen.

"There is worse, sir."

"Worse?"

Nodding, Peter said, "Yes sir. Koppy knows the farm. The farmer had half a dozen guns, including a pistol. He was quite well off and liked to hoard his money. The men have coins and they will be much better armed." The lieutenant nodded. The deserters were now more mobile and would not need to beg. Other farmers could suffer the same fate. The soldiers would not appear as deserters but would be dressed well in the farmer's clothes. Peter had not finished with the bad news and his voice was laden with dread, "There were three men who worked on the farm. Koppy did not like them. That may be because they were Gcaleka but as we have not found their bodies and Chappy says that five of the horses were laden with men I think we can assume that they now have allies. We hunt five armed men and not two."

161

The contrast between the two officers was striking. I handed them their tea and saw stark realisation on the face of the adjutant while Lieutenant Bromhead was more concerned with the amount of milk I had put into the cup. Lieutenant Melvill would make a good officer and be a credit to the regiment while, I suspected, Lieutenant Bromhead would just see his time out and the regiment would know little of his passing.

"Then we have to move and move quickly. It will mean pushing our horses but I would have these five before they can do more damage to innocents like the Huys. A good report, Peter. Have you never thought of transferring to the regulars?"

He laughed as he sipped the scalding tea, "No sir, I am a farmer. I don't mind playing the soldier now and then but I hate all the yes sir, no sir. When this is all over I shall return to my farm, marry Elsa and raise children rather than callouses on my backside."

That elicited a frown from Lieutenant Bromhead and a smile from the lieutenant, "Quite." He looked at me as he sipped his tea. "Good brew this, Roberts, proper sergeant major's tea. These poor people won't need their tea. Take whatever those evil men left and be ready to ride. We go a-hunting!"

Chapter 13

My legs and buttocks were still chafed from the day before and as I saddled Copper, Peter noticed. "Sore?"

I nodded.

He took a jar of leather polish from the shelf above the stall. "Rub this on the saddle. Don't worry that it will make a mess of the uniform." He turned and said something to Koppy who laughing left us. "Koppy will fetch some cream to ease the pain. He is amused that your white skin should turn red."

"I am glad that my discomfort brings pleasure to someone."

I had seen the jar in the kitchen. Koppy handed it to me and Peter said, "Smear it liberally where it hurts. It stinks to high heaven but it works."

I dropped my trousers and the two scouts knelt to stare at me. I am not sure that they had ever seen an Englishman do this. It was disconcerting but I ignored their attention and opened the jar. It did smell disgusting but as soon as I applied it and felt the relief then the smell seemed of no consequence.

"What are you doing, Roberts? Time is wasting."

"Sorry, Lieutenant Bromhead, just coming." I pulled up my breeches and placed the cream in my satchel. I led the two officers' horses outside.

Lieutenant Melvill sniffed, "Stinking smell, what."

"Sorry, sir, that is me. I applied some cream to my thighs."

Laughing he said, "Resourceful man. The lieutenant and I were born to the saddle. I can only imagine what it must be like for you. Well, bear up and off we go."

The forage and the grain had helped our horses. The four local horses would not have enjoyed the luxury many times in the past and they took off as though it was the start of the Derby. I had watched the others ride and I adopted the same style. Despite the speed, it was much easier to ride and the cream helped. The trail was easier to see as there were six horses that we were now following and they were shod. It meant we did not have to stop as frequently for they laid a clear trail. Stop we did for Lieutenant Melvill did not want to burn out the horses too quickly. We found water and let the animals rest while we refilled our canteens and ate some biltong.

It was in the early afternoon that we heard the firing from up ahead. It was in the distance but close enough for us to hear it. Koppy turned and spoke to Peter. "Koppy says that there is another farm five miles up the road. An old farmer, George Davenport, lives there with three servants. He has no family."

Even the dull Lieutenant Bromhead did not need a picture drawing and we dug our heels into our horses' flanks. In my case, all thought of pain was gone for I vividly recalled the sight of the dead farmer and his wife. The land here rose and fell. There were stands of trees but they were mainly where there was water. The undulating nature of the land meant we could never see that far ahead. Had we chosen to waste time and ride to the high ground then we could but we relied on our two guides to get us where we needed to go quickly. As with the farm where we had found the bodies, the farms in this part of the world were also built close to water. I could not see a farm on the skyline and that meant it would be lower down the slope. Although the two officers could have ridden on ahead they wisely kept to the pace of the slower local horses and as mine was the slowest I was gradually being left behind.

I reached into my satchel and pulled forth a mint. I now had enough confidence to be able to lean forward to reach Copper's mouth, "Good boy, a little harder, eh?"

The brave little beast responded well and we kept closer to Blackie. Blackie and Copper seemed to have grown close. They had been tethered together at our camp and stabled to share the same hay rack at the farm. I think Blackie went a little slower to help his new friend. We crested the rise and, in hindsight, that was a mistake. Our prey was still at the farm but the sight of our horses alerted them and we saw five men mount and lead the sixth horse. I recognised Llewellyn and Madog, not that we needed any confirmation. The five men took off west. I know that we had needed to ride quickly but it was clear now that we were too late and worse, our enemies were now mindful of pursuit. Hitherto they had not tried to disguise their trail but now they would.

The scene we found was as distressing as the first farm. The difference was that the bodies were all in the cobbled and gated yard. The white farmer had been shot as well as his three workers. There was a fourth body whom Koppy identified as one of the men from the Huys' farm.

"Roberts, check the house, although I think it will be deserted."

With my carbine ready I entered the house. Our arrival had managed one thing. We had disturbed them in their work. They had taken from the single-storied building but only from one room and the rest was undisturbed. They had left things I knew they would have found useful. When I emerged I saw that the bodies had been covered with tarpaulin and that Koppy and Chappie were no longer there.

"We have no time to bury these people. We will do that on the way back. I want to catch them before they can hurt others. That brew of tea we had at the Huys farm might have cost us dear."

Koppy rode in and shouted to Peter who translated, "He says that one of the men we are following is hurt. There is a blood trail. They have not taken the road but are heading across country." He pointed to a peak to the west. "They are heading for that piece of high ground and it is a rough terrain with plenty of places to ambush."

"Then we enter the lion's den knowing it is ready to feast." Lieutenant Melvill mounted his horse and pointed to the tarpaulin-covered bodies, "We owe it to the farmer and his men for they were men from our regiment who did this."

Chappy was waiting for us down the slope and we followed our two scouts across a landscape littered with thorn bushes, stones and suddenly gullies. It was a dangerous trail and I had to concentrate just to stay in the saddle. I learned to lean back when going downhill and when the trail twisted and turned up seemingly impossibly steep slopes then I had to lean forward. Peter was right, Copper was a sure-footed animal and I did little to guide him. I learned to allow him to pick his own way up the slope. It helped that I was at the rear and therefore not holding anyone up.

It was late in the afternoon when we saw the carrion birds circling. We could not rush any faster than we were for fear of falling foul of the landscape. This time we had not found as much water and we were mindful that our horses were our only hope of returning to the regiment. The birds descended and still, we did not see the cause. We climbed a steep rocky slope that saw Lieutenant Melvill's horse skitter and slide down an unstable patch of rocks. When we reached the top, we saw the birds and the cause of their flocking. A rider and horse had stumbled and fallen down the slope and lay a hundred yards away at the bottom. The birds and the rodents we spied did not cease from their feasting when we appeared. They knew that they were safe for we were far away. Lieutenant Melvill took out his field glasses.

When he replaced them in their case he said, "That must be the man Koppy said was wounded. His trouser leg is bloody. He is dead as is the animal. I would fire a gun to scatter them but they would return and that would tell our prey that we are close." He took out his canteen. "We will drink and rest for a while. The dead horse tells us that this is a tricky section. Let us not follow them into that valley of death, eh?"

By the time we eventually moved the sun was beginning to dip in the west. We now had the problem of finding somewhere to camp. The sunset and then the ensuing darkness enveloped us and we still had no place to camp. Lieutenant Melvill seemed to have the perfect nature to lead. He took command of the situation, "Dismount and lead your horses. We need to stop but I will not stop where we cannot camp."

Chappy was an excellent scout. He knew what we sought and he led us well. After what seemed like hours but was probably a shorter time, he found a dell where there was a covering of grass as well as a puddle left over from the last rain. Night had begun to fall and we could have gone no further in any case.

"We will camp here. Brent, have the scouts ensure that we have a secure perimeter."

Lieutenant Bromhead said, "Roberts, get a fire going."

"No fire."

"But Teignmouth…"

"I do not wish to let our prey know that we are close and from now on we whisper. Cold rations tonight. Roberts, we will tether the horses. Open some corned beef and we will have that with dried fruit." He stood with his hands on his hips and surveyed the rocks that rose above us. If they have ridden their horses up that slope then they may just be a mile or two away. Sound carries at night and whilst I do not think they are close I know not how far our voices will carry." He said it so quietly that we had to strain to hear and I doubted that the deaf Lieutenant Bromhead would have heard a word.

One of the items left at the Huys farm had been a bag of dried fruits. In a perfect world, we would have hydrated them but I knew they would help the corned beef to go down.

When I had opened the tin, I put the beef and the fruit in two dixies. I sliced the corned beef up and then I went to attend to Blackie and Copper. Lieutenant Melvill was still there with his horse and I saw the smile on his face when he saw me offer a mint to Blackie and Copper. He whispered, "You are full of surprises, Roberts. You are the first infantryman I know who cares so much for horses."

"That was Trooper, sir."

We fed and watered our animals, Peter did the other three. "Trooper?"

I told him of the cavalryman who had befriended me. We made our way back to the rocks where Lieutenant Bromhead was seated. My company commander asked, affably, "Have you a light, Teignmouth?"

I saw the cigar in his mouth. The adjutant sighed, "No smokes tonight, Gonville. It will give away our position." To emphasise his whispered words he took the cigar from Lieutenant Bromhead's mouth and shook his head vigorously. He sat next to me so that he could put his head close to mine and speak quietly, "Your story is interesting Roberts and explains much about your attitude. Most men join the army to escape. I can see that you have too but you were escaping the life of a factory worker and that is understandable. You should have joined a cavalry regiment."

I shrugged, "I joined the closest."

"And on behalf of the regiment can I thank you?"

I nodded and we sat in silence drinking water from our
canteens and eating corned beef and dried fruit. The chewing
helped my stomach believe it was eating a meal but the cold food
did not satisfy me. We all craved a hot meal. Perhaps it was the
reflective silence or just luck but an hour after we had finished
eating and when we were preparing to sleep that we heard first
the clink of a bottle and then voices. They came from the rocks
above us. The rock under which we had camped had an overhang
but the sides were just steep slopes. The top was a good three
hundred yards from us. Eyes widened in the dark and Lieutenant
Melvill held up his hand. I grabbed my carbine and silently slid a
bullet into the chamber. Having heard the voices once we were
able to pick them up more easily when they began again. I had
no idea what the two Huys' servants were saying but I picked out
the odd word or two from the two deserters. They had been
drinking.

The words did not come to us in sentences but in waves as
though the heads of the men were moving. The slurring did not
help.

"Ambush… bastards."

"Shoot down…"

The two servants' voices rose and then I heard clearly the
voice of Llewellyn, "Quiet, you bastards."

Silence fell. The adjutant stood and waved us all closer.
Having heard the words of Llewellyn we could not risk anything
louder than a whisper. "Peter, send the trackers all the way
around the rock. Have them cut off the deserters' retreat. I don't
want them hurt in a crossfire."

We waited patiently as Peter clicked and clacked his message.
The two men nodded and as soon as their backs were turned it
was as though they had disappeared.

He turned to Peter and me. I noticed that Lieutenant
Bromhead had his ear so close to Lieutenant Melville that he
knew he had to hear every word that was said, "We have had a
bit of luck. They must have chosen this high kopje to ambush us
when we came along in the morning. Let us use that to our
advantage. We will flank them. Gonville and I will go towards
the middle. Peter, take the right of the lieutenant and Roberts the
left of me. I know it means we will not see each other but we

have more chance of success if the enemy is surrounded. Be prepared to fire but do not fire until either they do or I command you."

We nodded but I thought he was wrong. Better to shoot first. We had not been in this country long but I knew that no one hunted a snake by warning it of an approach. The two officers took out their pistols and we moved into position. We waited for the signal to move. Lieutenant Melvill was giving Koppy and Chappy the chance to get into position. After what seemed an age, he waved us forward and Peter and Lieutenant Bromhead disappeared from view. The first four steps were easy for we had flattened the undergrowth making our camp. Lieutenant Melvill and I had to go to the left for the steep rock was almost vertical in the centre. I looked for rocks and I avoided them not only could they trip me up but anything could lurk beneath them. When I found anything to help to pull me up then I made certain that it was secure. It took time and halfway up I realised a flaw in the adjutant's plan. We would have no idea when Mr Bromhead and Peter were in position. It was too late to amend it now. The lieutenant and I were moving parallel to one another, I was glad I was carrying the carbine over my shoulder. The Martini-Henry would have been too cumbersome.

The closer we came to the top of the slope, the easier it was to hear the words from the camp. The two servants' voices sounded like insects and it was clear that they were on our side of the camp. We could hear the drunken laughter of the two deserters. We began to head further to our right for the ground flattened out and we were past the overhang. I knew what to look for, a rock behind which I could shelter. We could not see anything at first but, as the two of us drew closer to the camp and to each other I saw the horse line. The five horses were tethered there. They had been lucky not to lose the packhorse when they had lost their wounded man. As soon as we saw the horses the lieutenant signalled for me to crouch and I did so. We then moved from rock to rock until we were able to look down into the camp. I saw evidence of drinking. There were bottles close to all four men. We had not found any bottles on the two farms and I knew that farmers liked a drink. Perhaps that had been the reason the deserters had risked attacking the farms rather than simply disappearing.

Llewellyn and Madog were together and faced us on the far side of the camp and ten paces or so on our side of the camp were the two servants. The two deserters were both wearing good clothes, the garb of a gentleman. The two servants were closer to us and had their backs to us. I saw that while the rifles they had taken were close to them all, they would have to reach and grab them when Lieutenant Melvill arrested their attention. The lieutenant gestured for me to aim my carbine at the servants and I nodded, taking a bead on the back of the one to the left. He half rose. He did not make a sound but we both heard, as did our prey, the tumble of rocks from the far side of the camp. Either Peter or more likely Lieutenant Bromhead had made a noise and disturbed a stone. It sounded like a gunshot in the dark and had an immediate effect.

Llewelyn jumped up as did Madog and both picked up a rifle. It was not a Martini-Henry but a Sneider, the ones favoured by the farmers. It was the two servants who picked up service rifles. The four all looked in the direction of the sound which was away from us and Llewellyn shouted, "Show yourselves!" He had sobered up with the sound of the rocks.

Lieutenant Melvill had courage, probably too much for he stood and shouted, "Privates Llewellyn and Madog, give yourselves up ..." he got no further. One of the servants whipped his gun around to shoot down the adjutant and I just reacted and fired. The bullet smacked into his shoulder and gave the adjutant the time to drop behind the rock as the fusillade of bullets came our way. He fired two blind shots from his pistol as he dropped and already the smoke was filling the air before us. I had chambered a round and I aimed the gun at the rock close to the servant. I knew that, if possible, the lieutenant wanted prisoners. The bullet hit the rock and sent splinters into the face of the unwounded servant.

He dropped his rifle and stood, raising his hands in surrender, "I give up. Do not shoot!"

Lieutenant Melvill's voice was calm, "Walk this way and keep your hands in the air.

Madog shouted, "Cowardly cur!" And fired his gun at the back of the surrendering man. The enormous hole in his front told me that he was dead and, chambering another bullet I aimed at Madog. Bullets came from the other side of the camp. Mr Bromhead and Peter were now in position. The adjutant fired two shots at Madog and one caught him in the leg. The two men were trapped but there were enough rocks close by to give them cover.

Lieutenant Melvill was an honourable man and still trying to be fair to the deserters who in my opinion did not deserve fairness in any shape or form, "You can't escape. We have you surrounded. Give yourselves up and you will be given a fair trial."

Llewellyn laughed as Madog moaned, "A fair trial and a fine hanging! We will take our chances. We have plenty of guns and ammunition and a good place to hide. Do your worst."

The lieutenant nodded to me, "He is right. Perhaps we will just wait them out."

I pointed, "Sir, the man I wounded, he is still alive. If we wait, he will bleed to death."

Nodding he said, "You are right." He holstered his pistol. "Give me covering fire and I will try to bring him here. We know not yet what crimes he has committed."

"Be careful sir. Your life is worth more than any of these three."

Smiling he said, "Thank you, Roberts." He nodded and, raising my carbine I fired at the boot I could see protruding from the rock where Llewellyn and Madog sheltered. Mr Dalton might have been right and it was not that accurate at long range but this was just forty paces and I hit the heel. There was a scream and then two gunshots in return. The adjutant moved as soon as the two guns had fired. The servant was alive for he raised his head as Lieutenant Melvill, his pistol hanging from its lanyard, put his hands beneath his armpits. I fired a bullet at the rocks and it ricocheted.

I heard Madog shout, "It is a death trap boyo, let us surrender. My leg is hurting something fearful."

"The hangman's noose will hurt more. Have courage we know there is just a handful of them."

More bullets came our way. They were firing blindly by resting their rifles on the rocks and shooting in our direction. I saw flashes from behind the rocky fort and heard the cracks from Peter and Lieutenant Bromhead's guns. They had a better position and chips of rocks flew from the death trap that the deserters had chosen. A bullet managed to flick a piece of rock into Lieutenant Melvill's cheek as he dragged the wounded man the last few steps to safety. With three guns all hurling bullets into the enclave of rock and at such short range, it was inevitable that some would strike and we heard the cries from the two men as either shards of rock or fragments of bullets struck them.

After tying a dressing to the man's shoulder Lieutenant Melvill emptied his revolver into the rocks and then reloaded. I was like a press at Pritchard's which, once started would keep hammering and pressing plates of metal until stopped. I chambered, aimed and fired. I varied where I was firing to try to get a lucky hit on the rocks. After the lieutenant had emptied his pistol for a second time he shouted, "Cease fire!"

The smoke cleared and I saw a trail of blood seeping from behind the rocks where the two men sheltered.

"Sir, I can see blood."

"Cover me while I investigate."

I stood, "Sir, you are wounded, let me."

He put his hand to his cheek and it came away bloody. He had not known. Nodding he said, "Be careful. We have given them more chances than enough."

Instead of walking directly toward them, I headed for the horses first. I whistled and shouted, "Koppy, Chappy, you can come in now." I hoped they would understand me. I kept the gun aimed at the rocks and when I had moved far enough, I saw that the two men were both hurt. The guns, whilst still in their hands were on the ground. I shouted, "I think they are safe, sir."

I saw two figures rise from the rocks and saw Lieutenant Bromhead and Peter emerge. They, too, had their weapons aimed at the deserters. When I reached them, I saw that Llewellyn was already dead. He had been hit a number of times and bled out. A splinter of rock had removed his eye. None of us would know who had finished him off and that was probably a good thing. I kicked the rifle away from Madog. He too was bleeding badly. I heard footsteps and saw the two scouts as well as Lieutenant Melvill heading for me.

Madog gave a weak smile and blood trickled from his mouth. He had an internal wound too, "We nearly got away with it, boyo. We should have kept going, eh? That last farm was one too many. We did not need it but those lads we had with us said that the farmer was rich."

I laid my carbine down, well away from his hands. He was holding his stomach in, "If you hadn't attacked the girl then none of this would have happened."

He leered, "She was pretty. I was fed up with tired old whores." He suddenly winced, "Give us a last drink, eh boyo? Ease the pain and the ending."

I saw a bottle of an amber coloured liquid just out of reach and handed it to him. He drank deeply. It was whisky and he consumed at least a gill. "Do you need us to write to anyone?"

He shook his head, "Llewellyn was the only family I had. Sad, isn't it?"

The bottle fell from his hands, his eyes closed over and he died.

Lieutenant Melvill said, "That was well done, Roberts." He looked at the others. "Anyone else injured?"

Lieutenant Bromhead shook his head, "Sorry, Teignmouth, it was my boot that shifted the rock. I am damned clumsy."

"In the end, it didn't matter. Let us light a fire and cover these bodies."

"First, sir, let me see to your cheek." Nodding he sat on a rock as Peter and the two scouts moved the two bodies across the camp to where the dead servant lay. I took the bottle Madog had drunk from and said, "This may sting, sir." I used Madog's neckcloth to wipe the alcohol across the wound. It was not a deep one. "Here, sir, if you keep this pressed against it the bleeding will stop. I will get a dressing from my pack." Mr Dalton had given each of us a small medical kit. By the time the other three returned and began to build a fire I had finished.

"Good work, Roberts, now you had better tend to the wounded man."

Peter said, "What wounded man?"

173

I pointed, "He was in the rocks close to where the dead man lay. Did you not see him when you fetched the dead man?"

Just then we heard a cry. We all ran to the place we had left him. I looked around but could not see him and then Peter pointed, "There, at the foot of the cliff. Is that a body?"

The bloodied white bandage Mr Melvill had applied told us that it was. The man had tried to escape and fate had delivered the justice the dead farmers demanded. As we headed back the adjutant said, "He could have lived."

Peter said, "Perhaps he feared the punishment. Whatever happened no one would employ him as a servant. Once he ran his life was over."

We lit the fire and put on a dixie of water. Peter grinned as he said, "You have played the nurse, Jack, let me play the cook, eh. Have a pipeful, you have earned it."

I found as I lit my pipe that my hands were shaking. This was not like the battle of Ibika where I had stood shoulder to shoulder with Alf and Fred. Here I had been almost alone and men were firing bullets at me. The bullets we had fired into the rocky death trap the deserters had chosen told me how much luck was involved in survival in such battles.

The next day we loaded the three bodies on the backs of the horses and headed back. We picked up the broken body of the fallen man and by night time we had reached the farm where we had left the bodies. While they had been undisturbed by animals, thanks to the shelters we had made for them, they still stank and we buried not only them but also the two servants we had on the horses. The colonel would want the deserters brought back but the two dead men needed burying. We slept that night under a roof but I did not enjoy the sleep. I knew that the ghost of the old man who had been murdered and his dead workers would haunt it. The next afternoon saw us at the Huys' farm but none of us wanted to spend another night in a house of the dead and we pushed on towards our camps knowing that we had a better road ahead of us. We reached our camp at nine o'clock at night and both we and our horses were exhausted.

Despite the hour, the colonel was roused and I saw the delight on his face when he saw that we had been successful and that there were two deserters draped over the officers' horses that had been stolen. "Thank you all. You have saved the reputation of this regiment and I am grateful. None shall ever speak of this again and no record will be kept." He glared at us. "Understand?"

We all nodded and I said, "Yes sir." I heeded the Colour Sergeant's advice.

"Roberts, you may have the day off tomorrow."

"Thank you, sir."

When we were outside, I handed Copper's reins to Peter. The rest of his regiment had already left and he would be joining them. I handed him the carbine and the bullets I had left. "Take this as a leaving present, Peter, I have learned much from you and without you, me and the other boys would have fared badly."

"I can't take this. Will you not get in trouble?"

"I might but I want you to have it."

He took it and clasped my hand, "And I have learned much from you. Take care, redcoat."

Lieutenant Bromhead had already gone as had the two scouts but the adjutant remained and he had witnessed the interchange, "That was a kind gesture, Roberts. You know, in normal circumstances you would have been mentioned in despatches for your action. There might have even been a medal but as the colonel made clear, there was neither attack nor any murder. Know this. I shall keep an eye on you and if it is in my power then I shall see you promoted."

"Thank you, sir." That seemed unimportant at that moment.

As I headed for my tent mates, I felt that I had a friend in high places for the adjutant was well thought of. Mr Bromhead might be a dull blade but Lieutenant Melvill was as sharp as they came.

The next morning I dressed in my uniform once more and it felt strange and constricting after the loose khaki one I had worn for the last few days. Leaving the slouch hat in the tent I headed back to the commissary and handed it over to the orderly. He looked at me suspiciously, "Where is the carbine you were issued?"

I looked down at the table, "Sorry, I lost it in the passes. We were in wild country."

He snorted his disbelief, "A likely story! You will have a stoppage of pay until you leave the army, old son. Name, rank and number."

"1173 Private Jack Roberts."

Just then Mr Dalton strode up, "Is there a problem, Hargreaves."

"Yes Mr Dalton, this soldier claims he has lost his weapon."

The old soldier nodded and smiled, "Roberts, is it?"

"Yes, Mr Dalton."

"Lieutenant Melvill told me that he was impressed by you on your recent," I saw him choosing his words carefully, "scouting expedition. Hargreaves, I believe that we can write off the carbine as an unfortunate loss due to action in enemy territory. I am certain that Private Roberts will take better care of his rifle. Isn't that right?"

Grinning, I said, "Yes, Mr Dalton."

"Now run along and enjoy your day off."

Returning to our tent I knew that the adjutant had told him what I had done.

I enjoyed my day off. I had my boots to clean after the rough treatment I had given them scaling the rocky slope and I had underwear and socks to wash. That evening, after their patrols and their work and when we had eaten, I told them of the chase. The colonel might want the story kept quiet but these were my friends and deserved to know what had happened to our nemesis.

"So you don't know who it was who actually killed the two of them?"

"No Fred, and I don't want to know. We fired a lot of bullets and I am not sure that anyone did the job. What has been happening here?"

"Nothing much. We just patrol. There are still no warriors in the villages. Easy duty."

And so it continued. We had our first winter in South Africa and by the time spring came the rebellion was over and the leaders were punished. After a month or so we were marched north towards Zululand. We travelled under a hot early summer sun. Governor Bartle Frere and the war office in London had decided that was where the next trouble would come from and we had proved ourselves as a reliable regiment. When new boots were issued, we knew that we would be marching and march we did.

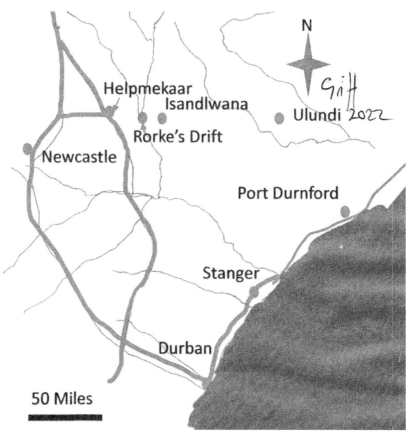

Zululand 1879

Chapter 14

Helpmekaar December 1878

Since the capture of the deserters, my life had changed. Mr Bromhead was still aloof but less so with me and he even paid me to look after Blackie. The extra money would come in handy. Taylor was the most useless soldier in the regiment and, even worse, he was a drinker. Mr Bromhead's deafness meant he was unaware of the slurring of Taylor's words. Indeed, so long as his uniform was kept smart, his leather polished and his food fetched when he needed it then Taylor could do as he wished. Blackie was a different matter and I was paid, while we awaited the arrival of fresh troops, to groom him and occasionally to exercise him. My collection of coins was growing. Lieutenant Melvill had also not forgotten me. I was used, on three occasions, to help him recover deserters. These were not in the same class as Llewellyn and Madog, in every case it was more that they were absent without leave rather than deserters but, in the colonel's eyes, it amounted to the same thing. We were not even away from camp for a night but it showed the trust that the adjutant had in me. However, it did not endear me to many others in the regiment who saw me as the adjutant's hunting dog. I had a couple of run-ins with other soldiers who thought I should not be recapturing men who simply wanted a drink and a whore and who would return when they were satiated. That I had been ordered seemed immaterial. The confrontations, however, were verbal. I had continued to grow since joining the army and having already dealt with the bully Llewellyn, none were willing to risk my fists.

My tent mates and I became even closer. Until the rest of the 2nd Battalion arrived we were the only representatives of the 2nd Battalion. We recognised other officers and sergeants but we were not close to the 1st Battalion. Life was good as we awaited the arrival of the army. We had beer, plenty of food and there was a rum ration. I did not drink all of mine and Henry did not touch his. He used some of his as a way of keeping wounds clean and any of the rest of our tent knew that they could enjoy more rum if they wished. I quite liked a glass of rum but I mainly used my rum to keep my tobacco moist. It also helped it to taste sweeter when I smoked. We had no patrols but still suffered the daily drills and the marches. Our boots were now in a very sorry state. We had repaired them as best we could but now the soles were so thin that it was hard to find a place to drive in hobnails.

Lord Chelmsford had been a good commander for when he had come to Gcalekaland, he had put down the rebellion quickly and efficiently with the troops he had brought there. The general who had led us, or rather, not led us at Ibika was no doubt languishing in England telling lies about what he did. We were more confident in Lord Chelmsford, even before he had arrived, rather than his predecessor.

A letter arrived for me just before Lord Chelmsford's reinforcements landed. It was from my mother.

Liverpool April 1878

My dearest Jack,

I hope that this letter finds you safe. I was overjoyed when I received your letter which came just before Christmas Day last year. It was the best Christmas present any of us could have wished for. I have had to wait until now to send this letter as I did not know where to send it. Aunt Sarah managed to discover that your regiment was heading for Durban and so I am sending it there in the hope that there will be just one Jack Roberts and you will receive this.

You will be pleased to know that your brother and sisters are growing well and all are happily employed and well thought of at work. That is pleasing for a parent as it shows I have brought them up right. They do not bring in as much money as when you and your father were working but it is enough and we are content. I still see your sisters each Saturday and Billy comes with me. He looks sharp in his suit and

*attracts many admiring glances from the girls.
It is good to regularly see the town where I grew
up and I have fond memories of it all. When we
are together it is you of whom we speak. Your
brother admires you greatly and it will not
surprise you to know that you are the favourite
of both of your sisters. We all want you home
safe.*

*The newspapers mentioned a police action in
South Africa but as I did not see your name
published amongst the casualties then I hope and
pray that you are well. How do you cope with
the wild animals? It must be fearful for you to
hear lions and other such terrifying creatures.*

*Your nan was ill this winter but you will be
pleased to know that she recovered well and both
she and your Auntie Sarah send their love.*

*I will end now and Auntie Sarah will try to
get this letter posted for me. We all love you and
pray that God watches over you. Come home
safe, my son.*

Your loving mother

I had smiled when she spoke of lions. Thus far the only wild
animals I had seen had been Madog and Llewellyn. I had been
remiss and not written and so when I had finished reading the
leader I penned a reply and went to the port to pay a sailor to
post it for me on his return to England. I would have sent money
to help the family but I did not know the sailor well enough to
trust him. I would hoard the money until I returned home and it
would make my family's life easier.

The ships brought not only fresh troops with the new
commander but also the rest of the 2nd Battalion. We had awaited
their arrival at Durban. When the ships docked and they
disgorged the new troops there could not have been a greater

contrast with the rest of the regiment. The officers excepted, all
of our uniforms had faded so much that we looked to be dressed
in pink and pale blue. We were all tanned and bearded. When the
rest of the 2nd Battalion marched ashore they almost gleamed.
We recognised faces but more than half of the men we saw were
recruits and they looked it. They were still awkward in their kit.
We had been that way too. Our replacements were not the only
ones to join us. As well as the militia horse, the 90th Foot, 1st
Battalion the 13th Foot, the 2nd Battalion 3rd Regiment of Foot,
and the 99th Foot also landed and would give us more Imperial
troops for our next campaign. There was a naval brigade with
heavy guns as well as a rocket battery. We knew we would be
heading into Zululand and the sheer numbers told us that this
was not the police action that had been the Xhosa rebellion. This
was an invasion and I was mindful of Peter's words. The Zulus
were a more formidable foe than the amaGcaleka had been.

The replacements and reinforcements were given just a
couple of weeks to acclimatise to the land and then we set off for
Zululand. The long march to the starting point for our regiment
was over two hundred miles. The old hands, the ones in the
faded uniforms, coped far better than the replacements. We saw
the contrast more than any of the other veterans for we marched
with our battalion who were all in new uniforms. Lord
Chelmsford had divided his forces into four and we were in the
centre column. Our colonel commanded our column and
therefore marched according to Queen's regulations. It was
easier for the older hands than the new ones. South Africa had an
unforgiving climate. We learned about the battles won by Lord
Chelmsford from some troopers from the Natal Native Police.
We had served with them in Gcalekaland and they homed in on
our faded uniforms when we had a water stop. We had tried to
give advice to the new men but being new men they resented it
and many suffered on that long march. Necks, faces and hands
blistered in the sun. Canteens were emptied too quickly and they
had not the sense to seek shade when it was offered.

"You boys will find this a little harder than Ibika, my friend."

The native policeman spoke to Henry who nodded, "We
served with Nicholson's Horse and they told us that the Zulus
are a more formidable enemy."

Fred asked, "What I can't see is why we are here at all. I mean we have an eight-day march to reach their land. Why? That is miles beyond Cape Colony."

I could tell that the native policeman was all in favour of the war from his words, "Land. The Zulus have good land for their herds and they still make war along the border. I have a farm north of here in Transvaal and I want my family safe."

"But what has that got to do with Queen Victoria?" Fred was like a dog with a bone and he would not let it go. I knew, from Trooper, that kings and queens did not think of wars in the same way as soldiers. They never had to go and fight. The war in the Crimea had been over which church would be the senior one in the Holy Land. To me, that had been a far more pointless war than this one.

"Your queen, Empress, I believe she calls herself, sees herself as the protector for all the colonists and that suits me." He laughed, "You boys make much better targets in your red uniforms than we do and besides you get paid better than we do."

There was no malice in his words and he was right. We were a much better target.

One advantage of such a large column was that we were well supplied on the road north and there were no attacks. So long as we were to the west of the Tugela River then we were not encroaching on Zulu territory and their pride, intact, we would be left alone. Once we crossed the river at Rorke's Drift we would be in Zulu territory and they would not take kindly to that. I was already composing my next letter to my family and I would tell them of the confusion of such an invasion as this. All we knew was the little world in which we marched. When I had lived at home we rarely bought a newspaper and news tended to filter down to us. Mother had written that she had hoped her letter would reach me. Had my mother invested in a newspaper she might have learned more.

The men of our section in the 1st Platoon were all that we saw until we stopped and erected tents. We marched together and camped together. We sang songs as we marched together and we shared whatever bounty came our way. Mr Bromhead rode far to the fore and any information we had came from the native horsemen or the sergeants and they were close-mouthed. We would be told what was needed of us as and when it was necessary. It was like my family at home. We were not privy to everything that we, perhaps, should have been.

When we reached the starting point for three of the columns, Helpmekaar, we found a huge well-organized camp. There were three columns there, ours, Colonel Durnford's and Colonel Pearson's. Colonel Pearson would carry on north to Transvaal but the other two would cross the river. We would be based, at first, at Rorke's Drift and after that…when we needed to be told then we would be. Lord Chelmsford, so the rumour ran intended to invade from a number of points simultaneously in the hope that we would spread the Zulus thin. In the event it was a vain hope but, to us, it sounded a plausible rumour that might just work.

Captain Spalding, we learned, had been seconded by Lord Chelmsford when he had arrived and he had helped our general greatly. The result was that, when he returned to us, he had been promoted to Brevet Major confirmed. We had been under the direct command of Major Spalding all the way from Durban and had addressed him as Major Spalding since before Ibika. He was a good officer and I had more confidence in him than in Lieutenant Bromhead. The lieutenant was a sound officer and although I now knew he was courageous I had learned when I had followed him and the adjutant on the deserter hunt, he seemed to lack common sense. I would back him to stand firm and not surrender but I did not think that he would be able to outwit an enemy. Major Spalding, like Lieutenant Melvill, was a clever officer. I was happy that if we were with Lieutenant Melvill then we would be looked after. Colonel Durnford led his irregulars and they headed towards Rorke's Drift first. They would be heading further east towards Isandlwana. The Zulu capital was at Ulundi, well to the east and in the heart of Zululand. Lord Chelmsford, we surmised, was heading there. We followed a day or two later.

It was not far to the river, a mere ten miles, but the one hundred yards crossing of the river was more daunting than one might have wished and felt like the bubbling river was a small sea. Cavalry and wagons could easily cross it and there was a ferry. I saw that engineers had begun to build a bridge to facilitate the crossing however we were not afforded that luxury and with rifles held above our heads, we waded into the water and crossed. I confess that my mother's letter had put in my mind the idea of wild beasties. We had seen no crocodiles and I did not even know if they lived here but the thought was in my mind as we crossed the bubbling waters. The waters threatened to sweep us from our feet and I was glad that I had such strong arms and legs to withstand the force of the water. When we put our boots on solid ground, I was happy to be alive, wet but alive. We passed an engineer officer and some native levies. They looked to be building a redoubt to house guns. I saw that it was in its early stages and that the lines had just been laid out for the trenches, pits and mounds. The levies did not look to be happy to be working. The redoubt was comforting for it meant that at some time in the future they would be putting artillery there and that pleased us.

Rorke's Drift had been built by a man called Jim Rorke. Living so close to Zulus he had made it a defensible dwelling. Although now a mission station it was stoutly built. Approaching from the south we saw two well-built buildings. One looked like a house while the other was some sort of store. Close to the store was a well-constructed kraal. We had learned this was the name given to paddocks for animals. The one closest to the store had a single gate and a good wall. Blackie would be well protected. Further to the north and east was a much larger kraal with a low wall and it was filled with native cattle. They would be slaughtered as and when they were needed to feed the army. I saw tents erected between the house and the store and that was where we were marched. There were walls as well as rocky patches that looked like jagged teeth guarding the north side of the structure and looming over everything was the Oscarberg Escarpment. It was covered in trees and dominated the valley.

As usual, the officers left the sergeants to organise the erection of the tents but we were old hands at that now and we soon had them up although the ground was hard having been baked by the summer sun. There was a stream nearby and our first task was to fetch pails of water and fill the water butts. I saw that the house had been taken over by the medical section and the stores by Mr Dalton. I wondered how long we would be here if such arrangements were being made already. It seemed to me that we were fortifying an outpost in Zululand. The army had not needed to make a defence of Helpmekaar but we were now in Zululand and as we had close to Fort Murray, we were making a fort. The difference was that we did not have high ground and, as far as I could see, there was too much cover close by. I knew how adept warriors were at hiding almost in plain sight. That night, after we had eaten and we were seated before our tent on some logs we had found and were smoking, Henry speculated.

"This looks to me, boys, like our base. From what that native policeman told us we are now in Zululand. That river crossing needs to be defended. I am guessing they will leave a few companies here to defend it. The rest of us will head east to fight."

Alf shook his head, "I hope, then, that the battles take place close to here."

"Why is that, Alf?"

"Simple, Fred, this is where the hospital is situated and we have seen how wounds can go bad in this climate. I would like to get here sooner rather than later if I cop one." We all worried about wounds going bad and losing a limb. That had been Trooper's greatest fear when he had been speared at Balaklava.

Alf was right and there were already men in the hospital. Some had been injured on the march while others had illnesses such as dysentery. The hospital was their only hope. Surgeon General Reynolds, as I knew from personal experience, was a good doctor and not a simple sawbones who would take off a limb as soon as look at it.

Over the next days, more troops arrived and we set about making the camp comfortable and life an easy routine to it. We dug latrines and we still drilled and when we were not we repaired walls and made the two buildings and kraals defensible. When Lord Chelmsford arrived then everything changed. He was there but days before he issued his orders and our column began to head north and west, into Zululand. To Lieutenant Bromhead's chagrin, we were left to guard the mission while the rest of the regiment packed up their tents and headed east towards Colonel Durnford and Isandlwana. We were left with

Captain Stephenson and his troop of Natal Native Horse. I knew that the lieutenant had little time for the local horsemen but he could do little about it as Brevet Major Spalding commanded. Lord Chelmsford had left his chosen man to command our fort. As soon as the main body had left there was an officer's call. Colour Sergeant Bourne had the rest of the company stand to. We were sent to watch the river and ensure that the native levies continued to work. As we passed Lieutenant Chard, the Engineer officer in command of the work, the officer said to Corporal Allan, "Try to keep them working, corporal."

"Will do, sir. Do you want my lads to lend a hand?"

He smiled, "I think you would be better occupied keeping your eyes open for Zulus."

"Zulus, sir?"

"I do not think that the Zulus will take kindly to a huge army invading their land. They may well decide to get their retaliation in first and we are an easy target." He pointed to the redoubt, "At least until I get the fort built."

"Hitch and Roberts, get yourself upstream a bit and keep a watch on the hills to the east."

"Right Corp."

We both knew how to move in this land now and used solid stones as we made our way along the riverbank rather than risking tufts of grass in which any manner of nasty creatures might lurk. There was a large stone to the side of the river. No doubt it had been swept downstream in some storm in the past and it afforded a good vantage point as it rose a good eight feet from the land. I clambered up, using Fred's hands to help me and then I reached down to pull him up. We both wore clothes covering our necks although, as we faced the sun, it was our faces that would suffer. Luckily our skin had become tanned and toughened after two years in South Africa. We both slipped a bullet into the chambers of our guns and peered east. We had no idea what we were looking for except that any movement towards us represented danger. Feathers that in England had seemed innocuous were now a sign of danger.

"What do you think, Jack?" Fred was garrulous to the extreme and filled any silence with questions.

"About what?"

"Will there be a battle?"

"I reckon so but this time we have so many soldiers and guns that I can't see these Zulus emerging triumphant. Peter Brent warned me about the Zulus. It will be harder than with the Gcaleka and the new lads will have to learn on the job but the general seems to know his business."

"And we will miss it."

I laughed, "You will miss the likelihood of getting killed?"

He shook his head, "It's not that, Jack, it is, well, when I leave the army and I have a family, I want to be able to tell my children what we did. At the moment it doesn't sound much. Ibika was not a real battle, was it? We did not cover ourselves in glory. We stood there and opened fire. The enemy never even got close to us. My dad was at the Battle of the Alma and he told me how the redcoats stormed the heights and won the battle. He was so proud of that day. He would show us his arm where the Russian bayonet sliced it open and I thought how glorious it would be."

I nodded understanding a little of what he was saying but I was not convinced. Trooper's wound had changed his life. Of course, he had not married and had not been able to regale a son with his tales of glory. It suddenly came to me, on that bright January morning, that he had told his tale, he had told them to his surrogate son, me. Until that moment I had not thought of a family. How could I? I was in South Africa and any wife I might take would be in England. I decided that when my enlistment was up then I would return home and find a wife. I smiled to myself. I was making such an undertaking seem simple and it would not be. I would be in my late twenties when my time was up. Perhaps there would be no women who would take me on. For the first time, there was a pang of regret at my enlistment.

He nodded at me, "You, at least, have the story of the deserters with which to regale your children. Even Lieutenant Bromhead was impressed by you."

I was surprised, "He was impressed?"

"One duty he was the duty officer and came along with Lieutenant Coghill. They had a quiet cigar close to me and Lieutenant Bromhead sang your praises." He laughed, "You know that with his deafness he cannot speak quietly. Lieutenant

Coghill said that his friend Lieutenant Melvill had said the same thing. You should have had a medal for that."

I remembered the colonel's word. A medal would have meant divulging all that the two deserters from the 24th Foot had done. Like their bodies, the secrets were buried in Gcalekaland.

We were kept on duty all morning and then we were summoned back to the compound. It had been transformed in our absence into an ant's nest. Mr Dalton was busy with his men arranging the ammunition boxes and others were reorganizing the sacks of mealie in the storeroom. Brevet Major Spalding and Lieutenant Bromhead were striding around the compound with Colour Sergeant Bourne behind them. The major was pointing out features of the mission station.

Corporal Allan said, "Get food as soon as you can. We may be busy this afternoon. It looks like that officer of engineers was right."

After we had eaten Taylor came over to me. He annoyed us all for he seemed to have little to do and we all treated the little man with contempt. "Private Roberts." Everyone else called me Jack but not the little man.

"What do you want, rodent?"

"Mr Bromhead wants you to exercise Blackie."

I stood, "Well it is clear you can't do it, isn't it?"

"I don't like horses."

"What do you like? Apart from the bottle."

Ignoring the insult he went on, "The lieutenant said to hurry."

I knew that he would not have done so but I was happy, in any case, to spend time with the horse. We had found some apples on the way west and I had secreted a few of them. The summer heat had wizened them but Blackie would still enjoy them. The lieutenant nodded as I passed him and the major. I felt Colour Sergeant Bourne's eyes upon me.

Entering the kraal I took the rope to lead the horse. I gave him the apple while I attached the leader, "Come on old boy, you will be getting fat just standing around." He neighed. Horses seemed to understand me. I walked him twice around the kraal and then began to run, not fast, for it was too hot for that and I kept to the centre so that the horse ran further than I did. I ran him until he had a slight sweat and then walked him to cool down. Tying the leader to a rail in the kraal I began to groom him, singing as I did so. He enjoyed it. My singing was low and I was able to hear some of the conversation between the officers.

"We don't have enough men here, Bromhead. We are exposed. I know the general needed the guns but he could have left us one. Lieutenant Chard could have built a redoubt. Perhaps Captain Stephenson's rider will fetch one of the companies we left at Helpmekaar."

"Do we really need them, sir? Surely General Chelmsford is more than capable of subduing the Zulus. We have more regulars this time than in Gcalekaland."

"You are guilty, Mr Bromhead, of counting your chickens. We have never fought this enemy so how we do know what they can do? No, another company and a defensive wall are what we need. I hear that Mr Dalton has some experience of building forts, let us go and consult with him."

Having finished with Blackie I took him and tethered him in what shade there was. As I closed the gate, I saw Taylor with a bottle and I wondered why Mr Bromhead tolerated him.

The next morning we were given our orders and it was to begin to move mealie bags and ammunition boxes to make a defensive position joining the two buildings and the kraal. Mealie bags were also placed so that we had what was, in effect, a laager. Lieutenant Chard had a horse and he saddled him. I was not sure if he was unhappy that his advice had not been sought but, for whatever reason, he absented himself and decided to go for a ride. Technically, although outranked by Major Spalding, he was not under his command and as he could do no more work on the redoubt until his men arrived, I suppose it was understandable. The native contingent who had been his workers were now building the walls of boxes, wagons and mealie bags. The reason he gave was to ride to the main column and see his junior officer and his sappers.

The work suited me better than most. Hauling heavy mealie bags and ammunition boxes was like the work I had done in the iron gang at Pritchard's. It was repetitive and, to my mind, not too difficult although some men found it hard. Whilst some of the others moaned and complained I just got myself into the rhythm of it. I found that humming a song helped.

Fred shook his head, "You are too bloody cheerful, Jack. How can you enjoy this? It is not soldiering."

Sergeant Windridge had his tunic off and was labouring alongside me, "If the major says to do it then it is soldiering and Roberts is doing what all good soldiers do, making the best of it. Now try to keep up, Hitch."

"Yes, Sarn't."

What had seemed a disorganised jumble began to take shape by the afternoon and I could see what Mr Dalton, who was also labouring, intended. If we were attacked there would be a four-foot wall all around us. The buildings could be defended and with loopholes in the walls would become strong points. Colour Sergeant Bourne was constantly at his side, seeking clarification of the plan. The two men seemed to get on well. I suppose Mr Dalton having been a senior sergeant for so many years had much in common with Colour Sergeant Bourne. We were all surprised when Lieutenant Chard galloped his horse in. The horse was lathered and showed that the lieutenant had ridden him hard.

Major Spalding and Lieutenant Bromhead were not stripped and labouring. As officers, they were supervising and shouting our orders to the rest of us. They turned as the engineer galloped in, "Trouble Mr Chard?"

Dismounting he saluted and said, "Could be. When I was at the main camp at Isandlwana my chaps told me that Zulus had been seen to the north and west of the camp. They seemed to think that a fight of some sort was in the offing."

Lieutenant Bromhead grinned, "Good oh. Now we shall show them."

The major shook his head, "It may be, Lieutenant Bromhead, that the big fight will not be with the main army but with us. After all, why take on almost two thousand men when there is a choice morsel like us. It may be nothing but I will ride to Helpmekaar. I shall order that jumped up captain in command there to send me another company. I should be back before tomorrow evening, all things being equal." He turned to me, "You, Roberts, isn't it?"

"Yes sir."

"You have a way with animals. Go and saddle my horse." I hurried off and by the time I had obeyed the orders and returned the major was ready. "Lieutenant Chard, you are in command until I return, I suggest you continue to improve the defences. We may not need them but it is as well to be prepared, eh?"

No one seemed concerned that there might be an imminent battle but we worked all afternoon with renewed vigour. By the evening we were exhausted but we had a defensive wall into which Lieutenant Chard had incorporated the two wagons that were at the station. It was truly a fort and looked more like one than the first we had built close to Fort Murray.

"Do you reckon we will have to fight, Hooky?"

"It might come to that, 716, we just don't know. The major is a good chap and I like his preparations. By the time he returns with another company, we will have double the numbers and with the native contingent we might be able to hold out." We had worked out that we had well over two hundred men with which to defend the mission station.

Fred said, from the dark, "Nah, Colonel Glyn and the lads will sort out the old Zulus, you mark my words. A Martini-Henry, a few field pieces and our horsemen will sort them out."

I wondered.

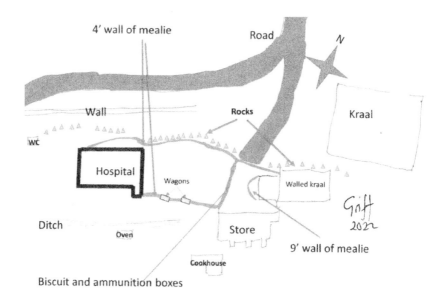

4' wall of mealie

Road

N

Wall

Rocks

Kraal

WC

Hospital

Wagons

Walled kraal

Ditch

Oven

Store

9' wall of mealie

Cookhouse

Biscuit and ammunition boxes

The Mission Station at Oscarberg 1879

Chapter 15

Rorke's Drift January 22nd, 1879

The day began much the same as the previous one had ended and we were set to work on the defences. Lieutenant Chard took men to continue working on the redoubt. It now seemed that we might need it. The difference came just after noon when we heard the rumble of artillery from the north and east. Everyone stopped what they were doing and stared into the distance until Colour Sergeant Bourne shouted, "No one told you to stop working! Get on with it." No matter what danger there might be we always had one constant, Colour Sergeant Bourne.

The three officers all gathered together along with Mr Dalton and Colour Sergeant Bourne for an impromptu meeting.

"Well, the battle has started. I bet those guns put the wind up the old Zulus."

I shook my head, "You don't know that, Fred. Remember what Peter Brent told us; the Zulus move as fast as horses. Unless the gunners are sharp then they might only get a couple of rounds off before they are overwhelmed. Remember Ibika." That battle had been won not by artillery but by steadfast rifles and a swift charge by the cavalry.

There were still civilians in the mission station. Reverend Smith, who acted as our chaplain, and Otto Witt, the missionary in charge of the station, were there. Along with Surgeon Reynolds, they volunteered to ride up the Oscarberg escarpment from where they would have a better view of Isandlwana.

We were due for a break and it was as we sat to enjoy hot tea and corned beef sandwiches that two things happened at once. Surgeon Reynolds returned from the escarpment with the chaplain and Otto Witt in tow and four colonial cavalry riders galloped in, their horses lathered and terrified.

The leading trooper pointed behind him and blurted out, "The camp at Isandlwana has been taken and men massacred."

The second trooper had lost his hat and looked frantically around as though seeking more men than he could see, "No one can stand against their numbers."

Surgeon Reynolds pointed at the man's mount and said, "That is Surgeon Shephard's horse."

"Yes, sir. He is dead. The survivors are under the Command of Captain Essex and are heading for Fugitive's Drift. We are joining them."

Before they could be stopped the four men galloped off. Even I knew that four more guns might help us. I saw, for the first time, that Lieutenant Bromhead had learned to command, "Roberts, go and fetch Lieutenant Chard from the river."

Surgeon Reynolds said, "Tell him to hurry, we saw Zulus coming from Isandlwana."

"And have him bring the men too, Roberts."

"Sir."

"Come along Surgeon Reynolds, let us make the hospital so that we can defend it."

I ran to the river where the pontoon was just making its way from one bank to the other. A sergeant from the Buffs regiment, Sergeant Milne, was in charge of the native levies hauling on the rope.

"Lieutenant Chard." He looked up. "Lieutenant Bromhead asks if you would bring the men back to the camp." I saw the frown and I went closer. He was not deaf like Lieutenant Bromhead and I would not need to shout. "The Zulus have massacred the column, sir, and are advancing here."

"Thank you. Sergeant Milne, moor the pontoon in the middle of the river and get here. There may be trouble."

"If you like, sir, I can stay here with eight men and we could hold the Zulus off."

Smiling, Lieutenant Chard said, "I think your eight rifles would be of more use around the perimeter, Sergeant Milne, but your offer is duly noted."

"Sir."

"Off you go, Private, I think that Mr Bromhead will need you to help him rather than waiting to see if we make it safely back to the camp."

"Sir."

Lieutenant Chard was a no-nonsense officer.

As I reached the camp, I saw two riders rein in and hurl themselves from their mounts. Lieutenant Chard was right behind me. I went to pick up my tunic, helmet and rifle from where I had been working and the two men, seeing an officer broke the news to him.

"Lieutenant Adendorf and Sergeant Vane, sir. We have just come from Isandlwana. The column has largely been wiped out and there is an impi of four thousand Zulus heading this way even as we speak."

Lieutenant Chard had followed me quickly and was still fastening his tunic. He nodded, calmly, "Sergeant Vane, be so good as to carry on to Helpmekaar and report the news to Major Spalding. Ask him for more troops."

The sergeant threw himself on his horse and galloped off. Lieutenant Adendorf said, "Perhaps I should go with him."

"No, Lieutenant, we need every man we can get." He turned to me, "Where is Lieutenant Bromhead?"

"I believe he is at the hospital, sir."

He hurried off and entered the hospital. I began to fasten my tunic. It was when I was fastening the top button that I saw Lieutenant Adendorf chewing his lip and then, after looking around to see where Lieutenant Chard was, he sprang into the saddle and followed his sergeant."

He was disobeying an order and I had heard the command clearly given. I ran after Lieutenant Chard and found him at the entrance to the hospital. "Sir, the lieutenant has ridden off. I believe that he is following his sergeant."

He shook his head, "Rats leaving a sinking ship, eh? What is your name, boy?"

"Roberts, sir."

"Stay here. I may need you?"

Just then Otto Witt and the chaplain rode in. The missionary just said, "There are thousands of warriors coming for you. I must join my family. God Bless you but I fear that I will return to a blackened mission station and all of your corpses."

With that cheery thought, he galloped off. The chaplain had handed his reins to his servant while he went into his tent. I am not sure what he had planned but whatever it was it was forestalled when his servant threw himself on the back of his horse and galloped off after the missionary.

Lieutenant Chard said, "Colour Sergeant Bourne, we need a lookout on the top of the hospital for it affords a good view of the north."

"Sir. Hitch, get yourself up on the roof and sing out if you see anything."

My friend, his rifle slung over his back, climbed up the ladder that led to the low roof over the entrance to the hospital and then crabbed his way to the apex where he straddled the roof and then unslung his rifle. He called out, "Colour Sergeant, horsemen approaching from the south."

I was close enough to Lieutenant Chard to see the relief on his face. Lieutenant Bromhead came out and the officer of Engineers said, "They may be reinforcements. We could do with them. How many men do we have in total?"

The lieutenant frowned and Colour Sergeant Bourne said, easily, "There are eight in your party Lieutenant Chard, thirty-five wounded in the hospital, one colour sergeant, one lance sergeant, four corporals, three lance corporals, sixty-eight private soldiers and two drummers." He waved his hand at Captain Stephenson's native contingent, "and one hundred of those fellows." He could not hide the derision in his voice.

Hooves drummed and the one hundred troopers from Sikhali's horse under Lieutenant Vause rode in. He saluted. As a colonial, he was outranked by both of the regular officers, "Lieutenant Vause from Fugitive's Drift. I came to help you evacuate the mission station."

The two regulars looked at each other and Lieutenant Bromhead said, "Quite out of the question. We were ordered to stay here and defend the stores and the animals. Besides we have thirty-five men in the hospital."

Lieutenant Chard pointed, "Take your men to beyond the Oscarberg and warn us of the enemy's approach." I could see that Lieutenant Vause was reluctant but he had been given an order and he led his men away. "I think we can let the men rest now, Lieutenant Bromhead. The mealie bag wall is four feet high and that will provide cover. I want Surgeon Reynolds and his orderlies brought to the store. That is a safer place for them."

"Of course. See to it, Colour Sergeant."

197

"Sir. Roberts go and inform the surgeon of Lieutenant Chard's decision."

As I ran off, I heard Lieutenant Bromhead say, "Almost nine hundred of our men killed, it beggars belief."

I heard Lieutenant Chard say, in reply, "There may be survivors and if there are then we are here for them. This will be a more secure sanctuary than Fugitive's Drift."

I ran to the hospital where Henry and some of the others from our section were making loopholes in the walls. I saluted and said, "Surgeon Reynolds, Lieutenant Chard wants you moved to the store. He thinks it would be safer."

"And the patients?"

"He didn't say, sir."

He peered towards the Oscarberg, "Might be a good decision for this is the direction they will take but the store will not be as comfortable as this place." He turned to his orderlies, "Fetch all the equipment and medical supplies and come with me. You had better come too, Roberts."

Waving to the lads I picked up the medical bag the surgeon handed me and ran towards the storeroom. It was a mere forty yards and made me realise what a tiny place we had to defend. With two hundred or so rifles we could deter an enemy but could we hold out?

I helped the surgeon make a temporary operating theatre in one of the better rooms and then I was dismissed. I went outside and was just in time to see Lieutenant Vause ride in. His men were not with him and he looked wild, "You have no chance to make a stand, Lieutenant. There are thousands of them and my men won't stand. I am sorry." With that, he dug his heels into his horse and took off.

What happened next was shameful. Captain Stephenson, who commanded the native contingent, looked on helplessly as his men all downed tools, grabbed their rifles and fled. The captain threw himself on his horse and galloped after Lieutenant Vause.

"Stop!"

Waving an apologetic hand the colonial officer whipped his horse. Some of B company who were resting picked up their rifles and fired at the backs of the retreating men. They brought down three before Lieutenant Bromhead shouted, "Cease fire!"

Only one of Sikhali's Horse remained, Sergeant Moody, who said, "Sorry sir. The captain is young..." his voice tailed off apologetically and he nodded, "I shall stay."

The lieutenant was making the best of a bad job when he said, "Thank you." He turned to Lieutenant Bromhead and Colour Sergeant Bourne. "We have too great a perimeter to guard. I want a wall of ammunition and biscuit boxes building from the storeroom north to the road. I know the men are exhausted but we need a place we can make a last stand."

Mr Dalton said, "I will have my lads help. We are all in this together now. Come along Chaplain, we can use your arms for something other than making the sign of the cross."

The Colour Sergeant's voice boomed out, "Right my lucky lads, you have enjoyed a rest now help Mr Dalton shift the ammunition."

I went to help but Lieutenant Chard said, "Stay here, Roberts, I may well need you as a runner." He smiled. "You seem a calm sort of chap."

Lieutenant Bromhead said, "Roberts might be young but he is a veteran. Lieutenant Melvill thought him the best man in the regiment." The colour sergeant's rolling eyes told me what he thought of that but I swelled with pride and then felt guilty. Where was Lieutenant Melvill now? Had he made it to Fugitive's Drift or was he lying with the rest of the regiment just a few miles away?

I knew that the men who hauled the heavy ammunition boxes were tired but there was an urgency to their work. No one had explicitly told them of the threat but we were no fools and knew that four thousand Zulus represented a real threat. We had barely managed to finish the wall when Fred shouted from the hospital roof, "Here they come. There are thousands of them and they are as thick as grass."

Lieutenant Chard and Lieutenant Bromhead had already walked the perimeter assigning men to their firing positions and now the bugle sounded to stand to. Where was I supposed to be? Colour Sergeant Bourne saw my dilemma and shouted, "Get to the hospital and join your butties, there's a good lad."

I needed no urging and I ran to the hospital. Fred apart, the rest of the section were standing with guns poking through improvised loopholes. Henry smiled when I entered, "Well if we are all going to die, I can think of no better company. Welcome, Jack."

"Where do you want me?"

He looked around and said, "Fred will be lonely up on the roof, you and Alf go and help him. If it gets too hot then come back down here."

"The lieutenant wanted the patients moved to the veranda, Hooky."

"Well, that will have to wait until we have the opportunity, eh? Now run along you two." Hooky was in his element. He was in command and he knew what to do. He should have had a promotion before now.

As I climbed up the straw roof, I saw that the Zulus were making for our south wall. There was cover there for them. What they could not know was that our south wall was strongly made and two wagons had been embedded amongst the mealie bags, two wagons which were sound strongpoints. I had not heard the order to open fire but men were firing and it seemed, to me, judicious for me to do so too. Lying against the roof with just my helmet and rifle poking over the top I took aim and fired. I say, take aim, but in truth, the aim was just at the mass of black and white shields that came at me. I could not have picked an individual had I tried. The other two were firing and I could hear the crack of rifles from the loopholes. Henry and the others were doing as we had been ordered and defending the patients. We got into a rhythm. Two would fire while one reloaded so that there were always bullets coming from the three of us. When we reloaded, we dropped our heads below the roof for cover. It was as I did so that I saw Mr Dalton, who was directing men to fire from the wagon wall, get shot in the back by men using rifles on the Oscarberg. That the hits were lucky at that range mattered not to the men who were hit. He was tended to and did not go to the surgery but continued to direct the fire of men from his wall. He was an old soldier and I knew from Trooper just how tough they can be. We had lost men. At least one, Mr Byrne, one of Mr Dalton's men, was shot in the head and his body lay in a pool of blood. While the wounded would receive attention the dead would lie where they fell. It gave me the determination to keep firing.

My experience in the war against the amaGcaleka had told me who were the best targets, the chiefs and, as the Zulus took cover, I stopped aiming at the broad mass and chose to aim at the chiefs. Now that they had come closer they were easier to identify. We were having great success until I heard a cry and Fred dropped his rifle and clutched his shoulder. He had been wounded by a lucky bullet from the Oscarberg. It was an ugly wound for the bullet was homemade, I could tell that from the size of the hole.

"Fred, get yourself down. You can do no more here."

Nodding and a little pale he slid down the roof to join Henry and the others. As he reached the end of the roof and looked down, he shouted, "Coley is dead." Harry Cole was the first in our section to die and it made me work even faster to move the bolt. I ignored my burnt hands and kept firing.

Alf said, "Oh, no, the buggers have realised that this is a straw roof." He fired and I saw a warrior with a flaming assegai fall. There were others who were copying the dead warrior. They had attached burning grass and straw to their spears and were intent upon throwing them at the roof. The ones in the hospital could not see the danger and so there were now just two rifles firing at the spears. We dropped a warrior with each bullet we fired but inevitably some got through and as soon as the burning spears hit the tinder-dry hospital then it burst into flames. It was not a gradual glowing that grew into a fire, the straw was so dry that the whole section that was set alight roared flames into the air.

"Get down, boyo, we have done all that we can."

It was one thing for Alf to give that command but the flames took hold so quickly that it was easier said than done. As we slithered to the ground Lieutenant Bromhead appeared with five men, one of them was Sergeant Windridge. I saw why. The door from the hospital was now exposed to a Zulu attack. The patients should have been moved before and now might be too late.

"You two fix bayonets and join me. We have to ensure that the patients can be evacuated from the hospital."

I saw Cole's body as well as Joe Williams and two other patients. They had been speared by Zulus who now lay dead. We could hear the Zulus in the hospital and the muffled sounds of bullets being fired and men fighting for their lives. I could only imagine the horror of it. The roof was now afire and there would be danger from a fiery death as well as a violent death at the hands of Zulus. We had to guard the one door through which Henry and any others who were still alive in the hospital might escape. Lieutenant Bromhead was using a rifle and whilst he was a good shot, he reloaded more slowly than the rest of us who had endured the Brecon drills. Those drills saved our lives. We peered over the mealie bags, fired, ducked down to reload and poked our heads up again. Some of us were marginally faster than others so although there were just eight of us we kept up a continuous fire. I had wrapped a neck cloth around my barrel and I was able to hold it more easily. Even so, we had to put our bayonets to good use. We were forced back from the wall of mealie bags as the sheer weight of numbers poured forward. It took time to extricate wounded and sick men from the hospital and so Lieutenant Bromhead had us fall back but in good order. It was as we did so that a Zulu chief, with ostrich feathers in his hair, ran at Lieutenant Bromhead. I still had my next bullet in my hand and so I lunged at him with my bayonet. He was a good warrior, how else had he become a chief and he deflected it with his shield exposing me to a lunge from his assegai. When we had trained at Brecon, I had learned to use the stock of my rifle and I pushed it towards the assegai. Miraculously the tip of the savage spear went into the wood and stuck. I saw the surprise on the chief's face and before he could react, I whipped my lunger across his body, the tip tearing into his throat. I chambered the round and pulled the spear from the stock of my rifle. I raised and fired, almost at point-blank range as a Zulu attempted to have revenge for the dead chief.

"Fall back!"

I saw Henry Hook dragging Private Connelly from the burning building. Henry had a wicked-looking wound over his eye and his face was bathed in blood. Connelly had been taken to hospital with a broken leg and it was now clear that he had two. Henry had not been able to be gentle when rescuing the patient.

Henry's rifle was slung around his back and he needed both hands to drag the wounded man back to the main line of defence. Only Alf and I were close enough to help and we did not hesitate. We ran forward, disobeying the lieutenant's order to fall back and fired at the mob of Zulu warriors intent on getting to Henry and Connelly. I fired my bullet and it knocked one to the ground. Alf did the same and then made the mistake of attempting to chamber another round. I did not and I used my bayonet. I struck with such force at the nearest Zulu that my lunger went through the hide shield and tore open his middle. While Alf managed to shoot one Zulu a second thrust his assegai into Alf's side as my friend tried to reload his rifle. He raised it to finish off Alf but I beat him to the strike and I skewered him. Alf tried to crawl back to the safety of Lieutenant Bromhead and Sergeant Windridge and so I stood my ground.

"Come on you bastards! You have to get through me first."

There were three of them and every moment I held them up would buy more time for my comrades to escape. My life did not matter and, to be truthful, I was now convinced that there were so many Zulus that defeat was inevitable.

I saw the eyes of one flicker to Alf and knew he was distracted. Taking my chance I struck him in the thigh with my lunger. A second thrust his assegai at me but I used the trusty stock of my Martini-Henry to block the blow. It was all in vain for the third did for Alf and my friend and tentmate was skewered as he lay on the ground. I was enraged and sometimes that gives a man energy and strength he does not know he possesses. I swung my lunger so hard that I almost took the head from one Zulu and although the second managed to stab me in the left arm I whipped my rifle around and severed his throat. Panting I chambered a round. I could vaguely hear Lieutenant Bromhead shouting, "Roberts, get back here now. That is an order."

I ignored it and looked at Alf's body. He was clearly dead and we had not said goodbye. Fred was wounded and I did not know how badly. I raised my rifle and fired at the next Zulu who had dropped down to the ground before me. He fell and I reloaded.

"Jack, get back here now! That is an order." It was Henry's voice and I obeyed. I walked backwards until I was with the rest of Lieutenant Bromhead's section. The massive Sergeant Windridge was helping Henry to drag the moaning and semi-conscious Connelly to safety.

The Zulus were now in the hospital but as I learned when I reached Henry, all those who were alive had been rescued. The Zulus seemed intent on mutilating the bodies of the dead. I saw one hacking at Alf's body and their distraction allowed us to make it back to the recently constructed defences of biscuit and ammunition boxes. We clambered over the mealie bags and I took my position on the firing line.

Mr Dalton had been shot in the back but he was still working. He and the chaplain were dragging an ammunition box around and when he reached me, he tugged my leg and held out a handful of cartridges, "You are a brave lad but there is a time to run and a time to stand. This battle is not yet over. Trust to God and your rifle and we will emerge victorious."

The chaplain said, "Amen."

I was given a second handful and I filled my almost empty expenses pouch. 716 was next to me and I said, "How was it inside the hospital?"

He shook his head, "Brutal, boyo, we had to cut holes in the walls to escape. We left some good boys behind. Sergeant Maxwell is dead. Poor Fred is in a bad way."

I nodded. I had seen the hole. Even if we survived this battle then he had no future in the army and I wondered what he would do.

"Here they come again. Face your front and independent fire at will." Colour Sergeant Bourne's voice was reassuring.

As the afternoon turned to night we kept firing at the faces that appeared from the dark. This was not the sustained attack we had endured at the start and I wondered if these steely warriors we fought were also tiring. Colour Sergeant Bourne took one in two men to build a redoubt for Lieutenant Chard and we had to spread ourselves even thinner. We would have a last line of defence: a nine feet high redoubt made of mealie bags and with a good wall behind it. It might save some of us but the men who had been taken from the wall were missed. Sergeant Milne of the

Buffs brought us something even more valuable than ammunition, water, for we were desperate. Had we wanted to, we could have opened one of the biscuit boxes before us and eaten but food was the last thing on our minds. Our canteens were all empty and while there was a river close by it had a barrier of live Zulu warriors to protect it.

Suddenly a chief shouted something and a hundred or more Zulus ran at us. They were shouting 'Usutu!'

Sergeant Windridge and a wounded Corporal Allan raced to join us as we shouted that we were under attack. My barrel was now so hot that I had been forced to tie a second of my neckcloths around it to stop my hands from being burned anymore. I raised my rifle and fired without even thinking about it. I did not see the men I shot. It was impossible to tell who shot who. The gleaming Zulu bodies kept appearing no matter how many we dropped. Some men, further along the line, were hit and taken to the veranda of the store which was now being used as a makeshift hospital but the four of us were a solid block in the middle of our section of the wall. Our bullets miraculously kept the attack at bay. I only had to use my bayonet once when a warrior who had been feigning death on the Zulu side of the wall, suddenly rose above the boxes with a raised assegai. Alf's death was on my mind and the bayonet rammed into his head and emerged from the back. It seemed to signal the end of the attack and, as the sun quickly set, night descended upon us.

It was not total darkness for the hospital burned and that helped us for the Zulus were unwilling to be silhouetted against its flames. The Zulus on the hillside could no longer fire on us and we had respite there, too. The blindly fired bullets had been a nuisance but as Fred had found out, a deadly nuisance.

When the attacks on the north and east walls intensified Colour Sergeant Bourne came to fetch us. He looked at Corporal Allan, who was wounded, "Have you seen the surgeon, Corporal?"

"Yes, Colour Sergeant. I can still fight and I have seen what the Zulus do to the wounded."

"Right, come with me. We need you lucky lads to bolster the defences on the north wall."

We saw the medical orderlies, some of whom were wounded themselves taking men to have their wounds tended to. This time we were spread out along the line and I found myself next to Henry and Shadrack Owen.

Henry smiled, "You did your best for Alf. I tried the same for poor Harry Cole but…"

I raised my rifle and fired at the Zulu who rose from a pile of wounded men just twenty yards from us. "What happened?"

Henry shot into the pile of apparently wounded men and three rose to run at us. Our training kicked in and all three died. "He panicked. It was hot in the room thanks to the fire and the Zulus were close but we were doing well. He opened the door to try to escape but they were outside the door and they butchered him. I shot the ones who killed him and then closed the door but…"

Shadrack reloaded his gun, "Harry was a nice lad but he was scared of his own shadow. He was not cut out for the army. Not like you, Jack, you are a born soldier."

I shook my head as I fired at another Zulu head that appeared in my sights, "I am not sure. Is it always like this?"

Sergeant Windridge was four men down and he had heard my words, "I have never seen anything like this. It is a miracle that we are still alive and I will say one thing for these Zulus, they are brave men. All we can do is face our front and keep doing our duty until the end."

Henry said, "Aye, and our numbers are shrinking. Still, if we pray to God he may help us."

I glanced behind me, "And our little fort is getting smaller too. It is just thirty yards to the surgeon and the wounded men."

Henry shot at another Zulu and said, "It looks like Mr Chard is making plans for that. It looks like he has built another fort."

To our right was a nine feet high stack of mealie bags, ammunition and biscuit boxes. Wounded men were being used to help make it even stronger. There were firing steps inside and it would be a place to make our last stand. I think that we were all praying that Major Spalding would return with another company or two from Helpmekaar.

"That is where we will make our last stand, I am thinking."

Our rifles were good weapons but they were so hot that some ceased to function. The rifling became fouled and cartridges softened and jammed in the breeches. So far it had not happened to us but I knew that it would and I had a plan in mind already. When my rifle eventually broke down, the barrel blocked I said, "Henry, Shadrack, cover me, I am slipping over the barricade to fetch a couple of rifles."

Although we had not lost many men some had dropped their rifles over the barricade and had been unable or unwilling to rescue them. I spied two of them.

"Don't be daft, Jack, use your lunger."

I took the bayonet from my rifle and, grinning, said, "I will." I dropped my helmet to the ground and rolled over the barricade. I hoped that if I was seen the Zulus would assume I had been hit by one of their bullets although they were so inaccurate that so far few men had been hit by them. I landed on the bloody body of a Zulu. I waited in the dark and looked around. Bullets still cracked and Zulus still ran at the barricade. Waiting until there was a lull I crawled towards one rifle and grabbed it with my left hand. I held it in the air and a hand took it from me. The second was a little further from the barricade and I crawled towards it. I was seen and Zulus ran at me. My comrades did not let me down and they fired bullet after bullet at them but as I grasped the rifle strap a Zulu hand grabbed me. Another one had been feigning death. I was only saved by my lunger and my quick reactions. He used both hands to grab me around the neck. I drove my bayonet up under his ribs and twisted. This time he did die and I rose and ran for the mealie bags. As others shot at the Zulus, Shadrack pulled me over the top.

"Lucky boy!"

I nodded knowing he was right. It was midnight when the main attack came. I only knew the time because Mr Dalton had just come by with more ammunition and I had asked him the time. He had told me it was almost midnight.

Cries of 'Usutu!' 'Usutu!' 'Usutu!' rang out and the most determined attack since the sun had set was unleashed. I had a rifle that was cool and a full pouch of bullets. I fired my new rifle like a man possessed. The others were the same but, inevitably some Zulus used the bodies of their dead and wounded to climb up onto our barricade and raise their assegais to spear us. With our bayonets attached our rifles were more than four and a half feet long. We drove them up into the groins, thighs and stomachs of any warrior who fearlessly leapt above us. My world shrank to the two or three men around me and the Zulus who were trying to kill me. I know that I was lucky but I had learned how to load while lunging so that I was able to keep the warriors at bay. Not ever strike with my bayonet killed. In fact, I doubted if I killed more than one or two with it but the long, sharp blade caused terrible wounds and incapacitated many warriors. After a ferocious fight of half an hour or more it was over.

As the Zulus fell back, I said, "Sergeant Windridge, I think some of these Zulus before the barricade might be playing dead,"

"Let's find out."

We all stood and, leaning over the barricade, fired bullet after bullet into the apparently dead Zulus. More than a dozen rose but were shot before they could escape. I doubted that they would try that trick again. We returned to our watch and awaited Sergeant Milne and his water cart. When he came we filled our canteens and were then told that the rest was for those in the new hospital. Until we could get down to the river to refill the water cart, we would have to eke out the water in our canteens.

I turned to Henry, "It is going to be a long day."

He nodded sagely, "And I wonder if we shall see another dawn.

When dawn came, we looked for the next attack. None of us had slept for it had been too dangerous to do so. Lieutenant Chard seemed indefatigable and he had men clear the thatch from the storeroom roof so that it could not be fired. We had learned the cost of not doing so in the hospital and the smell of burnt bodies still drifted over to us. On our section of the wall, we were ordered to repair any damage to the boxes and mealie bags. When that was done Colour Sergeant Bourne came over to us. We all looked like dishevelled wrecks but he looked ready to stand by Colonel Glyn's side at a Queen's Birthday parade, holding the colours.

"Sergeant Windridge, take your section and pull down the walls of the burnt-out hospital. Mr Chard does not wish to afford the Zulus the opportunity to use the building for cover. We will cover you from here."

"Colour Sergeant, how is Hitch?"

It was almost an impertinent question and even as the words came from my mouth, I awaited the tirade I anticipated would follow. Instead, he gave a little sad smile, "Hitch is alive but his days of soldiering are over, Roberts. The surgeon took scores of pieces of metal from his shoulder bone." I nodded. "Now cut along and do as you are ordered."

We slung our rifles and hurried over to the walls. You could still feel a little residual heat from the burnt-out building but you could touch the walls. They were cooler than a Martini-Henry in the height of battle. We laid our guns down and used the pieces of timber that had fallen to the ground. With two men to a timber, we rammed the walls until they tumbled to the ground. As they did so, I saw charred bones. They could have been the patients or Zulus it was impossible to discriminate and I shuddered at the thought of their deaths. Alf had been killed quickly and I don't think he suffered pain but to be burnt alive was too horrible to contemplate. We returned to our rampart.

It was seven o'clock when the Zulus appeared to the southwest of us. There were hundreds of them and they were beyond the range of our guns but still in sufficient numbers to warrant the bugle ordering us to stand to. I chambered a bullet and rested my rifle on the mealie bags. It seemed an age as they kept moving north but once they had passed us and kept going, I almost cheered.

Henry said, "They looked more tired than we are."

716 asked, "Do you think it is over, Hooky?"

For once Henry seemed stumped for words, "I honestly don't know, 716. We are not being attacked now so let us enjoy this moment, eh?"

It was eight o'clock when a sharp-eyed sentry on the new hospital roof shouted that he could see red uniforms crossing the river. We stood to, for it could have been a trap and they might have been the Zulus who had defeated the 1st Battalion and taken their tunics but when the mounted horsemen rode in, followed by Major Spalding, then we knew it was over.

Chapter 16

Mr Dalton appeared along with Colour Sergeant Bourne. They had with them the brandy that had survived the battle. "Take out your mugs and let us toast the dead eh boys?"

We cheered and held out our tin mugs. To my great surprise, I saw Henry hold his mug out, "Henry! You are tee total."

He nodded, sagely, "And after this, I will return to a more sober life but I believe that what we endured warrants the taking of a little spirit and besides, I would like to honour our dead. We shall be going home but all that they will have is a grave in this bone dry, desiccated land."

We were each given half a mug of brandy and some downed it in one after we had all said, "To the fallen."

Hooky, 716 and I sipped ours not to savour it but to reflect on the moment. We each knew that we should not be alive. The odds, like they had been with Trooper at the charge of the Heavy Brigade, had been against us and yet, amazingly we had survived. I know that I thanked God for he must have been with us.

When we had finished the brandy Hooky nodded and said, "Well, I have had my one drink and I am content."

We were almost forgotten as the relief column established its own camp. Our stout defences were demolished and that released the two wagons to carry the wounded back to Helpmekaar. Surprisingly Blackie and the other horses, although terrified, had survived unscathed after the battle. We were ordered to hitch up the wagons and then help the wounded into them. We had lost very few men but almost half of the company who had survived were wounded. My scratch was nothing and I had kept quiet about it. I would tend to it myself.

Hooky and I helped a very distressed Fred into the wagon. He had been given some laudanum to numb the pain but I could see he was in discomfort. "Well, my time in the army was brief, eh, boys? I wonder what I shall do."

I smiled, "Open a pub. You can tell tales like no one I have ever met."

"Perhaps." He grinned, "Although I suspect I might drink all the profits." He looked at the three of us, the last of his tentmates and said, "I shall miss you all. You were my family these last couple of years. You, Jack, I owe much to. If you and Alf had not come to my aid then who knows what Llewellyn and his animals would have done. If you are ever in Islington then look me up."

"I will, Fred, I promise."

The wagons left under cavalry escort and we tramped behind as we marched to an almost deserted Helpmekaar. Major Spalding had emptied the garrison. We were comfortable there and enjoyed our first hot meal in what seemed like a lifetime.

It was after a night in a bed and with no sound of battle to disturb our sleep that Colonel Glyn and the other survivors of the disaster at Isandlwana arrived. There were not many of them. The colonel and some of the men had been with Lord Chelmsford and not in the camp when the disaster occurred. They all looked harrowed for they had passed the bone strewn field of Isandlwana. The dead would need to be buried but that would be for another day. Of Lieutenant Melvill there had been no sign. I had hoped that when I saw the red uniforms arriving from the north he would be with them but that hope was dashed.

We were ordered to a parade and a gaunt Colonel Glyn addressed us. "Firstly I have to thank you all for what you did at Rorke's Drift. The honour of the regiment was saved and it is you men, officers and warrant officers who saved it. There are no words. I must tell you that the colours have been lost along with the two men who tried to save them, Lieutenant Coghill and Lieutenant Melvill."

My heart sank to my boots. I had feared the words but hoped, beyond hope itself that he had somehow survived. Even as the pronouncement was made, I prayed that the colonel was wrong and that the lieutenant was with the other survivors at Fugitive's Drift.

"However there are rewards for those before me." He smiled, "Lord Chelmsford has requested that the Queen make the award of the Victoria Cross to the following officers and men of the 24th." He smiled, "I do not doubt that she will accede to the request. Others will be awarded medals but today is all about the

24th Foot. Lieutenant Chard, Lieutenant Bromhead, 1240
Corporal Allan, 1362 Private Hitch, 1373 Private Hook, 716
Private Robert Jones, 593 Private William Jones and 1393
Private John Williams."

I could not help grinning. My tent mates had been rewarded.
Hitch's stories would be enriched by the purple ribboned medal
that was the highest honour in the British Army.

The colonel had not finished, "If I had my way then each of
you would be given a medal. However. it is in my remit to
promote some of you and I shall do so now. Officers died and it
is in the nature of battle for the brave to reap the reward.
Lieutenant Chard, you are not a member of our regiment but you
commanded this company and I am pleased that Lord
Chelmsford has gazetted you to the rank of major." The
normally serious Engineer could not help smiling for he had a
double promotion. Lieutenant Bromhead is promoted to the rank
of captain and, until this campaign is over will be a brevet
major." I smiled as Mr Bromhead cupped his hand around his ear
to hear the words. "Colour Sergeant Bourne is promoted to the
rank of second lieutenant." We were all pleased for him but
Colour Sergeant Bourne's face remained expressionless.
"Sergeant Windridge will be the new colour sergeant." I was
pleased for our sergeant. He was a good man and his resilience
and strength had helped us in the battle. "Finally, for his services
at Rorke's Drift, not to mention Gcalekaland, Private Roberts is
promoted to the rank of corporal." I was stunned for I had not
expected anything.

There were murmurs and Lieutenant Bourne shouted, "Quiet
in the ranks!"

"Finally, you will all be going home, as shall I. The regiment
needs to be rebuilt and the men before me will be the steel in the
backbone of the new 24th. The wounded will be taken by wagon
and the rest of the regiment will march tomorrow. You may
dismiss the parade, Colour Sergeant Windridge."

As soon as we could we set about congratulating each other. I
knew from Trooper that there was no greater honour than the
medal that so many of our battalion had earned. The battle had
changed us all but the medals would change the lives of others
even more. We said our farewells to the wounded and my parting

from Fred was hard. He and Alf had been my best friends. Henry had his wife and the others, 716 and Shadrack were privates whilst I would now be a corporal. Everything would change. Would it be for the better?

Things changed for me sooner than I thought that evening when I was summoned to the colonel's office. There Brevet Major Bromhead and the colonel awaited me. "Roberts, we have a request to make."

Mr Bromhead said, "Actually, Corporal Roberts, it is I who have asked for you."

The colonel frowned and then nodded, "We all know that, like your comrades, you need some leave but the colours are lost and lieutenants Coghill and Melvill are missing. Whilst it is unlikely that they are alive Captain Bromhead would like to recover both the colours and the bodies or if they still live, then the men. He has asked for you. This is purely voluntary and you need not go."

I blurted out, "I would like to go. I liked Lieutenant Melvill and if he is alive, I should like to find him and bring him home safely, sir."

The colonel smiled, "Commendable and it shall be duly noted on your record. Who knows, you may attain the third stripe in a year or so."

As we left, I reflected that the third stripe was immaterial as far as I was concerned.

Once in the open Mr Bromhead said, "This time we have a decent horse for you and a scabbard for your rifle. Some local cavalrymen will be our escorts."

"Do we know where the colours were lost, sir?" It seemed easier for me to talk about the loss of a colour than the adjutant. If I said the word lost then he might be dead. I know it was superstitious but a man cannot change the way he is.

"We will head to the Buffalo River and start there for the two officers were reported as having started down the Buffalo Valley. I have to warn you, Roberts, that whilst Lord Chelmsford is heading towards the Zulu capital Ulundi, there are still bands of Zulus wandering the land looking for stragglers. This may be dangerous if you wish to reconsider."

I smiled, "No, sir, I owe a lot to the adjutant. I will risk it."

I returned to the barracks to pick up my blanket, satchel, gun and ammunition. They all looked up and Henry said, "Where are you off to?"

"Going to find the colours. If I don't see you before you leave then I will see you in Brecon."

His face betrayed his fear but his words were comforting, "You take care, you hear. We would like you back, Corporal." I nodded. Henry handed me some corporal's stripes. "Lieutenant Bourne dropped these off for you."

716 handed me a little packet, "Here is a needle and thread," he grinned, "Corporal."

I grinned back, "And don't you forget it."

They all stood and gave me a comic salute. I left the barracks with a smile on my face.

The men who awaited us were from Sikhali's Horse. From their shamefaced looks, I guessed some had been amongst those who had abandoned us. Mr Bromhead also recognised some of them. His voice was harsh as he commanded, "Find us the Buffalo River and keep us safe. The men of Sikhali's Horse owe this regiment that much, at least."

The young lieutenant nodded and said, "Yes sir and may I congratulate you on your medal."

The withering stare forced the young man to lower his gaze. I saw Blackie and next to him was a fine chestnut whose reins were held by a young trooper. There were three pack horses and I guessed that they had a grisly purpose. The trooper was of Dutch origins and he had a thick accent, "His name is Goldie."

"Golden?"

"Goldie."

I nodded, "And for the record, my rank is corporal, trooper." I said it gently. I was not reprimanding him.

He smiled, "Corporal. Goldie is a good horse but he takes some handling."

I nodded, "Thank you."

I slid my rifle into the scabbard and hung my helmet and satchel from the saddlebags. After tying my blanket to the saddle I donned the slouch hat I had retained after the deserter hunt. As Brevet Major Bromhead was wearing fatigues and a forage hat I did not think that he would object. I left my canteen attached to my belt. My uniform was now so faded that I would not stand out as much as I would have done when I stepped ashore at Cape Town.

I stroked the horse's head, put my foot in the stirrup and hauled myself up. He did not like the weight and tried to buck. I pulled hard on the reins and spoke firmly to him, "Steady Goldie." I leaned forward. It was a risk but I took it and slipped a mint into the horse's mouth. As with all the other horses I had mounted, it worked.

The trooper nodded, "Well done, Corporal."

I just nodded, grateful that I had not been embarrassed before the ten troopers and their officer.

We headed back towards Zululand and sought the river. There were many rivers crisscrossing this land and they fed into each other. The result was that in places they were ankle-deep while in others they needed a horse to cross.

Lieutenant Bromhead had obviously thought all of this through. I smiled for although his words were also intended for the officer and the troopers his eyes were on me, "We will begin north of Fugitive's Drift. My reasoning is thus. If the colours and the bodies had been carried as far as that then they would have been reported."

I was the one who answered him and in that moment the pecking order was established. I was the one who would help the newly promoted Mr Bromhead and the militia were just our escorts. "That makes sense, sir."

We headed for the Buffalo River. The mission station was to the east of us and Isandlwana further east than that. I wondered how Lord Chelmsford would defeat these warriors. As the morning drew on I thought about the courage of the Zulu warriors. Even in the face of a barrage of lead they had come on and kept coming on. As we stopped at noon to water our horses, I said, "Mr Bromhead, how can Lord Chelmsford defeat the Zulus? I know he has a larger army but Peter Brent told us that the Zulus have an army of fifty thousand warriors. We have nowhere near that number."

He looked east and smiled, "He has learned from the mistakes of Colonel Durnford and Colonel Pulleine." I knew that he was privy to more information than I was. "They will move in boxes

of men and wagons with cavalry guarding the flanks. It will
enable them to bring great firepower to bear on each attack. Of
course, it will slow their advance to a crawl but this is a
marathon, Roberts, and then there are the weapons. I hear he has
Gatling guns with him."

"Gatling gun?"

"A wheeled machine gun that can fire more than two hundred
rounds per minute. Imagine that Roberts. Our company could
manage that, just about, but how long could we have kept it up
for. The guns cut down swathes of men and they don't overheat
as quickly as our rifles. I hear they were very effective in the
American Civil War. Lord Chelmsford will win but it will take
time and sadly the 24th will not be there at the end."

He looked sad and I realised that only a couple of officers had
survived. I had known a few of the men who had died but all of
his friends had perished. When we returned to Brecon, he and
Colonel Glyn might be the only survivors. It was a chastening
thought.

It was the middle of the afternoon when we saw, in the
distance, the camp at Fugitive's Drift. The wounded survivors
would have been taken south towards Greytown and then
Dunbar. The ones who remained were just guarding an important
crossing of the river. The water was deep but it would only deter
a man on foot and Captain Bromhead led us across the river. The
cool water was pleasant rather than chilling and I allowed Goldie
a couple of mouthfuls of water before I pulled up her head and
continued to follow the captain. We picked our way over land
without trails. The route we took was rock-strewn and often we
had to climb away from the river because of some rock or other.

We were already beginning to think of making a camp when
Captain Bromhead pointed and shouted, thickly, "There,
Roberts, do you see?"

I looked to where he had pointed and I saw the red and blue.
The two colours were caught in a cleft of rocks in the river.
There was no question about who would go for them. They were
the colours of the 24th and a soldier of the 24th would fetch them.
I dismounted and handed my reins to one of the troopers.

"Be careful, Roberts."

"Sir." I placed my slouch hat on Goldie's head.

As a boy, I had enjoyed exploring and climbing and the steep sides did not daunt me but I stood to assess the safest route. Once I had it in my mind, I took a serpentine path and descended making sure that I only moved one limb and that the other three were secure. There was no need for reckless speed. The two flags had lodged with their spikes caught beneath a rock and when I finally reached them, I knew that I would have to drop into the water, up to my waist. I did not think that there were creatures lurking beneath the water that might hurt me but I did not know for certain and doubt is a fearful thing. I steeled myself and stepped into the water. I waded upstream, against the current until I reached them. I was keenly aware that every eye was upon me. I took the Queen's colour first and tugged at it. It came away and I held it aloft.

I heard a command from behind, "You two, go and help him."

While I waited, I studied the regimental colour. It was at a slightly different angle and I suspected I might have to employ another strategy. The Queen's Colour taken from me, I reached down and pulled at the flagstaff. It would not budge. Ducking my head beneath the water I saw why. A rock, the size of my fist, had lodged between the flagstaff and the boulder. Reaching down I tugged away the rock and then, as my head emerged from the river, I pulled the colour free. It was not their colour, the militia did not have them, but the troopers and their officer all cheered as the regimental standard rose above the river.

A trooper waited to take it from me but I shook my head, "Thank you but I shall manage."

It was a struggle but I eventually clambered back to the horses. I was dripping wet but it had been worth it. The colonel would be pleased and I knew that Lieutenant Bourne, not to mention Colour Sergeant Windridge would both sleep easier knowing that the colours had been recaptured.

I handed it to Captain Bromhead, "The colours, sir."

He nodded and said nothing. I saw why. His eyes were wet and heavy and had he said anything then he might have broken down and he would not do that in front of the militia. I turned to the Militia lieutenant, "Should we camp here, sir? It looks as likely a spot as any but you know the land." There was a natural dell and could be defended easily if we were attacked.

"Good idea, Corporal."

I retrieved my hat from Goldie and then began to unsaddle him. Captain Bromhead was left with the two colours and he gripped them as tightly as though they were alive. One of the troopers made a picket line for the horses and I tied Goldie to it. I went back to Blackie and took him there too. I slipped him a mint and then began to unsaddle him. I smelled smoke and knew that we would have hot food that night. I took off my tunic and placed it on Goldie's rump. There was enough heat from his body and the dying rays of the sun to begin to dry it and then I took off my boots and turned them upside down to allow the water to drain off. I took off my trousers and hung them on the picket line to drain. I began to shiver. It did not seem cold enough to warrant shivers and I put it down to the effect of the river. I slipped my blanket around my shoulders and sat as close to the fire as I could, with my satchel before me. I filled my pipe and as I gradually warmed up enjoyed a good smoke. I saw the corporal's stripes and thread in the satchel. When I had finished my smoke, I would fetch my tunic and sew them on and, by then we would have eaten and I could dry my uniform close to the fire.

Captain Bromhead brought the two colours and placed them close to the fire where they would dry and, I suspect so that he could continue to look at them.

"Can I get you anything, sir?" I had to speak up and my voice was so loud that some of the troopers turned to look. They would get used to his deafness.

"No, thank you, Roberts. I shall have a mug of tea when it is ready and enjoy a cigar."

He had changed since Brecon. The officer who was aloof and distant had endured much in South Africa and I suspected he would be all the better for it. The troopers made our meal. It was a hotchpotch of whatever was to hand. The basis, of course, was a tin of bully beef but they had added local ingredients such as dried meat, greens they had foraged and local herbs. With biscuit crumbled into it, the stew would be hearty and tasty. While they cooked it, I sewed the white stripes on the arms of my tunic. They stood out against the faded pink of my old tunic.

Captain Bromhead sucked on his cigar and said, "When we are back at Brecon, we shall all be issued with new tunics but I intend to keep mine. It will help to remind me of the defence of the Mission station."

The lieutenant ventured, "Sir, is it true that you held off an impi of more than four thousand Zulus?"

He laughed, "I confess that none of us had any time to count and it felt like ten thousand but I believe you are right."

"But how, sir?"

He nodded towards me, "Men like Roberts here with a Martini-Henry and a sword bayonet fought for each other."

I nodded, "And I believe that God was with us."

The captain nodded, "You are right, Roberts, for we lost far fewer men than one might have expected and tomorrow we seek other brave men. England will be weaker for their loss."

"I am not sure, sir. There are many more back in England. Perhaps the story of our stand might encourage them to join."

"You may be right." I wondered if he would be more enthusiastic when he went on his next recruitment drive than when I had first met him outside the Liverpool pub.

The next morning we continued our trail up the river. The two colours were tied to the side of one of the horses and were led by a trooper. It was shortly before noon that we saw the dead horse below us in the river. It was clearly dead and I could see where carrion had begun to devour it. We were forty feet up the side of the river and there looked to be no easy way down. We dismounted and went to the edge to see what else we could spy. It was one of the troopers who spied the bodies.

"Sir, down there, I see a flash of blue and a face."

We peered and saw the two bodies, jammed like the colours in the rocks. Mr Bromhead took his field glasses and confirmed that they were the bodies of the two missing officers. His voice was both dull and sad when he spoke, "Let us go down and retrieve them. God has guided us here and we can take them back and give a Christian burial."

I shook my head as I headed for my horse and my rifle, "Sir, I would not be too hasty."

He frowned, "Why on earth not, Roberts?"

In answer, I chambered a round and bellied up to the edge of the small cliff, "Sir, there were no birds pecking at the bodies when we rode up and none near the dead horse. Why not? Something is down there that has scared away the carrion."

I saw the militia lieutenant nodding.

"There is no rush, why don't we look at the ways down and see if we can spy out danger."

I knew he was not convinced but he nodded. The lieutenant assigned three men to hold the horses and the rest of the troopers took their rifles and joined me. I used the sight of my rifle to track along from the bodies. I was looking for something that should not have been there. It was the bird's feather that alerted me. Just twenty feet above the bodies in a cleft of rocks I saw an incongruous feather sticking up from the rocks. I had seen such feathers at the mission station and they had been worn by a chief. The angle was not a natural angle and it would just cost me a bullet to discover if I was being foolish or not. I aimed at the feather knowing that my bullet would ricochet off the rock behind and if there was, as I suspected, someone behind the rock then it might make them move. The technique had worked when we had hunted the deserters. I squeezed the trigger and the crack was so loud that it made the horses react and whinny. I chambered another bullet as my first cracked into the wall and a Zulu stood up and aimed a rifle in our direction. I was ready and my bullet smacked into his chest. A fusillade from the troopers followed as the rest of the ambush party of Zulus rose. There were more than twenty of them but only a couple had guns and when five more men were dropped then they fled.

"After them!"

Captain Bromhead was in the saddle before any of us and with his pistol in his hand, he led us east to cut off the escape of the Zulus. They were trying to get back to Ulundi. I knew that there would be no thought of taking prisoners. I sheathed my rifle. Only the two officers had pistols and if the Zulus had any sense, then they would make a stand. A carbine used from the back of a horse was a notoriously inaccurate weapon.

Goldie might have been a difficult horse to manage for some but was as brave as they came and she kept up with Blackie as we headed to cut off the Zulus from their escape. The captain was a good shot although the first man he killed was less than twenty feet ahead of him and was perhaps an easy kill. Peter Brent had told me that the Zulus were good runners and so I reined Goldie back a little. Tired Zulus would be easier to take. The result was that the lieutenant joined the captain and the two of them emptied their pistols as we gradually caught up with the fleeing Zulus. The lieutenant holstered his pistol and took out his carbine, using it one handed. The captain, his pistol emptied, drew his sword and it was he who slew the last Zulu. The man had a Sam Brown holster and he drew a pistol. The captain leaned from his saddle and as the pistol came up so the sword came down to split open the skull of the warrior. Both men, the officer and Zulu, showed incredible courage.

The captain reined in and dismounted. I took Blackie's reins, he was lathered and shaking. Captain Bromhead reached down and took the holster and pistol with the lanyard from around the dead Zulu. He looked up at me, sadly, and said, "I thought I recognised it. This weapon belonged to Lieutenant Melvill." He wrapped the belt around the holster and handed it to me. "I am sure he would wish you to have it. He was very fond of you and wished to see you advanced. Keep this in memory of him."

I was touched and took it with a murmured, "Thank you, Mr Bromhead."

We walked our horses back to the river. I led the troopers to retrieve the bodies of the dead men. They had been mutilated and I saw the anger in the captain's eyes when he saw what had been done to his friends. They had been deliberately left knowing that they would be sought. The Zulus would not understand the value of the colours but the two officers, both wearing pistols and with swords would be.

The lieutenant asked, "Where are the swords and the other pistol, sir?"

Shrugging he replied, "Probably taken by others. They will be lost forever."

We wrapped the bodies in the blankets we had brought and draped them over the two horses. We found a shallow part of the river and crossed. On the way back to Helpmekaar we found another four bodies. All were from the 24th. A combination of the carrion and the mutilations inflicted post mortem it was almost impossible to identify them but we managed to retrieve them and by looking through the tunic pockets worked out who they were. Their families would know what happened to their loved ones. It was a sombre party that returned to the garrison at Helpmekaar but we had gone some way to salvaging some honour after the disaster that was Isandlwana.

We caught up with the other survivors of Rorke's Drift at Durban. The reunion was emotional for the colonel had thought the colours were lost forever. Lieutenant Bourne sought me out, once we were aboard the steamship that would take us home. I was alone at the stern and reflecting on the changes in my life. The newly-promoted lieutenant made certain that we were alone before he spoke.

"That day, in Liverpool, I knew that you were underage but there was something about you that made me ignore it. You have proved yourself more than once and I am grateful to you for retrieving the colours." He touched the new uniform's epaulettes, "You can achieve this, Roberts. You have the right stuff in you. It will be a long journey but I believe that you could be an officer."

"Thank you, sir, you don't know how much that means to me."

As on our voyage out, the officers were kept apart from the non-commissioned officers and rank and file. We had, however, more room than on the way out. Apart from us, there were the wounded from the campaign since Lord Chelmsford had begun to head towards Ulundi. I was able to be close to my messmates. I was pleased that there was no awkwardness and there was no resentment at my promotion.

As we neared the cape and stood smoking at the stern rail Henry explained it to me, "You should have had a Victoria Cross too, Jack. The stripes were given to you because of that oversight. Me and the lads are happy to defer to you." He laughed, "There was always something about you that marked you as different. We all saw that from the minute you joined our section. It was why Ada asked us to keep an eye on you." He rubbed the whitening scar over his eye where the assegai had cut him. "You ended up looking after us. Your mad charge bought us enough time to get out of that hospital and Connelly and I are grateful to you and to poor Alf. We will not forget him."

The long voyage home gave us all the opportunity to go over all the events at the mission station so that by the time we disembarked at Southampton we were all content. We had talked it through and any blanks in the battle were filled. We could not have done any more than we did and that brings some comfort. This time there was no troop train to take us home. We were given travel warrants and travelled with ordinary passengers. We were assaulted by questions all the way back to the barracks. Each time we changed trains we were surrounded by civilians who had heard of the disaster at Isandlwana and asked about the war. That so many had died at Isandlwana had shocked Victorian England. They were used to victories and not massacres. The newspapers, as was their wont, had taken, it appeared, great delight in the disaster. It sold newspapers.

As we marched from the station in Brecon the streets were lined with the townsfolk waving flags and cheering. It made us marcher straighter and keep our eyes facing forward. I was now a Corporal and it was my job to ensure that they were all in step and obeying Queen's Regulations. Marching into the barracks brought home to us what we had done. The bright red and blue uniforms with the green collars we saw were in direct contrast to our faded, tattered and torn tunics and trousers. The helmet covers were no longer white but torn and stained yet they marked us as veterans and as we came to attention before the colonel and the new officers gathered around the new adjutant our eyes were drawn to the colours carried by Colour Sergeant Windridge and Lieutenant Bourne.

There was total silence as Colonel Glyn said, "Men of the 24th you have acquitted yourselves with great honour. These colours are a testament to that courage. Lieutenant Coghill and Lieutenant Melvill gave their lives in a vain attempt to retrieve them. That the colours are here and the bodies of those brave officers safely interred tells me that the future of this regiment is in safe hands."

I felt myself swelling with pride tinged with sadness at the deaths.

"Tomorrow, we start to rebuild this regiment and from the ashes of Isandlwana shall rise a phoenix that will stand as an inspiration for future generations. The 24th Foot!" We were all at attention but those watching, the new men, all cheered. I would be part of that start and I hoped that Trooper would be looking down and be proud of me.

Epilogue

We were issued new uniforms the very next morning. It meant we all looked the same and that was a good thing, although the tanned skin marked the veterans of Rorke's Drift. The new tunic already had the corporal stripes and there was no sewing involved. My helmet was still sound and so I was just given a new cover. The new boots were a necessity; the drenching in the river had done them no good at all. Captain Bromhead left the next day and I barely had time to exchange more than a salute. He would head to London to receive his Victoria Cross. The rest of us would have to wait until the end of the week before we could have a well-earned leave.

I found it harder to adjust to being a corporal than I had expected. Being saluted by my former barracks mates was hard. I got on well enough with the other non-commissioned officers but it was not the same. We had but a week to endure the change and I managed it. The food tasted different somehow. We had been away long enough to get used to the different taste of South African food. It was more heavily spiced than ours. I discovered that the mess food was blander. That was another difference. I now ate with the sergeants and corporals. Luckily, I had friends like Colour Sergeant Windridge who made me welcome. I was told that there would be formal dinners during the year and I would need to prepare myself for them. All in all, considering it was just a week much happened and time flew by. We all left together on Saturday morning. As some were heading south and I was one of the few going north we had to say farewell on the station forecourt and then I went to the eastbound platform. Had he still been there then Fred would have shared the train as far as Hereford. As it was, I was the only one heading there. The local trains for Monmouth arrived first and I waved off Hooky, 716 and the others. I found it as hard a wrench as it had been leaving my family all those years ago. Trooper had warned me of the attachment soldiers had with each other and now I knew what he meant. I had two families now.

I smoked my pipe as we headed north. I had the last of the South African leaf in it. I had bought another ounce of tobacco to replenish my pouch when we had passed the tobacconist shop in Brecon but I wanted a last memory of that exotic land before I reached home. I watched the green land slip by. Even the grass in South Africa had seemed browner. It was good to be home but I did not know how long it would be until I was sent away again. As Henry had warned me, "You take the time you have with your family and hold it tightly in two hands. We could be sent anywhere in the Queen's Empire. It was sage advice. I thought about Fred. He had been in a bad way the last time I had seen him. The homemade bullet had shattered bones and Surgeon Reynolds had told him that the long voyage back to England was the best form of healing he could have. He had no idea, when he left us, what he would do. I knew my task all too clearly. I had a platoon to train and I now knew what the training was for.

It was dark when I walked down the gangplank of the Royal Iris at Liverpool. People were both heading home from work for many people worked all day on Saturday and it was a shopping day. Others were heading to the pubs. I had my kit bag slung over my shoulder and I was big enough to be granted space as I headed home. I heard cheery comments as I passed. Lord Chelmsford had defeated the Zulus and Isandlwana was forgotten. Soldiers in red uniforms were heroes and I nodded and smiled at all the comments.

As I neared Auntie Sarah's the crowds had thinned out. I passed the pub where I had taken the fateful decision to sign up and then headed down their street. It was as I neared the door that I saw the black drapes that signified a death. Mother had said that Nan had been unwell but had recovered. Had she had a relapse? I silently opened the front door; no one locked their doors. I laid my bag in the vestibule and quietly entered the tiny narrow hall. I saw a glow from the back room and knew that would be where the family was gathered. I took off my hat and opened the door quietly for if they were mourning then silence was the order of the day. No one heard me and I saw the family, with their backs to the door staring into the fire. They were all there, even Nan. Who was dead? I had a moment to myself as I took in the family picture and then the slight draught I had created made Auntie Sarah turn around. I smiled but her reaction was not what I expected. She put her hand to her mouth and screamed.

All but my Nan stood and turned. Mother rushed at me and took my right hand in her two. She kissed it, "Jack! Is this you or are you a ghost come to mock us!"

My sisters ran to hug me and I enveloped them with my left arm. My mother's hands came up to cradle my cheeks almost as though she was testing if I was a wraith or real and I slipped my right arm around Auntie Sarah. "I am here in the flesh and, though I endured danger I am alive and whole. You thought me dead?"

Billy's hands found my right hand and he gripped it with both of his. He kissed the back of it, "The newspapers said that your regiment was wiped out in South Africa. We hoped upon hope that you were just wounded but as time passed and no word came, we believed the worst. When news came of Lord Chelmsford's final victory, we accepted that you had died." The boy I had left was now a man with a smart moustache but his smile was still that of my little brother, "You have been returned to us and for that, we shall thank God."

Auntie Sarah was still as organised as ever and she recovered first. She kissed my cheek, "You will be hungry and I shall need to make another bed up." Her teary eyes smiled, "It is good to have you home, Jack." The normally stoic Aunt Sarah had a catch in her voice I had never heard before.

Mother said, "You three go and find Jack's bag and bring it in here. Nan will want to see Jack."

She led me by the hand to the fire where a weeping Nan held her hands up for me. I bent my head and she hugged and kissed me on both cheeks, "Jack, Jack, Jack, we thought you dead."

"But I am not and how are you? Mother said that you were ill."

"I was but seeing you is the best medicine there is."

The back room had two good chairs, one was Nan's on one side of the fire and Mother led me to the other. "And now, you shall tell us how you escaped the massacre we thought had taken you."

Auntie Sarah returned with a bottle of beer and my siblings sat at my feet, close to the comforting warmth of a coal fire.

"Well, I know not what the newspapers said, but this is what really happened..." And so I told the story of my South African adventure. I had to tell it many times. They heard the version without the blood and the gore. They had the stories of heroism and brothers in arms fighting for brothers. When I took my sisters back to St Helen's I visited Pritchard's and retold it there. Every pub I visited during my leave had someone who was desperate to know what happened. The version I told them was the acceptable one. I did not speak of mutilated bodies or burning flesh. I told them the story they wanted to hear about how a tiny band of redcoats had held off thousands of enemies for almost two days and, in the process won more medals than any soldier of the Queen had won before. I knew that I was now two people: I was Jack, the lad from St Helen's and I was Corporal Roberts, soldier of the Queen.

The End

Glossary

amaFengu – the tribe displaced by the Zulus who later fought alongside the British
amaGcaleka – The name of the rebellious tribe who fought against the British in Cape Colony
appelliefie – Cape Gooseberries
Butty (pl butties) - 19th-century slang for close friends
en banderole – worn diagonally across the body
Half a crown - two shillings and sixpence (20 shillings to the pound, 12 pennies to a shilling)
Iron Gang - labourers in a workshop or factory used to lift and move heavy equipment
Kopje- a peak
Laager- an improvised fort made of wagons
Lunger - nickname for the sword bayonet
Xhosa – The name of the largest tribe in the southern part of Africa

Historical Background

I decided to bookend this novel with two interesting battles. The charge of the Heavy Brigade at the Battle of Balaklava is less well known than the Charge of the Light Brigade. That may be something to do with Tennyson's poem. It is strange that two incredible pieces of British military prowess, the Thin Red Line and the Charge of the Heavy Brigade should be overshadowed by a reverse, the fatal charge of the Light Brigade due to awful leadership and poor communication. RSM Grieve and Private Ramage were two of the first men to receive the new award of a Victoria Cross. That 300 men should charge uphill against 2000 men and win is incredible. General Scarlett led the charge and suffered five sabre wounds as well as a mighty blow which his helmet stopped. His ADC lost his helmet and had his head split open yet he continued to fight.

Like many people my age I first came to know about Rorke's Drift through the superb film Zulu. It inspired Keith Floyd to join the Guards! That too came alongside a British disaster, Isandlwana. Both the charge of the Light Brigade and the disaster at Isandlwana have much in common. Whilst the leadership and planning were appalling the behaviour and courage of the ordinary rank and file could not be questioned. If general Scarlett had commanded the Light Brigade things might have ended differently. He refused to obey Lord Lucan's command to charge without being formed into ranks because he was a good soldier and I can't see the short-sighted general riding up the wrong valley.

For those who expected this novel to be a rehash of Zulu then I am sorry to disappoint you. Great though the film was the characterisation was typical Hollywood. I used the Michael Glover book as my Bible for this work. Henry Hook was a teetotal Methodist who had been given a special service award not long before the battle. He was as far from the James Booth character as it is possible to get. His elderly daughters were so appalled at the portrayal of their father that they left the premiere in disgust. Lieutenant Bromhead was in his thirties and deaf. I make allusion to his dullness and that is what emerges from the accounts of the period. I have tried to colour him in but he is no Michael Caine. Similarly, it was Acting Assistant Commissary Dalton who was responsible for the building of the defences. He was played as a far gentler character than he really was. He was awarded the VC for his work. Lieutenant Adendorf was played as a local who fought with the British and that, too, was a fabrication. He fled before the battle began and was later arrested and executed for his behaviour.

The film got much right. The horsemen who should have stayed fled as did Captain Stephenson and his men. Hook and the others behaved courageously as they dug their way out of a death trap. The 9' high redoubt was built but not used and so the final cataclysmic slaughter did not take place. In fact, few men of the 24th died at the mission station. The main deaths came from the hospital. As for the Zulus, despite the portrayal in the film of seemingly thousands being killed, the estimate was that less than 1000 perished.

This book is about life as a soldier, ordinary soldiers. The soldiers of the Queen did not care who they were fighting they just knew they were fighting for their Queen and country. That idea may seem a little old fashioned now but I am not rewriting history I am trying to show what it might have been like to live in 19th Century Britain.

Many men joined the army as a softer option than the incredibly hard and dangerous work in the factories. I worked in an iron gang in the 1970s and I can attest to the hard work even then. I tended presses that reached 3000 degrees and needed the consumption of gallons of squash during each shift. How much harder would it have been a hundred years earlier? I was working an eight-hour shift while ten and twelve-hour days were the norm a hundred years earlier.

Anyone who has researched their family history in the nineteenth century and looked at the census records will know how even relatively well off factory workers rented or boarded. Four and five to a bed was the norm. We take so much for granted today but even in the 1950s life was hard and had a pattern. With coal fires, no bathroom, an outside toilet, no carpets and little money for food then it was closer to life in the 1870s. Offal was often on the menu and you ate what was there.

231

Nothing was wasted. Drinking beer and smoking were not considered unhealthy pastimes. There was a teetotal movement but it was only in the latter part of the nineteenth century that the water the people drank became healthy. Until then it was small beer that was drunk.

This series will continue but unlike my British Ace Series and my WW2 one, I will not be working my way through wars. I intend to look at how British soldiers served this country and how their lives changed as Britain changed.

Books used in the research:

- The Oxford Illustrated History of the British Army- David Chandler
- The Thin Red Line- Fosten and Fosten
- The Zulu War- Angus McBride
- Rorke's Drift- Michael Glover
- British Forces in Zululand 1879- Knight and Scollins

Griff Hosker April 2022

Other books by Griff Hosker

If you enjoyed reading this book, then why not read another one by the author?

Ancient History

The Sword of Cartimandua Series
(Germania and Britannia 50 A.D. – 128 A.D.)
Ulpius Felix- Roman Warrior (prequel)
The Sword of Cartimandua
The Horse Warriors
Invasion Caledonia
Roman Retreat
Revolt of the Red Witch
Druid's Gold
Trajan's Hunters
The Last Frontier
Hero of Rome
Roman Hawk
Roman Treachery
Roman Wall
Roman Courage

The Wolf Warrior series
(Britain in the late 6th Century)
Saxon Dawn
Saxon Revenge
Saxon England
Saxon Blood
Saxon Slayer
Saxon Slaughter
Saxon Bane
Saxon Fall: Rise of the Warlord
Saxon Throne
Saxon Sword

Medieval History

The Dragon Heart Series
Viking Slave
Viking Warrior
Viking Jarl
Viking Kingdom
Viking Wolf
Viking War
Viking Sword
Viking Wrath
Viking Raid
Viking Legend
Viking Vengeance
Viking Dragon
Viking Treasure
Viking Enemy
Viking Witch
Viking Blood
Viking Weregeld
Viking Storm
Viking Warband
Viking Shadow
Viking Legacy
Viking Clan
Viking Bravery

The Norman Genesis Series
Hrolf the Viking
Horseman
The Battle for a Home
Revenge of the Franks
The Land of the Northmen
Ragnvald Hrolfsson
Brothers in Blood
Lord of Rouen
Drekar in the Seine
Duke of Normandy
The Duke and the King

Danelaw
(England and Denmark in the 11th Century)
The Dragon Sword
Oathsword
Blood Sword

New World Series
Blood on the Blade
Across the Seas
The Savage Wilderness
The Bear and the Wolf
Erik The Navigator

The Vengeance Trail

The Reconquista Chronicles
Castilian Knight
El Campeador
The Lord of Valencia

The Aelfraed Series
(Britain and Byzantium 1050 A.D. - 1085 A.D.)
Housecarl
Outlaw
Varangian

**The Anarchy Series England
1120-1180**
English Knight
Knight of the Empress
Northern Knight
Baron of the North
Earl
King Henry's Champion
The King is Dead
Warlord of the North
Enemy at the Gate
The Fallen Crown

Soldier of the Queen

Warlord's War
Kingmaker
Henry II
Crusader
The Welsh Marches
Irish War
Poisonous Plots
The Princes' Revolt
Earl Marshal
The Perfect Knight

Border Knight
1182-1300
Sword for Hire
Return of the Knight
Baron's War
Magna Carta
Welsh Wars
Henry III
The Bloody Border
Baron's Crusade
Sentinel of the North
War in the West
Debt of Honour
The Blood of the Warlord

Sir John Hawkwood Series
France and Italy 1339- 1387
Crécy: The Age of the Archer
Man At Arms
The White Company
Leader of Men

Lord Edward's Archer
Lord Edward's Archer
King in Waiting
An Archer's Crusade
Targets of Treachery
The Great Cause

Struggle for a Crown
1360- 1485
Blood on the Crown
To Murder a King
The Throne
King Henry IV
The Road to Agincourt
St Crispin's Day
The Battle for France
The Last Knight
Queen's Knight

Tales from the Sword I
(Short stories from the Medieval period)

Tudor Warrior series
England and Scotland in the late 14th and early 15th
century
Tudor Warrior

Conquistador
England and America in the 16th Century
Conquistador

Modern History

The Napoleonic Horseman Series
Chasseur à Cheval
Napoleon's Guard
British Light Dragoon
Soldier Spy
1808: The Road to Coruña
Talavera
The Lines of Torres Vedras
Bloody Badajoz
The Road to France
Waterloo

Soldier of the Queen

The Lucky Jack American Civil War series
Rebel Raiders
Confederate Rangers
The Road to Gettysburg

Soldier of the Queen Series
Soldier of the Queen

The British Ace Series
1914
1915 Fokker Scourge
1916 Angels over the Somme
1917 Eagles Fall
1918 We will remember them
From Arctic Snow to Desert Sand
Wings over Persia

Combined Operations series
1940-1945
Commando
Raider
Behind Enemy Lines
Dieppe
Toehold in Europe
Sword Beach
Breakout
The Battle for Antwerp
King Tiger
Beyond the Rhine
Korea
Korean Winter

Tales from the Sword II
(Short stories from the Modern period)

Other Books
Great Granny's Ghost (Aimed at 9-14-year-old young people)

For more information on all of the books then please visit the author's website at www.griffhosker.com where there is a link to contact him or visit his Facebook page: GriffHosker at Sword Books

Printed in Great Britain
by Amazon

83285800R00139